I0573423

BEYOND THE GATES

Gates of Deceit • Book One

ERIN R. HOWARD

expanse Books

Published by Expanse Books,
an imprint of Scrivenings Press LLC
15 Lucky Lane
Morrilton, Arkansas 72110
https://ScriveningsPress.com

Printed in the United States of America

Paperback ISBN 978-1-64917-210-5

eBook ISBN 978-1-64917-211-2

Cover by Linda Fulkerson www.bookmarketinggraphics.com

I am a strong woman because a strong woman raised me.
Thanks, Mom. I love you.

PRAISE FOR ERIN R. HOWARD

Filled with twists and turns to keep you on the edge of your seat, Beyond the Gates is evocative of Divergent and The Giver while maintaining a uniqueness that draws you in. Readers will devour the book while seeking a path back to the safety of the Outpost with Renna, Miles, and the rest of the likeable cast of characters. Packed with surprises, chills, and plenty of heart-wrenching moments, this story of deception within and without the walls of humanity's last enclosures is well-worth reading for any fan of dystopian stories. Particularly those who thoroughly enjoy a thread of young love skillfully woven into its fabric.

— BRETT ARMSTRONG, AWARD-WINNING
AUTHOR OF THE QUEST OF FIRE SERIES

A riveting tale of finding truth and family against overwhelming odds. You'll be swept away and captivated by this world where thinking for yourself could get you killed.

— TABITHA BOULDIN AUTHOR OF
MADNESS IN WONDERLAND

ACKNOWLEDGMENTS

Here we are, a brand new book and a new series! I've wanted to write a dystopian series even before I wrote The Kalila Chronicles, and I'm so excited that you've taken this journey with me. I hope you fell in love with Renna, Miles, and Gabbi as much as I did.

To Jacob, thank you for always being my sounding board. You never seem to get tired of listening to my ideas or helping me come up with better ones. I love you.

Thank you to my children, who have to put up with me during my deadlines. You guys are why I write.

There are so many women in my life that I'm amazed at their strength, and this book is a reflection of that strength. Mom, Allie, Kenzie, Chastity, Tessa, Corie, and Jackee, I love you all. Thank you for always being there for me.

To Heather and Amy, I couldn't make it through this writing journey without you in my corner. I love you both.

To Susan, Nikki, and my Rag Tag writing group, thank you for believing in me and Beyond the Gates. This story is better because of you.

And a huge thank you to Linda, the staff, and everyone at Expanse Books and Scrivenings Press. Beyond the Gates wouldn't be what it is without you.

Thank you, God, for this gift of writing and the stories that you put in my heart.

Last but certainly not least, a huge thank you to all of my

readers! Your kind words and messages are why I keep writing. So please make sure you go to my website and join my writing community. I pray that God will use this new series to remind you just how strong you are and that He has a purpose for you. One that only you can do.

PROLOGUE

The sun beat down on her, warming her skin to an unbearable temperature. Her knees shook and she did the best she could to keep her nerves under control. No one uttered a single word this morning as she prepared to leave her house for the Monitors building.

She passed her family, avoiding their expressions as she followed the Guardian Officials. They escorted her down the dirt paths, walking past each residential home and business, while the people stared at her through closed windows.

Fourteenth birthdays were meant for celebrating at home, eating sweets, and opening a few handmade presents from her family. Instead, she paraded through the streets of the Outpost, her first day in her new role as Speaker.

Speaker!

The title weighed on her as if an invisible, gold-laden crown sat precariously on her head. It wasn't a role she wanted. Who was she to inherit such an honorable position?

The Guardian paused at the door and faced her. "Renna James, welcome to the Monitors."

He pulled back a heavy wooden door that creaked as it

opened. He gestured for her to go first. In the center of the old, outdated room were a desk, chair, and the intercom system. Her gaze swept around the room, but nothing else stood out as interesting. Just chairs, cables, and other technology that Renna had only read about in the Books of the Past.

"Take a seat."

Renna did as instructed, too nervous to ask what she had to do next. The Guardian bowed his head to her and left, shutting the door behind him.

Within seconds, it opened again, and a boy — perhaps a few years older than her — emerged, carrying a thick envelope. He stopped in front of the desk and handed it to her. "Welcome to the Monitors."

"Thank you." Renna raised a shaky hand and accepted the package, turned it over, and broke the wax seal of the Officials.

At least the march to the building wasn't an everyday occurrence. It was a special day—the first day—of a new Speaker's reign.

The Runner walked to the front door and waited, watching her. She adverted her eyes and pulled the parchment from the envelope.

You can do this, Renna.

She pushed the intercom button and spoke, praying her voice wouldn't falter. "Citizens of the Outpost, my name is Renna James, and I am your new Speaker. I do not know what happened to your previous Speaker, but I'm honored to take over this prestigious role."

Renna paused, panic threatening to take over. Something happened to Jovi? She forced her mind to focus on the paper and not on the sweet girl she grew up with. "Two Runners entered the forest last night, and both returned, with a new set of rules, effective immediately."

Clearing her throat, she continued. "You can no longer go into the meadow each morning after the Reading. The Gates will open for a brief period and then close and lock for seventy-two hours."

The Runner's gasp momentarily threw her off guard, but she continued. "You were provided a week's worth of essentials—and will only be given a week's supply at a time until your production quality improves."

Dread filled her stomach at the news. This wasn't how she wanted to begin her new position. "Medicine will need to be rationed until another shipment is available. Curfew is at 8:30 p.m. You may now leave your homes."

Renna waited for a few seconds, taking in a deep breath before she switched off the intercom. She rose from the desk and walked over to the Runner. "Do you know what happened to Jovi?"

"No. Do us all a favor and don't repeat that question. To anyone." He gave her a slight nod before opening the door and leaving.

The Guardian Officials who had escorted her before waited at the bottom of the stairs, and they repeated the same route back to her house. She was grateful for the escort this time because people stared at her from every doorway and sidewalk. Curiosity and shock lined their faces—their eyes asking the same question she wanted to know but couldn't voice.

Why was she the Speaker?

1

Day One

A shudder swept down Renna's spine as slimy earth oozed between her toes. Placing one foot in front of the other, she ran. The crunch of brittle leaves echoed her steps throughout the forest.

Branches slapped across her chest as she clumsily sprinted toward the safety of the Monitors. Debris littering the forest floor sent sharp stabs and stings along the bottom of her heels.

What a stupid, impulsive decision.

If she squinted, she could barely make out an old, rectangular concrete building that had seen better days—the Monitors' roof. Renna had to push a little more, and she would be safely within the perimeter of the Gates. Once inside, she could get back to announcing today's Life Rules to the Outpost. Just like every day for the last three years.

A fluttering of wings to her right drew Renna's gaze. Brown and white spotted feathers flew beside her, landing in a nearby birch tree. Attention caught by the majestic creature, Renna tried to slow her speed, but her toes tangled in the damp grass and vines and threw her off balance. Her knee protested the sudden restraint of the vines and buckled, sending her into a heap on the mucky ground.

Rocks nicked her palms as she slapped them down to break her fall, but it didn't stop her descent's momentum. Her face smacked the ground, sending the world into a flurry of circles. Clamping her eyes shut, she waited until the spinning ceased and her breathing steadied.

Already, the sting of the fall smarted around her eye. No doubt a beautiful array of colors would mar her face. The Outpost relied on her perfect vision. Any damage to her sight and, well—she shuddered at what could happen.

Slowly Renna opened her eyes, one at a time. Brilliant aqua skies filled her vision.

She could see!

She let out a high-pitched giggle and then clamped a hand over her mouth. Mud smacked her in the face, and she tried her best to wipe it off, but it smeared across her lips instead.

The owl *hooted* and flew over her in the opposite direction it had been heading. At least it was comforting to know that she was not seeing things after all. There really was an owl in the forest, and for her to see it, in the daytime—no one at the Outpost would believe her.

Although, she could never admit she had ventured into the forest beyond the meadow surrounding the Gates.

Reena's pulse skyrocketed. The Gates! She had to get back before the sirens blared. Scrambling to her feet, she broke out once more into a run, ignoring the aches and pains from fall-ing. She wasn't a Runner, so there was never a need for Renna to be outside of the boundaries of the Outpost.

The grey Monitors building crept closer into view as the forest began to thin. She had no idea how she would explain her muddy appearance, but she'd have to worry about that once she was securely behind her desk, waiting for the Runner to place today's rules in her hand.

Renna was about to break out into the clearing surrounding the Gates when something struck her from the side, knocking her flat on her stomach, forcing the breath from her lungs. For a few terrifying moments, Renna thought she would die. But as suddenly as the breath left, her lungs refilled. Renna brushed bits of dirt and grass from her lips as she tried to bolt up from the ground, unsure of what to do next.

"Wait just a minute!" Calloused hands reached out to stop her.

Renna tried to see who was behind her but only glimpsed clothing—no face. Judging from the voice, it was a man.

"Let go!" Renna wiggled and squirmed, attempting to strike her attacker, yet he overpowered her.

She kept kicking, hoping the man would get tired or give up. Finally. A curse filled the air as he removed his grip on her arm to block her persistent kicks.

"Be still," he huffed, "I'm trying to help you."

Help her? He had a strange way of showing help. She struck again, connecting with his body. It was the moment she needed to turn over.

She gasped. This was no man but a boy—one not much older than her seventeen years. She shook her head and stood before he could grab her again. Renna backed away from the teenager, but he threw his hands out, begging her to stay.

"Please, wait just a moment. You don't want to go back to the Outpost."

She raised her eyebrow. "I don't?" Was this guy insane? She took another step backward. How had she gotten herself into this situation? What was she thinking?

"You were out in the woods, right?" He gestured to the forest. "So you must have already been suspicious."

Renna paused. "Suspicious of what?"

The boy opened his mouth to respond, but the high-pitched wail of the siren cut off his words. Renna covered her ears to protect her eardrums from the sound. Dread filled her stomach at the signal. It was the start of a new day.

Who would read the day's rules to the Outpost?

Tears blurred Renna's vision as the long wail of the siren slowed and then finally stopped. Her hand instinctively touched the silver necklace dangling from her neck. The *S* pendant was cool against her fingers.

It was too late. The Gates were closed. She was too late.

"You're the Speaker." The boy gasped and Renna opened her eyes to see him backing away from her now.

"Where are you going?"

His face filled with regret. "I'm sorry, I can't …"

She stomped forward, irritation welling up inside at the sight of him retreating. "Wait! You can't leave me!"

He shook his head in horror and took off for the forest.

2

A glance over his shoulder assured Miles Butler the girl was not following him into the forest. Good. Miles didn't need the implications of bringing a Speaker back home with him.

He almost brought a Speaker home!

Miles absent-mindedly pushed a low hanging branch out of his face as he followed the familiar narrow trail from the Outpost to his encampment. His mind whirled. He could have epically messed everything up.

How had he not recognized the girl was a Speaker? She ran out of the thick of the forest as he waited for the right time to intercept her. But she tripped. He was about to make sure she was okay when she peered right at him.

He'd been mesmerized as her steely eyes widened in delight and a genuine laugh escaped her lips before she slung mud across her face, stopping the gleeful noise. Relief washed over him when he realized she wasn't fixated on him but on an owl in a nearby tree. By the time he glanced away from the bird, she was already on the move.

Again.

He'd run out of time to stop her.

Miles had no choice but to knock her to the ground and try to convince her to go back with him. The last thing he wanted to do was scare the girl, but by the time he got her to calm down, he noticed the initial dangling from a thin silver chain. A cursive S for Speaker.

The piercing shrill of the siren sealed their fate. It was too late to right his mistake. He let the girl's joy of watching an owl, a creature he'd seen countless times, distract him from his job.

His carelessness had also cost the girl, and she no doubt was scared out of her mind. Locked out of the one place she understood and had purpose.

Guilt wiggled its way in, but he pushed it aside with facts. The girl shouldn't have been in the forest. He had no way of knowing she wasn't a Runner. Each Outpost sent one runner out into the woods each night, and each morning, they returned with the rules for the Speaker to announce to the Outpost. Assuming the girl was a Runner was only natural.

"Hey! Don't leave, this is all your fault!"

Miles spun around, surprised at the feminine voice calling out from behind him. He scanned the area but couldn't make out anyone in the thick brush.

"Thanks to you, my people are stuck inside until the Gates open again!"

The Speaker. Miles sighed, dread filling his stomach. She followed him after all. He had to lose her and quickly. He sprinted down the trail, jumping over fallen logs and uprooted tree roots.

"Hey!"

She was chasing after him. Miles had to give the girl some credit. She was determined.

"Please stop!" The Speaker's voice came out in gasps of air, confirming she wouldn't be able to keep up with him. But he had to change trails, he could not lead her towards his encampment.

"I can't just sit outside the Gates for three days. The lock is on a timer. "

If he remembered correctly, she wasn't wearing shoes, so there was no way she could keep up with him off the path. Hating himself, he turned suddenly to the right, crashing through low hanging branches and uneven ground.

He glanced behind him and was shocked to see the girl was still chasing after him. Fatigue etched her face, but she barreled on and, every so often, flinched in pain. Still, she pursued Miles.

"I can't stay at the meadow. I have no trees to block the sun, no water, no plants—nothing." The more she rambled, the more Miles's stomach clenched. "Don't you know the forest is forbidden?"

The brush was becoming too hard to maneuver, and Miles had to stop sprinting and start walking carefully over a section of large rocks. The girl stopped calling after him, and Miles found himself confirming she was still there.

Then it happened. A short scream of pain, followed by silence. Miles stopped to debate whether or not to keep going. Taking a deep breath, he turned around. The girl was on the ground, clutching her foot.

Her hair fell in a tangled mess around her face, and tears streaked her dirty cheeks as she inspected her injured foot. What a jerk move. He couldn't stand to see someone in pain, and *this* was his fault.

What else could he do? His intervention took a Speaker away from her duty, which was unforgivable.

Now, leaving the girl on her own was just as inexcusable. He rubbed his hand over his face and quickly made his way back to her.

"You come to gloat?" Her voice was hard and cool as she glanced up at him.

"No. I didn't come to gloat." He bent down to look her in the eye. "I'm here to make sure you're all right."

She snorted, and her cheeks turned bright red.

"Can I see it?" He gestured to her hand clamped around her foot. Blood poured between her fingers.

"If I remove my hand, the wound will keep gushing."

"We need to tie something around it to add pressure and stop the bleeding." Miles pulled his pocket knife out of his back pocket, wishing he'd brought his backpack full of supplies. But this was only supposed to be an hour trip. And definitely not something that required medical supplies.

He cut a section of his t-shirt off the bottom. The girl's eyes narrowed, but she finally relinquished her foot for him to inspect it. More guilt punched him in the stomach. Dozens of tiny scrapes crisscrossed the sole of her foot, but a gash covered her heel. It wasn't too deep, yet walking would be a nuisance, and there was no doubt it would open back up.

"Will I live?" He glanced up to see her half-smile mixed with pain and accusation.

Taking his canteen, he did his best to clean her wound before wrapping the fabric around it and made quick work to knot it. "Yep." He cinched it, probably a little too hard, but she didn't say anything else. "Walking may be a little difficult."

"Just what I needed. More difficulty." She struggled to get to a standing position, so he reached out to help her. She shoved his hand away. "I can do it myself."

Miles sighed. "I was trying to help." Evidently, it was the wrong thing to say because the girl gasped.

"You were trying to help? You are the reason why I'm in this mess!"

The girl's charge stabbed him straight in the heart. He sighed, averting his eyes from her face back to her foot. Blood stained the side of the fabric, except there wasn't much he could do at the moment.

"I'm sorry." He bent down and tucked a strand of cloth back around the knot and then met her gaze. "I didn't know you were a Speaker."

The girl's eyes widened at his admission. "You know who I am?"

He had to tread carefully with his reply. How much should he tell her? Most people he encountered in the woods were already curious or at least suspicious about the forest. They had the seeds of doubt sprouting in their mind about the Outpost. But a Speaker would never trespass into the forest. Would never leave the comfort of the Monitors. So why did the girl? It didn't make any sense.

The girl's face changed from surprise to wariness. He needed to get the conversation on more neutral ground until he could figure out what to say. "I think you might need some stitches." He gently reached towards her foot. "It's a gnarly cut."

"Thanks to you."

Another stab, but she was right. He knowingly led her off the beaten path in hopes it would slow her down. Once she fell and called out for help, he couldn't ignore her pleas. No matter that she was a Speaker, and he was a Forest Walker.

A deserter of the Outpost.

And she was the one person who was off-limits. To harm or lure a Speaker away from the Outpost was a fate worse than death.

He stood and took a step away from her. He had to find a way to distance himself from this mess. "You're the one who followed me. It's not my fault you aren't wearing shoes."

"You left me outside the Gates. Just walked off into the forest and left me alone." She pushed back her hair from her face. "I had no choice but to follow you." She shuddered. "I couldn't have stayed out in the open for seventy-two hours!"

Ugh, this girl twisted everything. "You had to be back before the siren blared, not me." He didn't even try to hide his annoyance. She needed to take some responsibility for the situation. Did she not realize what would happen if she wasn't back inside before the siren ended?

Tears welled up in her eyes, but her tone was cold. "I wouldn't have been late if you hadn't knocked me down. Then grabbed my legs." She shuddered. "For a moment, I thought you were going to ..." Her voice trailed off, and terror filled her eyes.

All of the breath left Mile's lungs as the implications of her words filled him with nausea. "I could never do that to someone." He clenched his jaw so hard it ached. He only wanted to get her attention, but when she fell, she freaked out, and he'd only meant to get her to calm down. His stomach twisted at the thought of horror and panic she felt. "I'm so sorry you thought ... I only wanted to stop you from going back to the Outpost."

"Why stop me?" Her voice was quiet but no longer held the same venom and disdain it had before. "And why did you run away from me after the siren?"

Sweat dripped down his neck distracting him from her question. He spotted the sun slowly making its way above the trees. He was running out of time before he needed to be back. But what was he going to do with the girl? He couldn't leave her here. Not now. Not after she thought the worst of him, and not on her injured foot.

"Obviously, you can't stay here." He gestured around them. "We aren't exactly in the safest spot in this forest. Let's get you to my camp where we can stitch up your foot, and then we can talk."

The girl tilted her head, considering his words. It was the best he could offer at the moment. If they started now, he could help her walk back to his village and get her to the healer. He could find her some shoes, but he needed time to figure out what he was going to say to his village's leader, Thomas.

He grinned, hoping for a fresh start, and extended a hand, his leather bracelet moving up his arm. "I'm Miles Butler."

The corners of her mouth slowly lifted to a smile, and her eyes lit up. "Renna James." She slipped her hand into his, and Miles tried to ignore that it fit perfectly within his. He concentrated on getting her to a standing position and wrapped his arm around her waist to help take the weight off of her injured foot.

"All right, Renna James, one step at a time."

She took a couple of steps and then inhaled a sharp breath. "How many more?"

"A few hundred, give or take a few thousand."

"I was afraid you would say that."

3

Silence permeated the warm kitchen and made Gabbi want to fling open the closest window to see if it was as quiet outside as it was in the bakery. But she couldn't. Not until her younger sister's voice filtered through the intercom.

Stealing a glance at the mound of dough on the counter, she sighed. The ovens were ready, heating the small space to an unpleasant temperature. Why wasn't Renna explaining the daily rules?

Mother peeked her head through the double swinging doors of the kitchen, relief evident on her round face when she spotted Gabbi. "Did I miss The Reading?"

"No." Gabbi wanted to gesture to the ovens and mounds of dough overflowing the ceramic bowl, but instead just said, "Nothing yet."

She joined her by the counter, counting the empty loaf pans. "I'm sure everything is fine."

She wished she'd inherited her mother's optimism, but Gabbi teetered on the glass-is-half-empty opinion. "Of course."

Mother didn't reply but instead tied an apron around her waist. "Why don't you start kneading the dough?"

Gabbi's voice betrayed her shock. "We can't. What if it's not a bakery day?"

"It's always a bakery day." Mother gave her a look like Gabbi had suddenly sprouted another head.

"You know what I mean. We can't start our day until Renna reads the rules." She grabbed the nearest towel and wiped her forehead. How much longer was this going to take? Gabbi desperately needed the windows open. "We've had to close before."

"Not in a very long time."

It was true. Their little bakery had been passed down through the family bloodline for generations, and there was always a line of people waiting outside for them to open up. The sirens went off minutes ago, and Renna should have begun reading immediately. But nothing.

It didn't make any sense. Renna was a Speaker. And even though it shocked Gabbi they chose her family—her younger sister—for such a prestigious role, Renna had never flaked on her duties before.

Renna the perfect.

And Gabbi the overlooked.

That wasn't exactly fair. Or true. Gabbi was the oldest in the family of two girls, and her parents depended on her more than she wanted to admit. But for some reason, no matter how much she tried to be content, she longed for more. Anything but baking bread and stuffing pastries.

"Did your sister say anything to you last night?"

"I haven't seen Renna since suppertime." Gabbi reached for the bowl and turned it over. Mother was right. They would need bread. Even if the unthinkable happened and no one could leave their house, her family would still be hungry. She shuddered at the thought of having to stay in the stifling bakery. How could she miss her evening walk—she needed open skies.

"She usually says something before she leaves for the Monitors, but I didn't see her either." Mother's hands shook as she reached for a bar of soap.

Gabbi punched the dough down and kept kneading. She had to get the loaves ready and then move on to the pastries, and if she had time, maybe her mom would let her decorate the tiny round cakes today. They were already baked from the day before and sat on the counter, waiting for colorful flowers. Mother was a master at designing cakes and could pipe flowers faster than Gabbi, but never let anyone else decorate them. Instead, she set aside a couple for each of the girls to decorate for fun. Gabbi never wanted to admit it, but the only thing in the bakery that brought her a smidgen of joy was making a cake from start to finish.

"Is Father with you?" Gabbi strained to hear her father bustling around in the dining room, but there was nothing but silence.

"No. He's still at home. He wasn't feeling well this morning."

Gabbi's hands froze in the dough and she peered over at Mother. "How are we going to open the bakery without him today?"

"I assumed Renna would be here after The Reading, and we would call in Opal."

Just the three of them to run the entire bakery? No wonder Mother wanted her to get started without the go-ahead from The Reading. The bakery's demand required all four of them, plus occasionally help from Opal, a teenaged orphan from the children's home.

With Father ill and Renna missing, Gabbi had no idea how they would make it through the day, even with Opal's help. Gabbi moved the bread pans over to rise and glanced at the clock. Thirty minutes past The Reading time.

"What are we going to do if there is no Reading?"

"Gabriella James, I don't want to hear that come out your

mouth!" Mother opened the cooling unit and brought out the fruit fillings.

"I'm sorry, Mother. But it's after 6:30 a.m." Gabbi watched the color drain from her mother's face.

"I'm sure we will hear your sister's voice any second."

Gabbi sighed and grabbed a piping bag for the fruit filling. "I like this apple pie mixture."

Mother dragged her eyes away from the clock and back to the pastries. "Me too. The secret is in the spices."

"Great-grandmother Dottie's recipe?"

"The very one."

Gabbi filled the pastries in silence, counting how many of each flavor was needed in her head. With each passing tick of the clock, it became clear. No rules today. But why? An image of Renna getting fired from her job flashed in her mind, and the bag of filling slipped from her fingers, knocking a few pastries to the ground, sending bits of dough and fruit all over her apron.

"Gabbi," Mother chided as she raised her arm to deflect the flying pieces of pastry.

"Sorry!"

Mother suddenly burst into laughter, the sound a welcome reprieve from the mean thoughts of her sister. "Oh, Gabbi, you have fruit in your hair."

"At least it will smell good now."

"It might, but perhaps you should rinse it out."

"I think you're right." Gabbi pulled at the goopy mix of apple and cinnamon. "I'll be right back." Making quick work of untying her apron, she tossed it in the laundry bin before leaving the kitchen. The bakery dining room was eerily quiet. Rows of tables topped with yellow tablecloths and linen napkins stood waiting for customers who weren't coming.

She glanced back at the swinging double doors of the kitchen, but Mother didn't follow her. No doubt, she was already cleaning up the mess she had made. Before Gabbi could chicken out, she marched past the tables and toward the front door. What would one peek outside the curtains matter? She could get a quick glance of the street, just to make sure that something wasn't wrong with their intercom. Maybe it was broken, and there was a huge line of customers waiting on the porch and wrapped around the building. Like normal.

Or maybe she didn't want to look out the window. What if danger from the forest had finally made it past their walls and broken into the Outpost? Her heart thundered in her chest as she reached out a shaky hand to the blue and white curtain. What if everyone was gone?

They had rules for a reason. Stay inside, curtains drawn, until the Speaker announced daily rules brought in by the Runners. Everyone followed these, except her family. Her parents had petitioned the Guardians after Renna was born to move from their upstairs residence to a bigger apartment.

For a second, she wished they were back home instead of the stifling bakery. At least there, they would be more comfortable and could keep an eye on her father. If they were home, though, they would be in the same predicament as the rest of the Outpost—limited food supplies.

What were the people going to do? Would they get desperate and try to break the rules? Surely not. Except, there was a time before the rules even existed. When people disappeared into the forest and never came home. When food and medical supplies would suddenly stop for weeks for no reason at all. There was a time when no one left their homes for fear of being taken away, curiosity their only crime. Curiosity for what was outside the Gates, beyond the Outpost.

Gabbi wasn't old enough to remember the times before the rules, but her grandparents told her parents, and her parents told her.

Now, the rules were enforced above all else.

What if the Guardians were waiting for people to pull back their curtains and poke their heads outside? Gabbi took a step backward and let the fabric fall back into place. Their family would already be on the watch list because of Renna. They would be expecting her to come to the bakery to be with her family.

"Gabbi, these cakes aren't going to frost themselves!" Mother's voice cut through her thoughts of Renna and the shame she had brought to their family.

"Almost finished!" She shouted back, running toward the bathroom. As she scrubbed her hair, anger welled up inside of her. What would happen now? Never had a Speaker abandoned their post.

Her foolish, headstrong, curious sister.

She quickly threw her wet hair up in a bun and joined her mother in the kitchen as the three-chimed tone of the announcements belted through the bakery speakers.

Gabbi's heart picked up pace, meeting Mother's worried gaze. *Come on, Renna, please be there.*

"Citizens of The Outpost, you will remain in your homes until further notice. Anyone seen outside will be arrested." The voice was cold, impersonal, and threatening. Not Renna's reassuring and gentle tone.

Because it wasn't her sister at all, but a voice Gabbi didn't recognize. Which meant only one thing. Her sister was gone.

"Oh, Renna, what have you done?" she whispered, slowly looking away from the intercom and toward her mother, busy scooping purple frosting into a decorating bag. She turned to Gabbi, her face void of any emotion.

"You can pipe the violets on the tiny cakes today."

Tears fell from Gabbi's cheeks as she reached for the bag. Mother handed it to her and gave Gabbi a nod, then left her alone in the kitchen.

4

Renna made it all of ten minutes before Miles picked her up and started carrying her. He claimed it was because he was using more energy keeping her upright in the wild underbrush, but it was because they were going at a painstaking pace. She wanted to insist he put her down, yet it might take them hours at her current rate. Plus, every time she put pressure on the heel of her foot, it made her want to cry out in pain. He flinched every time she almost did. The process was a vicious cycle.

Renna tried to be an easy passenger for Miles, but the longer he carried her, the more she was in tune with his breathing and the determined look in his eyes as he carefully stepped over the uneven terrain. For a while, she refused to let her gaze sneak back to his face, but the forest wasn't any easier for her to concentrate on. Every sound made her tense. There was a reason her people were never allowed in the forest.

The forest was forbidden.

No one had ever made it back alive. Except for the Runners.

Looking at the forest only made her stomach twist and turn into knots, while looking at Miles only made her more aware of his arms around her. It was better for her to simply close her eyes and listen to his breathing.

"I believe you, you know."

"What do you mean?"

"Earlier, when I said I thought you were going to attack me." She watched as a crease formed on his forehead. "And you said you'd never do anything like that—well, I thought it was important to tell you that I believe you." Renna didn't know much about the boy, but she could easily see the guilt in his expression when he realized she was hurt and the repulsion all over his face as soon as she alluded to her fears. He instantly recoiled at her accusation, and one glance into his amber eyes told her he was telling her the truth.

"Thank you." His jaw worked, but he didn't say anything else.

"You're welcome."

Renna sighed, feeling a tiny bit better. Now if only she could work out the other questions welling within her. Like, why did he try to stop her to begin with? Why did he care if she left the Gates or not?

Didn't it surprise him to see her in the forest? Did people escape into the woods often? Was that why he said she must have already been suspicious? But suspicious of what exactly?

She should never have left the safety of the Gates. Especially without the proper gear. What must he think of her? Running through the forest without her shoes? Who did such a thing? The only people who entered the forest were the Runners, and they were decked out with the best of the best gear. Camouflaged clothing, backpacks filled with food and supplies, the finest weapons the Outpost had to offer, and of course, weatherproofed boots. They would never run out into the forest barefooted. She only wanted to feel the earth between her toes, feet sinking into the soft ground.

Her cheeks burned at the turn of her thoughts. She was

impulsive as a child. Abandoned her sacred post because she couldn't resist the call of wide-open skies and no boundaries. What must her parents think of her now?

Renna snuck a look at Miles and frowned. Sweat dripped from his forehead, causing his hair to stick up. He caught her stare and sighed, walking over to a nearby fallen log and gently setting her down.

"I can try to walk more now." Renna was careful not to let the bottom of her foot rest on the ground. "It stopped bleeding."

"I'm afraid that as soon as you put any weight on it at all, it will open back up." Miles sat beside her and sighed. "We aren't that far now."

"Are you sure? Because I see nothing around us but forest."

He gave her a small smile. "You just don't know what to look for." He patted the log. "There's all sorts of hidden secrets throughout this forest that lead directly to my village."

"You have a village?" Renna didn't even try to hide her surprise at his words. But confusion quickly chased the excitement away. "But you can't survive out in the forest."

"Obviously, you can."

"I mean, there are not any villages outside of the Outposts." She lowered her voice. "It's forbidden."

Miles raised an eyebrow. "That certainly didn't stop you from stepping out into the forest."

"I wasn't going to stay! I only wanted to ..." She let her words trail off, refusing to admit out loud what she really desired. Speakers were not supposed to want. Only to serve their people. But at this moment, with the way Miles waited for her to explain—with curiosity instead of judgment—she wanted to confide everything to him.

"Hold that thought." Miles stood and circled the log, looking behind them to the left. "Our help is almost here."

"Help?" Renna tried to turn to see what he saw, but she had no idea what he was suddenly so excited about.

"I told you. There are clues if you know where to look." His grin was contagious, and Renna found herself smiling along with him.

"Okay, I'll bite. What clue did I miss?"

"This particular log didn't just naturally fall at some point. It was carefully placed because from this vantage point, half a mile away, is our first security tower."

Renna followed the direction his finger pointed, but no security tower was visible. "I don't see anything."

"That's because it's up in the treetops."

"Like a treehouse?" Excitement filled her at the thought. Renna had read about them in the Books of the Past, but she had never seen one in person.

"Exactly." Miles gave her an appreciative nod. "We don't always have ways to communicate with the village while we are outside, but if we can get to one of the security checkpoints, they will send help. It's not a perfect solution, but it works in a pinch."

Renna nodded, squinting back toward the tower. Sure enough, two figures emerged from the trees. "Is that a horse?" Renna strained to get a better look, but there in the distance was a man riding a horse, pulling a second one behind him.

"Yes. No more walking or being carried."

Relief flooded Renna at the thought. She didn't know how much longer she could continue towards Miles's camp the way they had been. Renna wasn't used to being a burden to anyone, and depending on someone she had just met to carry her through the forest made her feel guilty all over again.

She should never have stepped one foot into the forest.

Her breath hitched in her throat as the Appaloosa stopped beside them. The spotted horse was beautiful, and she wanted to stand up and run a hand through its silky mane. But instead, she waited as Miles walked over to meet the rider.

A gruff voice called down from the horse, "You're late."

"There were complications." Miles quickly glanced in her direction, and she flinched. Burden and now a complication. Her self-esteem was taking a hit today.

"These trips always cause complications." The man grumbled and jumped down from the horse. In a quick stride, he swept Miles up in a hug. "I'm glad to see you."

"You can't get rid of me that quickly, Keegan."

Keegan took a step back from Miles and crossed his arms. "You're not hurt, are you?"

"No. I'm fine. But Renna cut her foot on the way to camp." Miles turned back to her. "Renna, this is Keegan. He's a little rough around the edges, but underneath he's a big teddy bear."

Keegan thumped Miles in the back of the head and handed him the reins. "If it weren't for me, you would have never made it in these woods, and you know it." Keegan walked over and extended his hand to her. "It's nice to meet you, Renna. I'm sorry you had to travel with this know-it-all."

Miles raised his eyebrows but didn't comment further. Renna didn't know why he chose not to mention who Renna was, but if Miles was going to keep quiet about her being a Speaker, then she would as well.

"It's nice to meet you too." Renna shook his hand and couldn't help but laugh. "It's definitely been an adventure so far."

"I'm sure it has." He sighed and reached out an arm to help her up from the log. "We will get you fixed up in no time. But first, we have to get you up there."

Keegan helped her over to the second horse, a chestnut-colored mare, and before Renna could react, he picked her up and heaved her onto the horse. Moments later, Miles swung up behind her.

The horse nickered and shook her head, and Renna tensed, unsure what to do next. There wasn't anything but a blanket on the horse's back.

"What's wrong?" Miles's voice asked in her ear. "Did your foot open up again?"

"No." Renna gently petted the mare, unsure of what to do with her hands. "I've never ridden a horse before."

"Toby is gentle. She's never bucked anyone off before, and she knows the way back home better than I do."

Renna gritted her teeth as the horses turned around and headed back toward the guard tower. "Why doesn't that make me feel better?"

5

Curious glances and flat-out stares greeted Miles and Renna as they made their way into the Forest Community. Miles was used to the cautious looks thrown his way when he brought in a new person. While the people were kind and welcoming, it took them a little time to warm up to someone new.

Renna stiffened in his arms and sat up a little straighter. No doubt trying to show that their unwanted glances didn't bother her. In their few short hours together, Miles figured she could handle the questions that would be hurled her way.

Usually, when someone came with him back to camp, they met with Thomas. Most were ready to leave the Outpost and didn't require a lot of explanation. Never had they had a Speaker in their midst. He was still unsure how to explain to Thomas what had happened.

They guided the mounts to the medical cabin, and Miles waited for Keegan to tie off his horse and help Renna down before joining them. The cabin was opposite Thomas's office, so Miles hoped he would have time to get Renna settled before he was summoned to give Thomas a report.

"I'm going to take the horses back to the stable and give them a treat." Keegan nodded to Renna. "I'll see you two later."

"Thanks, Keegan." Miles handed him his reins and then helped Renna navigate the stairs of the cabin and to an exam table in the corner of the room.

"Elaine?" Miles called out, gently helping Renna get her foot propped up on the bed. No matter how hard he tried to keep the injury clean, blood and dirt soaked the cloth.

"Miles, is that you?" Elaine entered the waiting area, a frown on her face. Her eyes widened, glancing at Renna and then back to him.

"We seem to need your help, Elaine." Miles gestured to Renna's foot and then stepped back so Elaine could get a closer look.

"I can see that." Another frown in his direction. "What did you do? Drag her through the mud and muck?"

Leave it to Elaine to speak the truth without even knowing it. "Renna cut her foot, and I told her that we could help her out." He grabbed a chair from the waiting area and placed it beside the bed.

"Renna, is it?" Elaine rolled a tool tray closer and slipped on a pair of latex gloves. "Let's take a look at this gash."

"Thank you." She gave Elaine a warm smile but stiffened as Elaine cut off the knotted fabric.

"Miles, I know I taught you better than this." Elaine sighed, inspecting the dirty wound.

Another ping of guilt hit him as he stared at Renna's foot. "I did the best I could with what I had."

"You went out in the forest without supplies?"

"It's my fault." Renna's voice interrupted before he could answer. "I don't think he meant to be out so long."

Miles didn't miss the way Renna came to his defense, and another wave of guilt washed over him. Would he ever stop feeling bad for what happened?

"Well, whatever the case may be, you've got a nasty cut. I'm going to clean it up and then put a few stitches in." She walked over to the cabinet and started loading her tray with more supplies.

Elaine grabbed a stool and placed it at the end of the exam table. With a sympathetic smile, she said, "This is going to hurt."

Renna's stomach clenched at Elaine's bluntness. "What did you mean that you taught Miles better than this?" Renna gave them both questioning looks before flinching once again.

"Elaine was kind enough to take me under her wing when I arrived here."

"We've been good for each other, really." Elaine glanced up from Renna's foot. "Since I'm the only one with any medical experience, I had this whole cabin to myself. When Miles appeared at the camp years ago, barely old enough to be on his own, it was the logical thing to do."

"Aw, don't let her fool you. She's worked me to death living here."

"Miles Butler, you do try one's patience." Elaine sighed. "Renna, please don't listen to these lies."

A grin broke out across Renna's face. "Oh, I completely understand. He's tried my patience as well."

"Renna, I like you." Elaine pulled out a long syringe. "That's why I'm going to numb your foot first before I start stitching."

"She says that to everyone." Miles couldn't help but interject. "But Elaine is great at her job."

"Well, he's right about one thing." Elaine patted Renna on the leg before injecting the needle. "I do say that to everyone."

"Great." Renna leaned back on the bed. "Can you just wake me up when it's over?"

"Are you sure you can sleep right now?" Miles scooted his chair towards the end of the bed. He wasn't the biggest fan of watching flesh be put back together.

"Is my face as pale as yours?"

"Probably." Miles laughed. "Elaine said she taught me, not that I enjoyed it."

"I think Elaine may be the only one who does." Renna sighed. "I'm amazed at people who can stomach this kind of work."

"It definitely takes a special person, and Elaine is the best."

"Why didn't you tell Keegan and Elaine who I really am?" Renna's voice was low enough that Elaine wouldn't be able to hear, but he couldn't resist taking a quick look in her direction anyway.

"Now's not the time to talk about that."

Her eyes narrowed. "Don't you think we need to get our stories straight then?"

It was a good point. The last thing they needed was their stories to diverge. Thomas would already question her appearance in the camp, and Miles needed a plan. Now was probably the best time to figure out the details.

"You were simply curious about the camp. You've heard rumors and wanted to see it for yourself." He offered quickly. It was vague, but maybe it would be enough.

"You know I have to go back." She blew a stray strand of hair off her forehead. "I can't stay here. My people need me."

"I know." He frowned. It definitely made everything more complicated. No one who came to the camp wanted to leave once they arrived. Thomas wasn't going to believe that for a second.

"And you're going to escort me back."

"I'm what?" He hissed, completely thrown off guard. That was not part of the plan. "I told you I would get you help, and I am." He gestured to Elaine, wrapping Renna's foot with a clean bandage.

Renna propped herself up on her elbows. "It's your fault that I'm in this mess. You're taking me back. Tomorrow."

He started to hiss back a retort but ended up just staring at her instead. How could someone frustrate him so much? No one else had ever come so close to leaving him without words. She wasn't being fair, but then again, he wasn't either. He was the reason she was in this mess. He was trained to know who to try to convince to come to the camp and who was off-limits. He should have left her by the Gates. No, scratch that. He should have never stopped her to begin with.

"Is everything all right?" Elaine's voice broke through his thoughts, and he turned to see a slight smile tugging up the corners of her mouth. She folded her arms. "Should I give you guys a few minutes to discuss whatever it is that's going on?"

"No, we're finished." Miles cleared his throat. "What's the word on her foot? All better?"

Elaine raised her eyebrows at him but then turned to Renna. "It's going to be pretty sore until the stitches dissolve. I'm going to give you a salve to keep on it, and you're going to want to pad your shoe so it doesn't put too much pressure on the wound."

"Thank you, Elaine. I really appreciate your help."

"A friend of Miles is a friend of mine." She handed a jar of medicine to Renna. "Why don't we take a look through my closet? I bet we can find some clean clothes and shoes."

Renna nodded. "That would be great, Elaine."

"That's my cue to leave." Miles stood up from the chair. "Thomas is going to want a report of my outing."

"Dinner is at six," Elaine called over her shoulder before sterilizing her tools and trays.

"Miles, wait." Renna swung down from the exam table, flinching as she got to her feet and limped a few steps toward him. "What are you going to tell Thomas?"

"I'm not sure." He lowered his voice in case Elaine could hear them. "But you should keep that necklace hidden. He'll know what it means."

Her fingers went up to the pendant hanging around her neck. "That's how ..."

"Yes, and Thomas will as well."

"What will happen if they know who I am?" Concern edged around every word.

"You know exactly what the rules are."

She winced, but then sighed. "Do the rules even apply in this place?"

Good question. He had been asking himself that question since realizing who she was. How could he answer her? Whatever he said would just prompt more inquiries, and Elaine was taking extra time putting away her supplies. Could she be eavesdropping?

"All they need to know is that you wanted to see the camp for yourself, but you'd never leave your family behind, so you have to go back."

Renna chewed on her bottom lip, taking her time before she answered. "Miles. I can't leave my parents behind. My sister. My people." Tears welled up in her eyes before she turned away. "They are all depending on me, and I failed them."

Without thinking, he gently reached out and lifted her chin. "You haven't failed them." Miles didn't know if it was the way she looked at him, regret mixed with sadness, or his guilt at his role in their situation, but he wanted to tell her he would get her home.

No matter what.

"I'm late to speak to Thomas." He let his hand drop along with the promise. Some things he couldn't promise no matter how much he wanted to.

6

Dozens of petite cakes lined the table and counters of the kitchen. The ovens were finally turned off, but that didn't stop sweat from dripping down Gabbi's neck and drenching her shirt collar.

What she wouldn't give to be able to open the back door of the kitchen and fling open the windows. Only a few hours into the lockdown and already the four walls of the kitchen were closing in on her. Gabbi placed the last cake with the others and wiped her hands on her apron before searching for her mother.

"Are you finished?" Her mother called as she went back to arranging the display cases.

"Yes. They're all ready."

"Perfect. I'm just about finished here."

Did her mother actually think they would be able to open the bakery? It wasn't likely. Especially since the alert came over the intercom earlier this morning. Gabbi debated whether to remind her of the announcement or to blindly play along with prepping the dining room for their nonexistent customers.

Gabbi finally started the process of filling the register. They never left the money in the drawer but instead tucked it safely away in the kitchen office. While their little Outpost didn't have much crime—if any—none of them could forget the stories of violence and theft throughout the rest of the Territories. Seven Outposts scattered across the Territories of the former USA, and this was the safest. It was harder to wrangle the crime in the larger Outposts, but here, most people wanted to work together and obey the rules. No one wanted any interference from the Territories' leader, Official Grant, to visit their small Outpost.

"Gabbi?"

She stuffed the rest of the money in their designated slots and closed the drawer before glancing over at her. "Yes?"

"Let's just bring in a few of the cakes for now." Worry lines creased her forehead. "We will just leave the rest in the kitchen."

"Good idea. I will go grab a few." Gabbi pushed through the swinging door and, once out of her mother's sight, closed her eyes and took a deep breath. Her sister's face flashed in her mind. *Renna, where are you and why didn't you take me with you?*

Gabbi was instantly ashamed of the unbidden thought. Her sister was so predictable. Stable. Dependable. Not a spontaneous bone in her body. If anyone were going to run away from the Outpost, it wouldn't be Renna.

It would have been her.

The sudden admission echoed in her thoughts until she had to bite her tongue to keep silent. Beads of sweat pooled around her hairline, and her knees shook as she moved away from the swinging doors toward the sink. She raised shaky hands and doused them in cold water, wiping handfuls across the back of her neck. *Pull yourself together, Gabriella.* There wasn't any way she could ever get up the courage to leave, but the idea sparked just enough of a flame that she desperately wished she could. What would it be like to leave the Gates behind? To have nothing but the blue sky and miles of earth beneath your feet?

Is that what happened to Renna? Did she have an urge to leave all of them behind? Did she think so little of her family and the Outpost that she could abandon everyone for whatever lurked outside?

No matter how mad she was at Renna, Gabbi couldn't believe—wouldn't believe—that her sister wanted that.

Because the only thing that awaited outside the Gates was death.

At least, that's what they were always taught. It's what was hammered into their minds at a young age. None of them ever wanted to venture out because of the cautionary tales of people who left and never returned.

"I thought you were bringing the cakes?" Mother's voice snapped Gabbi out of her reverie.

"Sorry. I needed a second to cool off."

"I don't blame you there." She crossed the kitchen and joined Gabbi by the sink. "I think I'll take some of that water."

Gabbi nodded and scooted out of the way of the faucet. She watched her mother for a few moments before finally moving to carry the cakes to the display cases.

"Thank you, Gabbi."

"For what?"

The water shut off, and Mother sighed. "For always being by my side and helping me. I may not always say it out loud, but I'm grateful for everything you do for your father and me." Her eyes filled. "For this bakery."

A stab—directly to her heart—would have hurt less than her mother's words. Wasn't she just moments ago, wishing she could trade places with Renna? Be free of the Gates for once and all? She would rather face death for the chance to see open skies than stay safely protected behind the walls. She didn't deserve her praise.

Gabbi found herself meeting her mother's outstretched arms and wrapping herself in a hug. What emotions must Mother be feeling? Her child was missing, and all Gabbi could do was dream of running away while condemning Renna for the same choices.

They might never see Renna again. Here Gabbi was thinking the worst of Renna when the simple fact was that she might not get to come home. Tears pricked her eyes, and she willed them away. Now wasn't the time to become a mess.

"My sweet girl." Mother leaned back and wiped a tear from Gabbi's cheek. "Why don't we go enjoy some lunch? Preferably something that doesn't require us to turn these ovens back on."

"That's a good plan." Gabbi sniffled and wiped her tears. "I'll bring the cakes out and join you in the dining room."

She waited until her mother was out of the kitchen before moving towards the confections. She would have to get her emotions under control and figure out the best way to help her family. But she wasn't sure what a nineteen-year-old girl could do from the confinements of her family's bakery. Especially when Father was home alone, ill, and the entire community was shut off from everyone else.

There had to be a way she could find out what happened to Renna. Someone connected to the Monitors who could help her. A teenage girl—a Speaker no less—doesn't up and disappear into thin air. Speakers were heavily protected. Highly valued; the Territories elevated the Speakers to almost a royalty status. The entire Outpost cared for them as if their own children.

It annoyed Renna and elicited the tiniest bit of jealousy in Gabbi. But now ... maybe that would work to their advantage. There had to be someone with information. Maybe someone spied Renna in the meadow last night. But that in itself would be another mystery. How could she be out of the Gates after curfew? Did she just not get back in time before the sirens blared and they locked again?

Had she gotten lost in the forest? Another problem altogether. Guards with weapons patrolled the forest at all times. Only Runners could come and go. Well, and the Territory Officials, but their visits to the Outpost were incredibly rare. There had to be something extremely wrong for them to leave the Headquarters. They chose to rule with an iron fist from afar.

Gabbi balanced the tray of decorated cakes on her arm and left the stuffy kitchen behind. Mother fidgeted with the intercom system. No doubt making sure it was working so they wouldn't miss the update declaring the lockdown over. This worry and strain couldn't be good for her mom. Once she started worrying about something, it seemed to slowly spread and cause her to lash out at everyone around her.

It was moments like this, when Gabbi could see the concern etched into her mother's face, that she had a hard time not being angry at Renna. How could she do this to their mother? There had to be a way to find out what happened and where she went. For Mother's sake, and her own sanity, Gabbi needed to figure it out.

7

Day Two

Renna wasn't sure what she expected the camp food to be like, but she was pleasantly surprised to find it piping hot and similar to the food she was accustomed to at the Outpost. Pancakes with maple syrup and two thick slices of bacon were handed to her when she walked into the dining hall. Her stomach welcomed the sight and she scarfed down the food in record time, all the while keeping an eye out for Miles. But he was nowhere to be found.

The open stares that graced her arrival the day prior were now just pleasant smiles and quick, curious glances. It was nice to sit by herself, with no one going overboard with their conversation, hoping to catch a few minutes of her time. At home, Renna didn't have much, if any, time to herself. An Outpost's Speaker was such an elevated position; it seemed everyone around her felt they had to talk to her. But deep down, Renna knew they didn't desire to converse with a seventeen-year-old girl, let alone to feign interest in her replies.

She finished her pancakes with one more big bite and put

away the dishes in an open container near the door. She followed an older couple through the door but stopped once they turned towards a row of cabins.

Where was Miles?

After Elaine patched her up, he left the medical building in a hurry and then was quiet all through dinner. He barely mumbled *goodnight* to her as he showed her his room, grabbed a stack of blankets, and then went to one of the infirmary beds. When she awoke this morning, he was already gone, and Elaine had a line of patients out the door.

Renna couldn't just stand in the middle of the camp. It would draw too much attention, and that was the last thing she wanted. She glanced around the camp one last time and started the walk back to the infirmary. Maybe she'd simply missed Miles when she went to breakfast. At the very least, perhaps she could busy herself helping Elaine until he showed up.

If Elaine didn't need help, she could prop her foot up to rest. Even though Elaine had padded her injured foot and loaned her a worn pair of leather boots, each step still sent a stab up her leg. This would be a long walk; the infirmary was all the way across the camp. To compensate for the ache, she hobbled, trying to work around the pain the best she could.

So much for trying not to draw attention to herself.

Renna half hopped, half walked to the nearest bench and plopped down, reminding herself to take deep breaths and push through the pain. She should have accepted the crutches.

Gabbi always told her she was too stubborn. But Renna hated to look weak.

The longer she sat, the more she tried to work up the willpower to stand and start walking again. A steady stream of people entered the dining hall. A few lingered outside, but Miles was still nowhere in sight.

Sighing, she stood and continued down the wooden sidewalk as angry voices carried out of the next building. Renna was almost past when she overheard her name. What in the world? Someone was talking about her, and they weren't happy. Straining to listen, she leaned towards the voices but couldn't quite make out what they were saying.

The mention of her name might have prompted her to move closer, but curiosity made her slowly peek through the window.

Two men stood on opposite sides of a large walnut desk. The man behind the table was tall, with wide shoulders, and carried himself like he was used to getting what he wanted. His face was hard and cold, but the wrinkles around his eyes suggested he was older than her father. The other male had his back to Renna, but she recognized his voice.

Miles.

The older man rounded his desk and sat down on the corner of it in front of Miles. His face was a blank slate as he spoke, and Renna couldn't quite make out what he said. Something about the rules.

A nod in return from Miles, and then he was gesturing with his hands, his tone rising in pitch, clearly agitated. The other man remained stoic as Miles ranted.

If only there were a better way she could hear their conversation, but the window was a straight shot to where they were sitting. All the man had to do was glance in her direction, and she would be discovered. She moved back out of view, resting against the building.

This was stupid. Anyone walking down the street could see her, and all she could hear were snippets of the conversation. It accomplished nothing, and what good would it do her to understand their conversation? It wasn't worth the risk of getting caught eavesdropping.

Her curiosity was simply trying to get the best of her. Again.

Pushing off the wall, she stepped towards the sidewalk, her foot protesting against the pain. She would have to hop back to the bench and wait for the throbbing to calm down. Shouts from inside the building startled her mid hop. The commotion drew her gaze away from the walkway to the front door, which swung open with such force that it crashed against the wall. Renna tried to right her balance, but her good leg buckled, throwing her toward the ground. She held her breath, bracing for the impact of smashing into the sidewalk.

"Watch out!"

Two hands grabbed her around her waist and stopped her descent, mere inches from the wooden planks.

"Are you all right?"

Mortified, Renna glared up at her rescuer. "I will be if you let me up."

"Renna! What are you doing here?" Miles helped her stand and let go, but she clamped her hands around his forearm.

"Wait, just a moment, please."

His face softened, and his gaze swept down to her foot that she held in the air. He nodded, wrapping his arm back around her waist for support.

"I think I may need those crutches after all." She grinned up at him, and he laughed.

"Come on, let's go see what kind of damage your stubbornness caused to your foot."

The walk back to the medical cabin didn't take nearly as long as it would have if she had to hobble back all alone.

He claimed a seat next to the first examination bed and unlaced her boots. "Let's see that foot." Renna grimaced as he gently pulled off her sock and revealed a red stain. "You seem to have opened it some." He ran a hand over his face and leaned back in the chair.

"Hey, are you okay?"

"I'm fine."

"You don't look fine."

"I don't think you need more stitches, but just more

padding." He focused his gaze on her and narrowed his eyes. "And crutches. No more walking on it until it heals."

She bit her bottom lip. Crutches would make it harder to walk through the woods and back home. "How long until I can walk without crutches?"

"Probably a couple of days."

A couple of days? She didn't have that kind of time. Today was already day two. Two whole days away from her people. Had they already been forced to stay indoors? What would happen to them if they couldn't get out for food? For the healer?

She needed a distraction. "Who was that guy you were talking to?"

Miles's head snapped up from repadding her foot. "You were spying on me?"

"I wasn't spying."

He raised an eyebrow at her statement, clean socks in hand.

"Okay, I wasn't ... until I heard my name."

Miles handed her shoe over. "What did you hear?"

She placed the boot back on her foot and made quick work of the laces. "Nothing, other than my name and something about rules."

"It's nothing to worry about." Miles opened a cabinet on the other side of the room and pulled out crutches. "I told Thomas I found you and that you want to go back to the Outpost."

"You sounded angry."

"These are the shortest ones I could find." He handed over the supports with a grin.

"Ha-ha." She eased off the bed and then put them under each arm. She wouldn't give him the satisfaction of letting him know they fit perfectly. "Back to your angry shouting."

"There wasn't any shouting."

"Come on, Miles. You can't fool me. You were livid, and you said my name. Doesn't seem like a coincidence."

"Look, we have rules just like your precious Outpost. We have jobs, a board of Leaders. But Thomas is the top of that board. What he says goes."

A sudden spark of fear hit her, and she instinctively fiddled with her necklace. "Does he know who I am?"

Miles covered her hand with his. "No, I don't think so." He gestured for her to tuck the pendant back in its hiding place. "But he doesn't understand why you want to leave."

"Did you tell him that I have to get back to my family?"

"Yes, and I think that's why he's concerned. Most people who come here, Renna, do not care about whom or what they are leaving behind."

"That's terrible. How can you just leave your family?"

Hurt flickered across Miles's face before it was replaced with a cold stare. "Not everyone has the perfect life." He pointed to where her silver S dangled. "And then chooses to run away from it on a whim."

She winced at his use of her position like it was something shameful. "That's really what you think of me?" Tears pricked the corners of her eyes, but she willed them not to fall. "No one has a perfect life, Miles. I'm not that shallow to pretend otherwise."

She took a couple of shaky steps towards the door, not quite getting the hang of the crutches. She yanked it open and then glared back at him. "And for your information, I didn't run away." She narrowed her eyes even more. "You tackled me."

8

"What did those towels ever do to you?"

Miles loosened his grip on the cotton fabric and let it fall back into the pile of laundry. "Sorry, Elaine."

She dropped a basket of clean sheets on the ground and leaned against the counter. "Are you going to tell me what's wrong, or do I have to drag it out of you?"

"I'm fine."

Elaine let out a chuckle and gestured to the shelves. "So that's why my infirmary towels are all rolled and stuffed in the cabinet like a four-year-old helped?"

He pulled out the offending towels and started folding them in half. "I didn't even realize I was doing that."

"Obviously, a certain brunette has your head somewhere else." She raised an eyebrow. "Is it because she's been hanging out with Benjamin and the other teenagers?"

Miles refrained from rolling his eyes. "No, it's not because of Benjamin." Did Elaine think he was jealous of a stable boy? It's not like his name was Westley.

"Well, lunch was a little tense today."

"You noticed?"

"I've had awkward conversations before, but you set the record for the most boring one."

"Boring is an exaggeration."

"Excuse me, I will amend my assessment." She tried to cover up her laugh with a cough. "It was the politest luncheon that I have ever attended."

"Is that a bad thing? One of your favorite selections from the Books of the Past is meal etiquette."

"No. But table manners were the only thing exchanged today. There was no discussion at all. And you enjoy the romantic comedy sections, but I won't tell your secret."

Miles rubbed his face and sighed. It was the most awkward meal he'd ever had. Every time Elaine asked Renna a question, she would answer, but she ignored Miles completely. After trying a few times to get her to talk, he gave up. "She's a little upset with me."

Elaine gasped. "Well, I never would have guessed. Especially with the way you bolted out the door after the dishes were cleared."

"Come on, stop teasing me." Miles sighed, stacking the towels correctly in the cabinet.

"I would, but it's just so easy." She gave him a warm smile and reached over to squeeze his arm. "Okay, I'm sorry. What's going on?"

What could he say that wouldn't give too much away? The last thing he wanted was to drag Elaine into his mess. It's not like he could openly tell her about Renna's job at the Outpost. "It's complicated."

She hesitated a moment before grabbing a sheet out of the wicker basket. She shook out the linen and passed one side over to him. "That clears it up a little bit."

He stepped back, smoothing out the edges to find the corners. "I thought you said you weren't going to tease me?"

"I never said that—you did."

"Elaine—"

"Fine. I won't tease you." She frowned, worry lines creasing her forehead. "I just don't like to see you upset."

Elaine would be the upset one if she found out that he insulted Renna. Guilt already weighed him down, and he didn't want her disappointment added to his burden. Miles joined his side of the sheet to Elaine's and let her finish the fold. "We just got into a little bit of an argument. I'm sure it will pass."

She set the sheet on the counter and grabbed another from the pile, holding out his end. "Has she met with Thomas yet?"

The fabric slipped through his fingers, and he jerked his head up. "Why would she meet with Thomas?"

"Really, Miles—honestly." She sighed, gesturing to the sheet on the ground. "Your head is in the clouds today. Everyone must meet with Thomas at some point."

"You're right. They do." Relief washed over him, and he hurried to pick up the sheet. He had to get his nerves under control before he slipped up. "No, she hasn't yet." Before they could formally join the Forest Community, each person had to meet with Thomas. He would ask them a whole list of questions, assess their strengths and weaknesses, and delegate them a job.

"Where do you think they will assign her?" Elaine grabbed the last sheet and an end toward him. "Has she mentioned what she did in the Outpost? What are her skills?"

"We haven't talked about that yet."

Elaine sighed. "You have to know something, Miles—you brought her here."

"Yes, I did."

"Where is she going to live?" Elaine arched an eyebrow. "She's under eighteen, right? She'll need a temporary steward."

"That's for Thomas to decide."

Elaine nodded and set the folded linen on the growing pile.

"True. We have a few older women who would be a good choice. I can speak to one of them if you would like."

"There's no reason to do that."

"Why?"

"Because it's not our decision!" Miles flinched as soon the words flew out of his mouth. Elaine didn't deserve his irritation, and he certainly wasn't doing a good job at avoiding suspicion. "I'm sorry, Elaine. I'm sure Renna would be happy to have you help find her somewhere."

"Renna's really gotten to you, hasn't she?"

"You have no idea." Miles's voice rose in agitation. "She's the most infuriating girl—" The clickety-clack of metal hitting the floor stopped him from continuing.

A girl's snicker came from behind, and Miles turned around to see two other teens from the Forest Community standing beside Renna. The boy was pale and holding a bloody rag to his palm.

What was it about this girl and bad timing? She constantly caught him at his worst. *Good going, Miles.*

"Did you slice your hand again, Roger?" Elaine asked, grabbing her apron.

"Yes, he did." The girl sighed. "Cook had him chopping vegetables."

"Miles, apologize and fix it." Elaine hissed under her breath as she brushed past him to check on the new arrivals. "Let's go take a look." She gestured for them to go into the other room and walked over to her supply cart.

He waited until Elaine and the others were out of earshot before taking a step toward Renna. "Look, I'm sorry—"

A flicker of hurt flashed across her face.

"About everything—"

Renna stared at him for a moment—her gaze nothing but ice—before she finally raised her chin slightly and walked away from him.

Again.

9

Day Three

Renna couldn't stand another tense meal with Elaine and Miles, so she got a sandwich from the kitchen and ate in silence in the barn. Well—almost silence. Toby munched loudly in her stall, occasionally stamping a hoof or flicking her tail.

Before long, Renna abandoned her measly supper and joined Toby at the stall gate, extending a hand to pet her nose.

"You can brush her if you want."

Renna glanced up in surprise, banging her elbow on the wooden door as she retracted her arm.

"I'm sorry. I didn't mean to startle you." A boy stood beside her, a brush in hand.

"It's okay ..." Her voice trailed off as she scrambled to come up with his name. He was one of the teenagers she met earlier in the day.

"Benjamin."

"That's right—I'm sorry. I'm trying to remember everyone's names."

"I'm sure it's a little overwhelming." He joined her at the stall door. "You want to help me with her grooming?"

"Sure." She stepped back with her crutches and waited until Benjamin led Toby out and secured her to a post. He passed Renna a brush, and she started on Toby's back, enjoying the calmness it brought.

"It's nice, isn't it?"

She glanced up from the horse and smiled. "It is. Is this what you do every day?"

"Yes. There's several of us that care and tend to the livestock."

They had livestock at the Outpost, but the horses there were for pulling farming equipment, not for riding. They fell into peaceful silence, and Benjamin let her braid Toby's mane.

"You're a natural." He stopped working and sent her a grin. "Should I be worried about my job?"

"I think your job is safe." She finished the braid and secured it. "Have you always wanted to work with horses?"

"Yeah, I guess you could say that. I grew up mucking stalls with my brothers." He laughed. "Okay, that part is not so enjoyable, but everything else is. What about you? What do you like to do?"

Renna froze. Why did she have to ask such a personal question? Renna hadn't planned what to say if someone asked her the same. Licking her chapped lips, she searched for something she could mention that would resemble some sort of the truth. She patted Toby's side. "My family are bakers."

"Really? That sounds exciting."

"That's one thing I sometimes miss." A voice interrupted from behind her. She turned around to see the same man that argued with Miles.

"Hey, Thomas. What brings you out here?" Benjamin asked, unhooking Toby and leading her back into her stall.

Renna didn't know whether to stay where she was or try to slowly hobble out of the barn.

"Good afternoon, Benjamin. I need to reserve a couple of the horses for a trip."

A trip? Renna's pulse quickened as her mind whirled with possibilities. What would one do on such an adventure? She hadn't had the chance to ask Miles what all went into his ventures out in the forest.

"Sure. Let me get the ledger." He slid the bolt into place on Toby's door and then flashed her a grin. "Be right back."

Don't leave me with him. Squashing down her fear, Renna slowly eased out of sight, hoping Thomas would forget her presence.

"Renna, right?"

She took a deep breath and did her best to keep her expression calm as she turned around. "Yes."

"Miles mentioned he found you on a scouting trip."

She nodded. "He did."

"What do you think of the Forest Community so far?" He flashed her a dazzling smile, and Renna could instantly see why he was the encampment's leader. He oozed charisma. At least this question wouldn't require her to lie. She hated the practice, and she wasn't any good at it.

"It's nice. I've enjoyed staying with Elaine and meeting everyone."

"Elaine is great, isn't she?" He cleared his throat. "We are delighted to have a healer here."

"Yeah, I bet."

"Well, you should be—" He gestured to her foot. "Glad that we had Elaine here to help, that is."

Her cheeks burned. "I'm very grateful to her for all of her help."

"How does one end up in the forest without shoes?"

How was she supposed to answer that? Not even Miles

pressed her for an explanation. "I ... wanted to run ... without my shoes on."

Thomas's brow furrowed. "You wanted to go without shoes in the forest?"

"Yeah, you know—it had just rained—and I wanted to feel the mud." Now her cheeks flamed, and sweat tickled her hairline. While it was the truth, it wasn't a reasonable answer for someone supposedly wanting to flee the Outpost. Leaving couldn't come fast enough.

"I can't say that I ever wanted to squish my toes in mud." There it was again—a charming grin. Was he used to that working on people? Did they not see through his pretense? Surely they didn't think him sincere. Of course, they must have if he was their leader.

"Well, it wasn't the best thought-out plan."

"No, I dare say it wasn't." His smile was still firmly in place, but his tone hid something else entirely. Renna couldn't put a finger on it exactly, but it unnerved her.

She forced a smile in return and opened her mouth, but Benjamin walked out of a nearby room with a large leather book in his hands.

"I'm back." He flipped the book open, and Renna had never been so happy to see someone in her life.

"Wonderful." Thomas pulled his gaze away from her and toward Benjamin, and she slowly started walking away.

"Oh, Renna—"

She paused, plastered a smile on her face, and turned. "Yes?"

"We will talk soon."

She nodded and whirled back around as fast as she could on the crutches and fled the barn.

10

Three days.

Gabbi hadn't seen her sister or father for three very long and miserable days. Nor had she stepped one foot out of the bakery. The intercom remained silent. Not a crackle or burst of static to show that Renna had made it back to the Monitors. In fact, not another word uttered since the initial lockdown, and Gabbi was weary of waiting for further instructions.

How long could they keep going without any word?

They stopped baking cakes after the first day. What was the point in making fancy sweets when they wouldn't be able to sell them? They were, however, making small batches of food that wouldn't easily spoil. Just enough for the three of them—although Gabbi didn't know how to get the food to her father. Mother had become quiet unless Gabbi asked her a direct question. She hated seeing her mother so sad. But there wasn't anything more she could do to help her.

Was there?

Gabbi glided a knife through the loaf of sourdough bread,

cutting two thick slices and piling them with cheese and turkey. They needed to use up all the loaf before it went stale.

Mother hid away in the small room at the back of the bakery. It was her father's office, and everything in the quaint space screamed her father, from the handcrafted shelves to the scratched wood floors. Gabbi rapped on the closed door and then stuck her head in. Mother glanced up at Gabbi and then back down at the black leather book open in front of her.

The ledger.

A handwritten list of every customer who had ever walked through the bakery's doors—name, household number, and housing number. Line after line.

Gabbi pushed open the door and set the plate beside the book. Her mother absentmindedly picked up the sandwich and took a bite. At least she was still eating, but only when Gabbi took the time to prepare and place it in front of her.

"What are you doing?"

Her mother's voice rose in surprise at Gabbi's question. "Did you know we have three hundred people in this Outpost?"

Gabbi claimed the seat in front of her father's desk. "No, I didn't."

"And almost every family comes in here for bread."

"That's a lot of bread."

Mother frowned. "That's not counting all the soups, sandwiches, and other hot meals we serve."

A rush of fear washed over her as she processed her mother's words. The Outpost provided standard housing. It was adequate to meet all basic needs. Living and sleeping areas, but it lacked storage. Cabinet space and pantries were a rare privilege. Most people in the Outpost kept only small amounts of food in their homes—just the staples—and then relied on the bakery to provide their hot meals. Her stomach knotted just thinking about it. "There's a lot of hungry people."

"Yes." Mother looked up from the ledger. "And they are counting on us."

Anxiety turned to panic. "What do you mean?"

"We can't let them starve."

"What can we do about it? We can't leave, remember?" Gabbi crumpled a fist full of her apron. Her mother couldn't possibly be considering leaving the bakery. First Renna, and now her mother? What was going on with her family?

"The people are our responsibility, Gabriella."

"You mean because of Renna?"

Mother dropped her sandwich on the plate and dusted the crumbs from her lap. "No, I didn't mean your sister, but I suppose you are right to some degree. We are somewhat responsible—"

"We are not responsible for Renna running away. That's on her." She didn't mean for her words to carry such a bitter tone, but they did, and she couldn't take them back now. "I'm sorry."

"Regardless of what may or may not have happened to Renna ..." Mother's eyes filled. "We are still the primary source of food for many. If we don't do whatever it takes to help them, who will?"

Gabbi sat back in the chair, trying to process exactly what her mother was suggesting. Never mind how they would get the food to the people, but they would be going against the leadership of the Outpost. Going against the lockdown. Against everything they were to taught to believe, respect, and fear. To go outside the bakery was more than defying orders.

It was treason.

Her mother sat across the desk from her and talked about committing treason. Like it was an everyday occurrence. If they were caught, imprisonment—or worse, banishment from the Outpost. Life outside the Gates meant death.

Gabbi had to convince her mom this was a crazy plan. "If we get caught, we would never see Dad again." She tucked a stray strand of hair behind her ear and lowered her voice. "Or Renna."

"I know, but how can you ask us to stay here and hide when we have so much, and everyone else is stuck in their homes with nothing?"

How indeed? Gabbi thought of her father, the orphan girl who helped them each day, her best friend Willow. What if it was weeks before the ban was lifted? Months? What if Renna never came home? Were they just going to sit back and let everyone famish?

No, she refused to believe that the leaders would let three hundred people starve to death. "The Outpost is going to open back up."

"You don't know that, Gabbi. What if they take too long?" Mother's lip quivered. "What if people are sick? Like your father?"

Guilt washed over her at the mention of her father. Hadn't she just been thinking how much they needed to check on him? But the idea of leaving the bakery soured her stomach.

Was she that much of a coward? But what her mother spoke of was much larger and more dangerous than sneaking out to get her father.

"Remember the stories of what happened the last time someone defied the Outpost and the rules?" Gabbi fidgeted with the strings on her apron. What if something happened to her parents? Or the leaders took her away?

Spending a few wayward moments daydreaming about the freedom to escape these walls was one thing. However, to do it … and reap the consequences of being caught … She would be forced away from her home. She couldn't even fathom it.

"Of course, I remember." Mother stared past Gabbi for a few moments before clearing her throat. "There wasn't a single person unaffected by the events the summer of my fourteenth year. And even though it hasn't happened since, we can't let the possibility of it happening again stop us from doing the right thing."

"The right thing?" Gabbi wiped sweaty palms on her jeans. "It's not as simple as right or wrong. Is it?" Gabbi hesitated before entertaining her mother's treasonous thoughts. "Let's say we decided to do this, and we go to the businesses and houses. There's no guarantee they would even let us in. What if they ... they rat us out?"

Mother's hand shook as she picked up her mug. "I have to believe they wouldn't do that."

"But you don't know for sure!" Gabbi threw her hands up in the air. "In fact, they might be so upset about Renna that they turn us in out of spite."

She slammed her mug down on the desk, the tea splashing over the rim. "Our neighbors wouldn't do that." Her eyes filled. "They are probably terrified. How would you feel if it were us out there, all alone, with no food in our house?"

Mother was right. She would be scared out of her mind sitting at home, wondering when the ban would be lifted so they could leave. She would spend all of her time worrying if they would get another meal.

"Think about your father. And the orphanage. All those kids. How long do you think they will survive on the rations they keep in housing?"

"How would we even go about this? It's not like we can just march out the front door."

Her mom's eyes sparked with excitement, and she stood. "Come on, and I will show you."

11

"Where do you think you are going?"

Miles didn't even have to look up from the workbench to recognize the deep bass tone belonging to Keegan. Miles sighed and shot a look over his shoulder towards the front of the supply room.

"I'm taking a hunting trip."

"Well, that's stupid."

"Gee, thanks, Keegan." Miles ignored the burly man and reached for the first item that he piled up on the counter to start filling his backpack.

"It wasn't an insult, and you very well know it." Keegan reached in the bag and took out the items Miles had just placed in it. "For one, you are not a hunter, and two, it's not your job. So, you want to tell me what is going on?"

Miles didn't take the bait. "They could use the help." He re-filled the bag, hoping Keegan would drop the matter.

"Nah." Keegan took out the water skin that Miles just packed. "I don't buy it. What else ya got?"

Miles covered his bags with his hands attempting to stop Keegan from snagging more items, but Keegan was just a tad faster and slid his hands under the strap, gripping and pulling it from Miles's fingers.

"Keegan! Will you just stop?" Miles lunged for the bag again, but this time Keegan lifted it up, high above his reach.

"Nope." Keegan pulled a bag of deer jerky out of the pack, took a bite, and tossed the rest on the counter. "Not until you tell me what in the world is going on in that head of yours."

Miles closed his eyes and took a breath. "Can't a guy just have the urge to go out in the woods and hunt an animal?

Miles glared up at the man who was more of a father figure to him than a friend. Keegan meant well, but Miles was not in any mood to put up with his theatrics.

Keegan fell silent before finally shaking his head. "Sure. If that person were a hunter. Try again." He dumped out the rest of the contents from the backpack at their feet, food and clothing scattering along the ground.

"Keegan! What is your problem?"

"Evidently, you are." He crossed his arms and leaned against the table. "I don't think I've ever seen you go hunting, so I don't buy your excuse. Something else must be bothering you. And if I were a betting man, I would say it's because of a certain person you brought back to camp."

"This has nothing to do with Renna."

"I never said it was Renna. You've brought back lots of people to camp." Keegan cleared his throat. "But now that you mention it, I have seen her hanging around the other young people, and you were nowhere to be found."

He pointed his finger at the older man. "You are one frustrating man, Keegan."

A wide grin covered Keegan's face. "I've been told that quite often, but we aren't talking about me. What's actually going on? If you've upset her, all you have to do is tell her you're sorry and that she's right. Women like to know they're right."

If Miles weren't so irritated, he would laugh at Keegan's advice. It was true, though, that Renna hadn't spoken to him since their argument at the infirmary. The role of a Speaker was not one to insult, and to do so was a grievous offense. He didn't blame her for not talking to him. Miles just didn't think she would go to such extremes to stay away from him. "Renna is definitely mad at me, but that's not why I'm leaving." He bent to retrieve the back-pack and the contents on the ground. "I can't talk about it."

Each time he tried to apologize, she would turn and walk away. Dinner with her and Elaine was nearly unbearable, and afterward, she would visit with the other teenagers from the camp. He finally gave up.

Keegan cursed in frustration and pointed a beefy finger in Miles's direction. "I told you that signing up to be Thomas's right-hand Tracker would be a bad idea. What has he got you doing, boy?"

"Nothing!" Miles gestured for Keegan to lower his voice and then took a minute to look around the supply room, but luckily, no one else was within earshot. "Really, Keegan? Watch what you say; you never know who may be listening."

Keegan snorted. "I wouldn't have to if everything was on the up and up."

Miles started to reply, but Keegan continued. "You know, I never understood why you took this job anyway. You are always leaving the camp and risking your life—for what? To bring back a handful of people to the Forest Community?"

Keegan's words stung. But Miles could not figure out how to explain why he enjoyed his job, so he finally just muttered, "I like being out there, Keegan."

"There's more than just animals in the forest, Miles." Keegan's voice held more than just a warning. It reeked of assurance. Like Keegan understood firsthand what was lurking out there. Keegan placed a hand on Miles's shoulder and squeezed. "If I can't talk you out of this crazy job, at least promise me you will always be careful."

Miles searched his friend's face, trying to catch any glimpse that he would let his guard down. Miles wanted to question him, but Keegan wouldn't answer. He never talked about his past. No matter how hard Miles tried to pry it out of him. It hurt that Keegan wouldn't open up more, especially since Miles had always been upfront about his life before coming to the Forest Community.

Finally, he nodded. "I always am." If he wanted to start his journey, he needed to go.

Keegan stared at him for a few more seconds before giving him a small smile that morphed him back into the Keegan that Miles knew and loved. "So, why is Renna mad at you?"

"It's complicated."

"Most things that are worth it in life are complicated."

Miles sighed, reaching for the backpack, but Keegan intercepted it and put it over his shoulder.

He would never get to leave at this rate. "Fine. I said something I shouldn't, but it's more about the fact that she wants to go back to the Outpost."

"So what? You want her to stay?"

Frustration boiled to the surface, and Miles blurted out what he hadn't wanted to talk about in the first place. "I didn't say that. But she shouldn't even be here, Keegan. It's all my fault she's here and that she's hurt—and if anyone finds out who she is ... " He let his words trail off, knowing that Keegan could fill in the missing blanks. Panic threatened as he glanced around the room again. He shouldn't even be talking about this.

Keegan's eyes widened, and his face turned red. Anger lined his face, transforming him back into the irritated father figure again. "Miles, you don't have any sense at all, do you?"

Miles opened his mouth to reply, but Keegan cut him off. "Taking a Speaker away from the Outpost is like murdering a

Guardian! There are consequences for your actions, Miles. For you, for the Forest Community. You might have well as have turned yourself in."

"Keep your voice down."

"It's a little too late now, isn't it?" Keegan folded his arms across his chest. "Why didn't you leave her as soon as you figured it out?"

"I tried!" Miles shut his mouth and waited for a moment before starting again. The last thing he needed was someone overhearing their conversation. "I tried to lose her. She didn't have shoes on, so I took the longest and hardest way back here. But she kept following me. Then she fell, and I almost walked away." He peered up at Keegan and sighed. "I was so close to walking away. But I couldn't leave her there."

Keegan's face softened. "Of course, you couldn't. I didn't raise you to be heartless, Miles. That's Thomas's doing."

It was the first time Keegan had ever mentioned being a parental role in Miles's life. "If Thomas finds out about Renna—"

"He can't find out about her." Keegan hissed, his voice taking on a tone Miles hadn't heard before. "No one can."

"I know, I know." Miles nodded, avoiding Keegan's gaze, and tried to devise some way out of the mess he had made. But nothing he thought of would help. The only thing that kept coming back to him was that he shouldn't have ever brought Renna back with him in the first place.

Miles's heart raced as memories flooded his mind. Thoughts about his family, the one he'd had before coming to the Forest Community. He promised himself years ago he wouldn't ever leave anyone behind. Bringing Renna back to the camp fulfilled that promise, even though it now held dangerous consequences.

Keegan handed over the backpack and lowered his voice, his demeanor changing before Miles's eyes. "Here's what you're going to do. You're going to go find Renna and get her away from all those teens before she slips up and reveals who she is."

"And then what?"

Keegan didn't miss a beat. "You take her home."

Take her home? Was Keegan crazy? Didn't he know that Thomas would never allow Miles to take someone home? "Keegan, it's not that simple, and you know it."

"You messed it up; you fix it." Keegan lifted a finger and planted it on Mile's chest. He lowered his voice to a whisper, gaze steady but pleading. "Get. Her. Home."

Miles blinked, trying to figure out what hidden message Keegan couldn't bring himself to say. He started to open his mouth to ask, but Keegan frowned down at him and pulled his hand away. "Always own up to your mistakes, Miles. Do the right thing."

"Seeing and doing are two very different things." He should help Renna, but actually getting Renna out was something he didn't know if he could do. "It's not always so easy to put into action."

Keegan shook his head. "No, it's not."

"Have you always done the right thing?"

Keegan's gaze drifted away from Miles for a moment before returning. "If I did, I wouldn't let you and Renna go out in the woods all alone." He gave Miles a small grin. "But I can tell this is something that *you* have to do on *your* own. So just do me a favor and come back in one piece."

12

Gabbi stared at the tunnel door in the storage room, her stomach churning at the thought of using it. She had a hand-drawn map from her great-grandfather in her hands, a backpack of supplies, and a flashlight. Now she simply needed the courage to climb down the stairs and get her father. It was crazy, scary, and a recipe for disaster.

So, what could possibly go wrong?

After the initial shock of her parent's secret—her grandparents had covertly built an underground tunnel—started to fade, her mother launched into a discussion on what they would do first. Obviously, that included rescuing her father before she began the impossible task of feeding the people in the Outpost.

But Gabbi couldn't get her legs to move.

There was no telling what lurked down in those tunnels after all the years of neglect and unuse. Pair that with the earthquake they had fifteen years ago—something Mother told her after she agreed to go down the dark passageway—and who knew what kind of damage there might be. The tunnel could be blocked off in places, and if that were the case, they were back to square one.

Gabbi gripped the straps of her backpack and took in a shaky breath. She agreed to go for her father, so she had to move. Any second, Mother would come through the cellar door and expect to go with her.

Even though Gabbi had argued—until she nearly lost her voice—Mother was adamant she would accompany Gabbi on this crazy journey. There was no way Gabbi would let both of them sacrifice themselves. She would never forgive herself if something happened to her mother.

She grabbed the small flashlight off the desk and clicked it on. She placed it in her pocket, with the light shining toward the ceiling so she could keep her hands free to pull the tunnel door open and closed. Gabbi was down a couple of stairs before she remembered the note she had hurriedly written. She climbed back to the top and propped it up on the barrel. Hopefully, her mother would do as she asked and not follow.

The stairs were steep, and Gabbi had to grip each rail to navigate. Each step creaked, and she did her best to keep a steady pace. Everything in her wanted to sprint to the bottom, but the stairs were so old; what if they were rotted?

Relief washed over her as her feet finally touched flat ground. She wiped her palms on her jeans before pulling the flashlight from her pocket and the map from her bag.

Mother was correct. The tunnel webbed through half of the Outpost and connected to the main businesses. But how was she going to get to the residential houses? Even if the business owners let her in and didn't immediately contact the Officials, it's not like she could walk out their doors. If that were the case, she would have left the bakery three days ago.

But that was a problem for later. She had to make it to her house and get her father to the bakery. One step at a time. Gabbi sighed and examined the map again. According to the sketches, to even get to her house, she would have to follow the passageway towards the Butcher Shop.

Satisfied but still uneasy, Gabbi followed the tunnel, keeping her flashlight directly in front of her. The small beam did not illuminate as much as she'd like, but it was better than nothing. Her skin crawled at the idea of navigating the dirt floor and narrow passageway without a light.

Dust and grime were everywhere, caking the walls and clinging to the air. The moisture tickled her nose, and it wasn't long before she was itching and had a full-fledged sneezing attack. She wasn't one to get easily scared, but the low ceiling and narrow passageway creeped her out.

Every now and then, she stopped to pull the map out, but it didn't clue her in on how long she had to walk to reach the center. Before long, though, other tunnels started coming slowly into view. As she neared the first one, she paused and peeked down it, but it was dark and quiet.

The next one to the right was also empty, but a beam sagged in the third and debris filled the entryway. Double-checking the map, she glanced at the passageway, relieved it wasn't the Butcher's.

But the Orphanage was down that corridor.

Her stomach flip-flopped. She wanted to go to the orphanage first. And now, she would have to clear the debris before attempting the dark tunnel. Even if she could clear the fallen items, how safe would it be?

Gabbi continued, trying to push the worry away for now. That would have to be something she solved once she got her father back to the bakery.

What if she wasn't able to get to him? Round and round, her thoughts cycled. Ugh, she was driving herself crazy. She had to keep pressing on regardless of what would happen, and she needed to force her mind to stop worrying.

Another tunnel came into view, and she rushed past it,

eager to get to the end. One more, the tunnel she needed should be next. As she neared the right passageway, her stomach churned, and her heart raced. This couldn't be happening. Not when she was so close. Her gaze swept over the mess of broken timber and stones.

The tunnel was blocked.

"No!" She reached the tunnel, her mind whirling in a hundred different directions. She could still do this. She could still get through and get to her dad. She just needed tools, gloves, and another set of hands.

Gabbi needed help. There wasn't any way she could clear this debris without her mother.

Or was there?

A stream of light toward the bottom of the pile caught her eye. It came through a hole about the size of her head. She got to her knees and hesitantly stuck her hand through the opening, feeling around the hole to see if anything was blocking the other side. It appeared as if someone began digging but stopped. Perhaps this would be the best spot to start? Or what if they stopped because it was unsafe?

She grazed something solid, but it didn't feel hard like wood; rather soft and clammy. It felt like … flesh.

What in the world? She yanked her arm back, but cold fingers clamped around her wrist.

13

"Help ... help me."

The words were strained and difficult to hear, but there was no denying the voice. Relief mixed with panic as she dropped to her knees. "Dad!"

"Gabbi? Is ... that you?"

"It's me." She flattened to the ground, trying to look through the hole, but all she could see were scraps of clothing. What was Father doing in the tunnel? And more importantly, how long had he been trapped down here?

"I'm glad to hear your voice." He coughed, and the sound pierced her heart. It was deep, rough, and sounded like it hurt.

"What are you doing down here?"

"I could ask you the same thing." His voice sounded annoyed yet pleased.

"I was coming to get you and bring you back to the bakery. And you?"

"I had to check on my family." Tears pricked her eyes at the protective tone of her father's voice. Even sick, he risked his life to be with them.

"Mom said you were very sick. I can't believe you left home."

His laugh turned into a raspy cough. "It sounded like a good idea at the time. I never thought the tunnel would be blocked. I tried my best to clear it, but I didn't have the energy to keep going. I must have a fever."

Gabbi's stomach roiled at the thought of him stranded out in the tunnel, sick, hungry, and alone. "I'm going to get you out, okay, Dad?"

"You'll need help, Gabbi-girl. The beam and rock are wedged pretty tight."

"What should I do? Should I go get Mom?"

Another round of coughs came from the other side of the beams. Then silence.

"Dad, are you all right?"

"I think you may need more muscle."

"There's no one here but me and Mom. Where am I going to find more help?" Gabbi did her best to keep her voice calm, but panic began to set in. "What about the butcher? Can't you go back and get him?"

"I can't. That was my first thought too, but when I was straining to remove the debris, a beam shifted and hit my knee. I think I twisted it."

"Why didn't you tell me you were hurt?" She gaped back through the hole, but she still couldn't get a good look at him.

"Gabbi, I need you to stay calm. We will figure this out together."

Her throat burned, but she managed to whisper, "Okay."

"Did you bring the map with you?"

"Yes. It's in my pocket."

"Good." He paused before continuing. "Get it out and tell me what is around this area."

Sitting up, she reached for the map and spread it across her lap. "The tunnel you're in leads to the butcher's shop."

Gabbi squinted in the dim light. "If you're heading my way ..." She turned to survey the surrounding area. "Then it goes to the Blacksmith. Past the Blacksmith is the Orphanage." Panic welled up. "But it's no good, Dad. That tunnel is blocked."

Father was trapped.

Silence hung in the air—as thick as the dust circling around her.

Dropping the map, she leaned back to the hole. "Dad?"

"The Blacksmith." Father's voice was almost too low to understand. "Cole and his son should be able to help ..." Another coughing fit took over, but he finally continued. "They will have the necessary tools."

"What if they don't want to help, Dad? What if they turn me in? You and Mr. Riley haven't exactly been on the best of terms."

"I know, but when it comes down to something that truly matters, he won't leave us stranded."

Gabbi traced the passageway on the map with her finger, skimming over the other places. Surely there was somewhere else, somewhere safer. "I think a thirty-year feud is something that matters as well. You think he will just set that aside?"

Movement and then more coughing came from her father's side of the tunnel. "There was a time when Cole and I were friends."

Gabbi laughed. "Yeah, before you stole his girlfriend."

"I did not steal his girlfriend. Your mother had already broken their engagement."

"You never told me they were engaged." She rolled her eyes. "No wonder he's held a grudge. And you know, growing up in school, his son always ignored me. Now I know why."

"Boys do that when they like a girl." Father's voice grew quiet again. "Gabbi, we need help."

"I know." She stuck her arm through the hole and squeezed

her father's hand. "I'm going to get them to come. Even if I have to promise free cakes for life."

Father laughed, but the action only set off another series of coughs. "Don't you dare. Your mother would have a fit."

"You're worth it." She gave him one more squeeze and then hoisted herself off the floor. "I'll be right back."

"Be careful."

She climbed to her feet, dusting off the dirt and grime before heading back in the direction of the Blacksmith's tunnel.

What was she going to do when she got there? Knock and hope someone answered? Should she turn the handle and go in? Gabbi found the correct tunnel, her mind running through possible scenarios, all ending with her being carted off to the Guardians of the Outpost.

It wasn't nearly as long as the passageway to the bakery, and before she was ready or had a solid plan in place, she was climbing the stairs to the trap door. Each one creaked underfoot, and her sweaty palms slid over the railings.

A chuckle worked its way to her lips at the thought of her appearance. Dust and dirt no doubt clung to her clothes and skin. And there was a moment back in the tunnel when she had walked through a spider web.

The trap door appeared a lot like the one at the bakery, and she wondered where it would be located in the Blacksmith shop. What if they were in another section of the building and couldn't hear her? What if they refused to help her?

Her breath started hitching in her throat, and Gabbi closed her eyes. She took in a deep gulp, held it, and then let it out slowly. She didn't have the luxury of what-ifs. She wouldn't take no for an answer. Not when her father's life hung in the balance.

Gabbi raised her fist to the door and knocked.

And waited.

Knocked again.

Gabbi felt stupid, standing underneath a possibly-defunct trap door, waiting for someone to open it. Putting her ear up to the wood, she strained to listen, to see if she could hear any movement on the other side of the door.

She sighed and knocked again, this time more forcefully. After a few seconds, a muffled voice grew louder, and then footsteps paused near the door. Gabbi debated on whether she should call out or knock again. Perhaps whoever was on the other side thought they were hearing things.

"Hello?" She called out, surprised at how calm and assured she sounded to her own ears. There was movement on the other side of the door, but Gabbi could not tell what they were doing.

"Hello?" She repeated, pounding again. Silence permeated the tunnel, and she was about to try turning the knob when the door swung open.

"What are you doing here?"

Gabbi took a step back and straightened, looking up at the Blacksmith's son, Zeke. Dust and grease covered his pants and shirt, but it was his green eyes that kept her attention. They were full of shock and amusement.

"Hi, Zeke. I'm Gabbi."

"I know who you are."

She nodded. Of course he did. They graduated from the small Outpost school the same year, and she was one of five girls in the entire grade.

He frowned and then glanced back over his shoulder, but she couldn't see what he was looking at. Finally, he turned towards her again. "We aren't supposed to be outside of our houses. If anyone sees you ..." His voice trailed off as he looked back behind him again.

Gabbi reached out and touched his hand, and he jerked his gaze back to hers. "I'm sorry, okay. I wouldn't have come, but I need your help. It's my dad."

His eyes widened. "Your dad is here too?"

She shook her head. "He's trapped under debris in the tunnel, and I couldn't get him out. Please, Zeke. I need your help."

He moved his hand out from under hers and nodded. "Stay here. I'll be right back."

"Thank you." She took in a deep breath and then released it. For the first time since stepping foot in the tunnel, she felt like she could breathe.

Zeke returned after an agonizingly long time, carrying a large brown duffle bag, with his father trailing behind him. Gabbi walked down the remaining stairs to flat ground and waited for them to join her.

"Gabbi, this is my dad, Cole."

She reached out to shake his hand. "Thank you, Mr. Riley, for your help. I'm really grateful."

He considered her outstretched hand before grinning and shaking it. "Come on, girlie, show me where he is."

She tried to keep her face blank as she pulled her hand away and wiped the grease on her jeans. "He's this way."

She led them down the tunnel and back to her father, explaining how he was sick and trying to get to them before he got hurt.

"Well, well, well." Mr. Riley called out, bending down, and looking at her dad through the hole in the debris. "Never thought this day would come."

"Oh yeah, and what day is that?" Her dad called back raspily. He coughed, and Gabbi's panic returned. They needed to get him out of there.

"The day you would finally sink so low that you had to ask me for help."

"Dad." Zeke cautioned, glancing at Gabbi. "Let's just get him out, okay?"

"No, it's okay, boy. Your dad's right. I have sunk as low as possible right now." He paused before laughing, a deep belly laugh broken by a fit of coughing. "Would be great, though, if you can get me out so that I can finally say to him what I've wanted to say for years."

"Well, why don't you say it now, old man?" Mr. Riley answered, holding a hand up to stop Zeke. "I, for one, would like to hear it."

14

Day Four

Her eyes flew open at the sound of her name whispered from the bedroom door, but before she could sit up to see who it was, calloused hands covered her mouth, keeping her from screaming.

"It's me."

She narrowed her eyes and pushed Miles's hands away from her face. "Really, Miles?" She sat up, pulling the tangled mess of the sheets up with her. "What is going on?"

"We have to go."

He couldn't be serious. She finally just got to sleep not long ago after tossing and turning. She yawned. "Now? It's the middle of the night."

Miles hurried over to his closet, pulling open the doors and throwing a few shirts and a jacket onto the bed at her feet before moving on to the dresser to grab socks and t-shirts. "I'm grabbing a few shirts for you too. They may be a little big, but it's the best we got right now."

"Wait. Tell me what's going on."

He crossed back to her side and then dropped to the floor and searched for something under the bed.

Did he finally get tired of her ignoring him? At first, she did it because she was hurt. His words about her abandoning her post hit home and stung. Obviously, she couldn't leave immediately because of her foot, and then, after a couple of days, she was ashamed they hadn't cleared the air from their fight. But she didn't know how to bring it back up.

She never expected that he would force her to leave, though. Especially at night.

"Miles, please." She swung her legs to the side of the bed. "I know you're still mad from the other day, but—"

He finished packing his bag and then knelt in front of her. His words were rushed and low, but his eyes never left hers. "We can't talk here. Get dressed and meet me at the far edge of the camp, opposite the side we came in with Keegan." He held out another backpack but didn't let go. "Put whatever you need in here." His gaze drifted from the bag to her throat. "I told you to hide that necklace. Do not wear it anymore."

"Miles, I don't under—" She stopped, seeing his face, a mixture of regret, worry ... and determination. Renna didn't know what spooked him so badly, but whatever it was, it couldn't be good for her. Especially if he told her to hide her necklace. She raised shaky hands, quickly unhooking the chain from around her neck. "Okay."

He sighed, relieved. "Give me a few minutes' head start. Don't talk to anyone. Better yet, don't let anyone see you." He squeezed her hand. "And be careful."

Too stunned to talk, she nodded, her thoughts whirling around in a tangle of possibilities. If he wasn't still angry at her and kicking her out, then what had happened? What had him so rattled and in such a hurry to leave?

Renna waited. The door clicked shut behind him before she

climbed out of bed. She gathered the few items Elaine had so graciously given her. An oval hairbrush, toothbrush and paste, and hair bands made up the small collection. She tossed them on the bed next to the pile of clothes Miles left for her. She picked up the shirts, running a hand over the soft, well-worn cotton before adding them to the bag. Next was a black leather jacket, and she hesitated before deciding to slide it on. She didn't know how fast a pace Miles would want to set out in the woods, and the last thing they needed was her slowing him down with scrapes from tree limbs and brush. She made quick but messy work of braiding her wavy hair. While her fingers were fast, they were also clumsy.

Packing took all of two minutes. The few items barely made a dent in the bag. She laced up her boots, careful not to pull too tight on her sore foot. It still ached but not nearly as much, and at least she shouldn't have to worry about it busting open anymore. Using the crutches had helped—as much as she didn't want to admit it to Miles.

Now, where to hide her necklace? The most obvious place was her bag, but she wanted it on her. It was silly, but the idea of not feeling the cool metal against her skin made her uneasy. She rolled up her pant leg, securing the chain around her ankle, before pulling her sock up over it.

Satisfied, she put the backpack on and paused at the door. Had she let enough time pass? Surely he was already in place waiting for her. Renna crept out of the bedroom, down the hall, and across the infirmary, careful not to wake Elaine. The cold and crisp air made her glad for the impulse to wear the jacket. The late summer heat beat down in daylight, but at night, fall was in the air.

She zipped the jacket as she walked, and her bag bounced on her back as she moved throughout the camp, trying her best to stick to the outer fringes and the shadows. As much as the quiet unnerved her, it was the perfect time to leave unnoticed.

Every cabin was dark and silent, with the windows shut and curtains drawn.

As the edge of the camp came into sight, her heart raced with anticipation. One long light shone in the distance, just enough to illuminate a hole in the fence. She frowned as she neared, wondering if the people of the Forest Community knew about this hole or if Miles made it for them to slip out.

"Miles?" Her whisper barely left her lips before hands grabbed her arm and drew her back into the darkness.

"Did anyone see you?"

She placed her hand on her chest. Wishing the action could calm her racing heart. "Stop scaring me." She hissed, taking in a deep breath. "But no, I don't think so."

Miles gestured to the spot where she stopped. "You were standing out in the open."

"Maybe you should have been more specific in your escape plans." Renna adjusted the straps of her backpack, annoyed she didn't think about moving out of the lighted area of the camp.

"I'm sorry." He rubbed a hand over his face. "I know this may seem crazy to you."

She held up her thumb and index finger. "Just a tad."

He nodded and surveyed the area before continuing. "I don't think anyone noticed me either. But I don't want to wait around to find out."

"Okay, so we go through the fence?"

"Yes, but be careful. There's a reason we don't use this side of the camp very much."

"What's on the other side?" Renna had a feeling she probably wouldn't like his answer.

"A twenty-foot ravine."

"A what?" Fear coiled in her stomach at his words. Didn't he remember just a couple of days ago she cut her foot open in the forest? Now he thought taking her to the edge of a ravine was a good idea? "Please tell me we aren't going down the ravine."

"Not on purpose, we aren't."

"Why doesn't that make me feel better?"

"Just stick to the fence edge and slowly maneuver around it until we get to the clearing. The ravine angles away after a few steps."

"Oh sure, easy peasy." She waved her hand in the air before following him to the opening in the fence.

"I'll go first. Wait here until I'm in position, and then I will talk you through it."

Nodding, she slipped off to the side as Miles dropped to the ground and slowly went through the gap.

"Okay, your turn." Miles's voice came from the other side of the fence, but she could no longer see him. He was in complete darkness, and Renna was going in blind. She crawled over the hole and stuck her leg through, trying to mimic Miles's exact movements.

Except Miles knew where he was going and didn't have Renna's balance issues. Her foot slid over the rocky terrain as the rest of her body came through the opening. She quickly tried to stand, hoping that would stabilize her and she would at least be able to get back toward the fence. But it just left her more unbalanced, her arms flailing around, desperate to grab onto anything.

That anything ended up being Miles.

His free arm wrapped around her, and she clung to him, her hands shaking and her pulse thumping in her temples.

Miles smiled, his eyes crinkling in the corners. "You made it."

Laughter bubbled up inside of her as she leaned away from him. "I wasn't anywhere near the edge, was I?"

He laughed with her, dropping his arm. "No, but you kind of freaked out. What happened to waiting for me to help you up?"

"My foot slipped, and I thought I was going over."

"You still have about ten feet before that happens." He gazed down at her and raised an eyebrow. "Are you ready?"

Heat burned her cheeks once she realized she was still holding onto him. She took a step backward and nodded.

"Good. I want to put as much distance as I can between us and the guard towers. They change shifts soon."

Miles picked up his backpack, threading both arms through the straps before walking to the fence post. He retrieved a bow and a sheath of arrows from behind a fallen log. "Do you know how to use a bow?"

"No. Not really allowed at the Outpost."

He nodded. "That's right. Well, once we get a little farther out, I'll teach you. You never know when you may need it."

"What is out there, Miles?" Renna pointed out over the ravine, a chill hovering over her.

"All sorts of things, but nothing like what you've been taught to fear."

"What does that mean?"

He sighed. "That will take a while to explain, and right now, we need to get moving." He reached out and grabbed her hand. "Come on, let's get you home."

15

Never had Miles experienced the force of someone's anger so much as right now. Renna had evidently gotten over her initial shock of being woken up in the middle of the night, and now they were back to where they left off the other day. Although, if the situation were reversed, he would probably be angry too.

He had insulted her in the worst possible way, basically saying she would wish for her people to suffer. It was cruel and untrue. It only took half a day with her to confirm she was loyal and would never abandon her position on purpose. So why did he say it?

Stopping, he took a second to inspect their surroundings. Something about this area set him on edge. Had they ventured that far off his regular route?

"Why are we stopping?" Renna's voice came out in huffs. A quick once-over squelched his suspicion that she had hurt herself again; she was not favoring her injured foot.

"I think it's time for a break." He scanned the area, looking for a place they could rest and get a better look at their surroundings. "There." He pointed to a tree whose roots were large enough for them to sit while under the cover of the branches.

"I can keep going."

"I'm sure you can, but I need a minute." He opened his canteen and took a sip, careful to keep his face blank. The last thing he needed was Renna suspecting that he didn't know where they were.

Or did he?

There was something vaguely familiar about this section of woods. He didn't pick the ravine side of the camp on a whim. It was the surest way to guarantee no one would see them leave, but he couldn't shake the feeling he'd been there before.

"What's wrong?"

He shook his head. "Nothing."

"There's something you're not telling me."

He froze at her words, his thoughts swirling as he scrambled to come up with some explanation.

"Something is bothering you."

He sighed in relief. This he could easily come up with, and it wouldn't be a lie. "I just don't like having to leave in the middle of the night."

"Why did we?" She frowned. "Last time we talked, I got the feeling that taking me home was the last thing you wanted to do."

Ugh, this girl purposefully got under his skin. "I'm sorry about what I said that day. I shouldn't have insulted you." Her eyes softened at his words. "I realize you wouldn't have left your post on purpose."

"Thank you." A grin slowly spread across her face. "But that still doesn't answer my whole question."

He handed the canteen over to her. "Drink. I can't afford for you to get dehydrated out here."

She rolled her eyes but accepted the canteen. "You're

stalling. Why the sudden change in plans? Why are you taking me back home?"

"You wanted to go back. Would you rather go on alone?"

She sat a little taller at the change in his tone. "No. I was just surprised, that's all."

Miles shuffled through the contents of his backpack, hoping it made him appear to be searching for something instead of wracking his brain for how far they had drifted off the path. But if he was being honest, it was probably better not to be taking the direct route. At any time, someone could find them, and he would be forced to admit why they were out in the woods. Word would get back to Thomas—

He couldn't even finish the directions of those thoughts.

"Can you at least explain what you meant back at Elaine's? When you said there are things out here that I wasn't taught to fear?"

His hands ceased their rummaging. Did he say that? What was it about this girl that made him slip up time and time again? When it came to Renna James, he always said way too much. He reached out for the canteen, and she handed it over. "I just meant you never know what you're going to find out here, okay? Come on. We need to keep going."

Renna didn't press the issue but followed behind him, her footsteps crunching the leaves and fallen twigs. Maybe it was a good thing they had veered off track. She would no doubt draw in every dangerous obstacle their way.

"Can you walk quieter, please?"

"Why? Is there something out here you're afraid of?"

Of course, she was back to shooting daggers at him. He could feel them launch his way with every word. "I'm always afraid, Renna."

He glanced over his shoulder to find that she had stopped walking. "What?"

She shook her head and caught up to him. "I didn't think you were scared of anything."

"Doesn't everyone have fears?"

A shy smile tugged at the corner of her mouth. "Sure. But you're always so cryptic. I can't figure you out, Miles Butler."

"Well, when you do, let me know, because I can't figure myself out either."

"Do you have me figured out?"

"You seem to have the ability to scramble my thoughts, throw me off guard, and annoy me more than anyone else." The words were out of his mouth before he could censor them, and he didn't even have time to wonder if he upset her again because she burst into laughter. "Not the reaction I thought you would have. Why are you laughing?"

"I'm sorry, I'm not laughing at you. It's just something my father says to my mother. They annoy each other so much, it's rather comical."

"Wait, are you saying that I annoy you too?" Miles grinned, the frustration melting away with her laughter.

"If there's one thing you can believe, it's that you've annoyed me plenty."

Light flashed behind Renna, and he instantly raised a finger to his mouth to silence her. Her eyes widened in alarm, but she didn't say anything. "Don't move." He whispered, waiting for the beam of light to come back in their direction.

"What's wrong?" She mouthed the words, but he shook his head, waiting for the confirmation that he wasn't losing his mind. He definitely saw lights coming behind them.

He wasn't wrong. The beams swept back in their direction but were luckily still too far off to detect them.

He reached out and grabbed her arm. "I don't have time to explain. But we need to hide. Now." He tugged her along behind him, letting go when he was sure she was following him.

He quickly turned them more to the left, veering off the path but not so far they couldn't get back. They sprinted, no longer worrying about how loud they were. Miles was now more concerned about getting to a hiding spot. Somewhere not in the open. He shouldn't have taken her out at night. It was stupid, but he was desperate. Keegan's warning to leave immediately weighed heavier than what could be hiding in the woods for them.

Every few minutes, he glanced back to make sure Renna was right on his heels. She was doing a good job keeping up with him, but fatigue was starting to show. He slowed his pace but kept going. He needed her to keep pushing long enough for him to find shelter. They were making too much noise, and it wouldn't be long before more patrols were alerted to their presence.

They passed a strange grouping of boulders, and Miles realized why this area was vaguely familiar. He slowed his pace, turned back, and ran to intercept Renna. He pulled her to the right, past the boulders and deeper into the forest. If he could keep her going just a little bit longer, then he could get her into hiding.

"How much longer?" She gulped between shallow breaths, and Miles reached out to loop his arm through hers.

"Not long, now." He breathed in her ear, barely a whisper. "Lean on me." He moved his hand from her arm and wrapped it around her waist, pulling her towards him.

She complied, letting him help take the brunt of her weight off her injured foot. He didn't even want to think what they would find when they stopped and checked it.

"Just a little bit more." He grunted between gulps of air. His legs burned and sweat dripped down his back despite the crisp air.

Finally, he came to a stop in front of a hill encased with rock and sighed with relief. From the looks of the boulders and tangle of vines, it hadn't been used in years.

"Miles, this doesn't look like a place to hide."

"It is, trust me." He let go of her and hurried to the front of the hill, pushing back the vines and running his hands over the rough stone until he found one about two-thirds of the way down. "Come here, I need your help."

Renna hobbled to his side, and he nodded toward his hands. "Put your hands here with mine. We need to pull the rock out."

"Are you insane?"

"Come on, it hasn't been used in years, so I need your help to pull it free."

She hesitated, her eyes widening in terror as lights shone on the top of the hill. They had to hurry.

"Renna!"

She hurried to his side and placed her hands beside his.

"On the count of three. Ready?"

She nodded, and Miles took a deep breath and counted. "One, two, three!"

They pulled on the rock, and it shifted slightly, but not enough to pull free from its resting place. More lights joined the one above their heads. "Again!"

They pulled again and again until the rock finally gave way enough for Miles to reach in and push it further out. "Come on."

"We don't know what's hiding in there." Her voice shook. "It's going to be pitch black."

"It's better than what is heading in our direction. I promise."

She looked between the cave and behind them, and Miles was afraid that any longer and she would bolt.

Shouts came from all around them, the voices echoing off the rocks and trees. They were out of time. They had to hide, or Renna would never step foot in the Outpost again.

He used his free hand and cupped her cheek, forcing her gaze back on him instead of the forest. "Renna, I'm begging you to get in. I have a flashlight, but I don't want to use it until we seal the entrance."

Tears pooled in her eyes, but she nodded and scrambled behind the rock, and he was seconds behind her. He slid the rock into place, praying he was fast enough to close it without being seen.

16

"Mama!" Gabbi pushed open the trap door to the bakery, calling out again for her mother as she climbed into the room. She moved away from the door to give room for Zeke, who half-carried, half-dragged her father up the stairs.

"Gabbi, you found him?" Mother froze in the doorway, her eyes widening as she took in the group. "Is he okay? What took you so long? I was so worried."

"He was trapped in the tunnel." Gabbi got a chair from the office so Zeke could help him sit down. "He hurt his knee, has cuts and bruises, but I don't think anything is broken." Gabbi placed a hand on her father's forehead. "And he has a fever."

"What were you thinking, trying to get here by yourself?" She chastised before wrapping her arm around Father's shoulders.

"You know that I had ... to get ... to my girls." Father wheezed the words in between bouts of coughing.

"And you," Mother pointed at her, "I can't believe you left without me. What if something happened to you, and I didn't know?"

"I couldn't get Dad out by myself, so I got help. It took us a while to get him out." Gabbi gestured to the two very uncomfortable-looking men standing in the back of the small cellar to shift her mom's attention.

"Thank you, Zeke." Mother's eyes filled as her gaze landed on Zeke's father. "Thank you both."

Mr. Riley shifted his weight and cleared his throat. "I can help you get him settled."

"That would be very kind of you, Cole. He needs rest and medicine."

Mr. Riley nodded and leaned down to help her father up. "Lean on me, old man."

"Who are you calling an old man? You're older than me."

"By a month." The men continued to argue as they slowly made their way out of the room.

"Gabbi, please get our guests something to eat." Mother paused at the door. "Did they resolve their differences?"

Zeke chuckled. "Your guess is as good as ours. They went from arguing to teasing each other."

Mother sighed. "I guess that's progress." She left the door open and hurried after the two men.

"Come on, the kitchen is this way." Gabbi motioned for Zeke to follow her, and she led the way out of the office. "I have leftover vegetable soup that I can reheat, and I know we have some cold cuts for sandwiches."

"Sounds amazing. How can I help?"

"There's bread over there in the pantry. And you can get out plates and bowls for you and your father in the cabinet next to the refrigerator."

"Aren't you going to eat with me?"

Gabbi carried the soup over to the stove to heat and then stacked cold cuts and cheese on a platter. "I should probably go check on Father."

"Are you sure you want to be there for that awkward conversation?" Zeke shook his head and put three plates on the table. "For a minute there in the tunnel, I didn't think my dad was going to help."

She nodded in agreement. "And I wasn't sure Father would let him. What was it, like fifteen minutes to get them to stop fighting?

"At least. That's why I started moving the debris on my own."

She grabbed a ladle from the hook on the wall. "I didn't realize how stubborn my father could be."

"They certainly seem to have that in common."

Gabbi filled two bowls of soup and then handed one to Zeke. "I am really grateful that you helped. I didn't know what I was going to do if you refused."

"Honestly, I was afraid if I did, you would have shouted so loud, it would bring the Officials to our door." He raised an eyebrow. "But I have the feeling that you would have figured something out and gotten him out of there without any problem."

Gabbi followed Zeke to the table and took a seat next to him. "Well, that makes one of us." She couldn't get the image of Father out of her mind when they finally removed the last piece of wood. Never had he appeared so vulnerable, and it had taken everything she had to keep herself from falling apart right there.

Zeke took a sandwich off the plate and then passed it to Gabbi. "Why do you doubt yourself?"

She paused before placing a sandwich on her plate as well. "I don't guess I realized I do."

He took a bite of the soup before replying. "Even in school, you always acted like you couldn't believe how well you did. Even though you were the top of the class."

"We both know I wasn't the top of the class." Gabbi shot him an annoyed look. "You were."

He leaned back in his chair. "Oh, that's right. But you weren't far behind me."

"I didn't know you paid attention to anything outside your work."

He took another bite of the soup. "I always paid attention. It's you who never glanced my way."

Gabbi's cheeks burned. Was he joking? She scrambled to come up with some other topic, but her mind kept coming up blank.

"So, how are you able to have a house separate from the bakery?"

The tension left her shoulders. "We get that question a lot. It wasn't until after Renna was born that my family petitioned to turn the downstairs into a dining room. The Outpost went through a growth spurt, and the line was so long to get in that it was getting difficult to serve everyone in a timely matter. Since the remodel took away our living spaces, they agreed to let us move into a small apartment."

"And your family didn't have any trouble getting it approved?" Zeke's voice changed from curious to hopeful.

Gabbi swallowed another bite of the soup before answering. Most business owners had to live above their shops. "It took a year or so for them to finally listen to my father's proposal. Why do you ask?"

"It's just my father says that he petitioned first with a similar idea to expand the Smithy."

"But his didn't get approved?"

"Nope." Zeke frowned. "Another reason to hold a grudge against your family."

"I'm sorry, Zeke—"

Zeke reached over and touched her hand. "No, don't apologize. It has nothing to do with either of us."

The door to the kitchen swung open, and Zeke pulled his hand away as Mr. Riley and her mother entered.

"Thank you for the help, Cole. He should rest now that he's in bed."

"Of course, Grace. I will always do what I can for you." Mother stared at Mr. Riley for a few moments before she cleared her throat and turned her attention away.

"Gabbi? Did you get lunch ready?"

"Yes." She passed a plate to Zeke's father and then stood up to speak privately with her mother. "How is Dad?"

"He's weak, but I think he will be okay." She pinched the bridge of her nose and shook her head. "I don't know what he was thinking, leaving the house so sick. Thankfully, he grabbed the medicine box before he headed this way."

"Good. So, we have the fever reducer?" Relief flooded Gabbi at Mother's words. She was afraid she would have to go back to the house for supplies.

"Yes, I gave him some. I wanted to bring him some soup and see if he could eat a little bit."

"I can take it up to him, so you can eat." Gabbi grabbed a bowl from the counter and filled it halfway with the warm broth.

"Thank you, dear."

Gabbi pulled her mother aside, glancing over her shoulder to make sure Zeke and Mr. Riley were preoccupied. There was still one glaring problem that she couldn't shake from her mind. "Mama?" Gabbi lowered her voice anyway, just in case. "Can we trust Mr. Riley not to turn us in for using the tunnel?" She didn't get the feeling Zeke would say anything, but from what she'd heard of Mr. Riley, she wouldn't be surprised if he tried to alert the Officials as soon as he got home.

"Why would he say anything, dear?" Mother patted her arm and leaned in closer. "He's one of the few people who didn't fully close their end of the tunnel."

"What?" Gabbi took in a sharp breath and tried to put the pieces together. "How many people know about these passageways?"

"Every family who has a trap door helped build and operate the passages. The Rileys are no different. In fact, his family was one of the first to suggest the need for them."

Gabbi tried to reconcile what she perceived of Zeke's father with what her mother was telling her. But it was hard to see past the grumpy exterior of the man sitting a few feet away. Even harder was imagining her family and other business owners banding together to build something so rebellious. Right under the noses of the other people of the Outpost and the Officials. What would it have been like to be there in the middle of such a monumental moment in the Outpost's history? A history she didn't even know existed until a couple of days ago?

Of course, wasn't she doing the same thing as her ancestors? She defied the order of the Officials and left the bakery. Every moment since she stepped out the door, she was breaking even more rules. Rescuing her father, going to the Blacksmith's, talking with and feeding Zeke and his father in their kitchen.

Gabbi watched as Mother joined them at the table, nodding at something that Mr. Riley said. Her gaze shifted over to Zeke, and she wondered what he thought about all this. Did he realize how much their families had in common? Did he know they built the tunnels together?

"Gabbi, are you going to give that soup to your father?"

She started at her mother's question, and Zeke turned to catch her staring at him. He gave her a lopsided grin, and Gabbi had to force her gaze away from him long enough to collect her thoughts and focus on what she asked.

"Of course." She turned and fled the kitchen, hoping she

was out of the room before her face turned bright red. Gabbi could already imagine what Zeke would say the next time she saw him. No doubt he would tease her about finally paying attention to him or some other such nonsense. She now understood one thing. How easy it was to be frustrated with a Riley.

17

Darkness surrounded Renna. Her heartbeat thudded in her ears, and she tried to calm herself, but panic was quickly winning out. She turned toward the entrance as Miles slid the rock back into place. She concentrated on the light until it disappeared.

Renna waited for Miles to turn on the flashlight, breath escalating with each passing second.

Surely, her eyes would adjust, and she could see something. Anything.

Why wasn't he turning on the light?

Finally, she could make out his outline. Renna took a few shaky steps forward, holding out both hands, breathing a sigh of relief when she made contact with his jacket. She wrapped her arms around him and buried her face in his sleeve, inhaling the scent of woods and sweat.

A low chuckle followed. "Renna, I can't turn on the light if you have my arm pinned."

"I'm sorry." She leaned back so he could get his arms free, but she didn't let go of him. He would just have to deal with it.

There was no telling what lurked in the shadows, and she wasn't going to be standing alone when they attacked her.

"Are you going to let go?"

"Nope."

Another chuckle, but he didn't argue. She had no clue how he managed to swing his backpack off his back, but it collided with her when he brought it around.

"Got it." A click, and then a semi-bright light illuminated the darkness. She glanced around the small space, her heart picking up in rhythm again. But as she surveyed the area, nothing lurked.

"If you let go, I can hang up a blanket over the entrance and turn on the oil lamp. Save the batteries on the flashlight."

She instantly let go and stepped back as heat rushed to her cheeks. "Here, I can help you."

He nodded, grabbing a thick wool blanket off the ground. Dust encircled them as he stretched out the blanket, handing her a corner. "There should be a nail for you to hang your side on."

She grabbed her end and, sure enough, towards the top of the entrance was a rusty nail sticking out from the stone.

"How did you know about this place?" She asked, wiping dust away from her fingers on her jeans. Miles was already at the back of the cave, shuffling through remnants of supplies. There wasn't much left, but it was evident from the old traps and makeshift furniture that someone used to live here.

She met him at the center of the cave. A circle of stone surrounded what she guessed to be some sort of fire pit. But instead of wood, there was a small tin can and a rack off to the side.

Hoping to discourage any insect still hanging around, she wiped off a tree log the best she could and took a seat.

"I used to live here." He mumbled in reply as he took a

match from his pack and lit the oil lamp. He kept the flame low and turned off the flashlight.

Renna studied the cave, trying to envision Miles living in the cramped space, using the animal traps to get food, and huddling around a small tin can fire to keep warm. She just couldn't wrap her mind around it.

"Did you live here alone?"

Miles took the empty spot beside her. "No. I was with my dad and uncle." His voice trailed off and she waited for him to elaborate. But of course, he didn't.

"What about your mother?"

His head jerked up, and his hand encircled the corded bracelet on his wrist. "She died when I was a baby."

"I'm sorry." She pointed to the leather on his wrist. "Did she give that to you?

"Yes."

"Did she make it?"

He pulled his sleeve down to cover the memento. "Yes."

So much for getting him to open up. She changed tactics. "How long do you think we will need to hide out?"

"A few hours." He sighed. "It might be best to wait for dawn."

"But you don't like that idea?"

He shook his head. "I thought it would be safer if we left at night to put as much distance as possible between us and the camp. But night isn't the safest time to walk through the forest."

She nodded, not knowing what else to say. She had a million questions, but Miles had evaded the ones she'd already asked, and she doubted that would change. Experience showed her that if Miles wanted to keep explaining, he would. No amount of prodding from her would make him open up more.

Renna had to put her life in his hands. The least he could do was let her in, even a bit. She hoped that he would trust her in time, because she couldn't shake the feeling he wasn't being completely honest with her.

"How's your foot?"

She started, lost in her thoughts. Shrugging, she flexed her foot. "Hurts, but I think it's okay."

He rolled his eyes, clearly not happy with her answer. "Give me your foot."

"Miles, it's fine."

He raised his eyebrow at her announcement. "Last time you said it was okay, you ended up not using the crutches and opened it back up."

"Fine."

He placed her leg on his knee, unlacing her boots, and removing her sock.

"Wait. I forgot to bring more bandages to change it."

"I grabbed them, so no worries."

Gratitude and something else settled over her at his words. Safety? Protection? She couldn't quite put a finger on it, but she was glad at least one of them was thinking. "What's the damage?"

"It actually looks pretty good." His gaze met hers, and he smiled. "It didn't open back up, thank goodness."

"That is a relief—hey, that's cold!" She wrenched her foot back at his touch, and Miles laughed, holding up a small container of salve.

"It can't be that bad." He grabbed her foot, bringing it back to his knee, and started wrapping it in clean bandages.

"You try putting that on your bare foot without being warned."

"I couldn't resist." He lifted her boot and tossed it in her direction. "All finished."

"Thanks."

"I would say anytime, but we don't need you getting hurt again."

A shudder swept over her as she slipped her sock back on and laced her boot—an image sprang to mind of her falling in the woods again, with whomever or whatever was chasing after them. Was it a person? A group of people? Some type of creature? Leaders always referenced the dangers of the forest, but none of the adults would talk about what specific threats were out there.

Death awaits you in the forest.

She had seen firsthand how her parents' faces paled at the mention of the forest, how they instantly clammed up and repeated the rule back to her and her sister if they ever asked. As a Speaker, she communicated daily with the Runners. She had seen their injuries, the sweat and dirt that caked their faces as they brought back supplies for the Outpost. She had witnessed the sadness when one of them would return without their partner. It never crossed her mind to question what the danger was before. But now, after everything she had experienced the last few days, Renna needed to know.

"Miles?"

He stared at her, concern evident in his expression at her tone. "Yeah?"

"How does your camp survive out in the middle of the forest?"

"The same as the Outpost. We have leaders and guards who keep a lookout for the entire camp."

"But nothing attacks your camp? I mean, you don't have any walls to protect your people."

Renna longed to pace while she waited for his answer, but she willed herself to be still. To not give him any reason to change the subject.

"It's not needed."

She scrambled to process his words. "What do you mean it's not needed?" Her voice grew louder with each word.

Miles grabbed her hands. "I need you to stay calm and remember that we have to be quiet."

Managing to nod, she did her best to squash the panic that was rapidly building. If Miles feared her response, then the explanation had to be bad.

"It's true that there are dangers in the forest. You have the typical wild animals that can hurt you, like coyotes, cougars, and snakes. But the main threat is your government. They want to keep you in the Outpost. They don't want you to leave. Ever."

"I don't understand." She ripped his hands from his and stood. She had to think, had to move. It was near impossible in the small cave.

"I know. It's not easy hearing the truth. It's hard for everyone I talk to."

Renna ceased the pacing and turned to face him. "That's what you do for your camp? For Thomas? You find people, fill their heads with all sorts of lies and convince them to leave their families?"

Hurt flickered across Miles's face. "I do not lie to people, Renna."

"How can I believe you?" Tears pricked her eyes. "I barely know you. I've lived my entire life at the Outpost. I'm a Speaker!" With each outburst, her confusion grew. His words, mixed with her experience, didn't make any sense.

Miles got to his feet and crossed the distance between them in seconds, placing both of his hands on her shoulders. "I don't know what I can say to make you believe me. And I know how important your people are to you, Renna."

"Did Thomas find out who I am?"

"No, I think we left in time."

"The people chasing after us, if they weren't from Thomas, then who ..."

Miles didn't say anything but dropped his hands from her shoulders.

Tears sprang to her eyes, clouding her vision for a few seconds. She did her best to look up at him. "If they aren't from your government, then that means they are from mine." The revelation hurt to speak out loud.

He clenched his jaw and simply nodded his reply.

She could barely get the words out. "They want to kill me."

Miles reached for her again, this time cupping her cheeks and bending to look her square in the eyes. "I'm not going to let that happen."

18

Day Five

Sunlight filtered through holes in the woolen blanket hanging from the cave entrance, illuminating dust particles swirling in the beams of light. Renna turned over in her sleep, but Miles wasn't ready to wake her.

He had no desire to reopen the conversation they had in the wee hours of the morning. Nor did he want to think about the promise he made her. A promise he had no business making, but Miles couldn't stand to see the hurt and fear in her eyes.

Miles made the mistake of getting too close to her, too wrapped up in her safety. Partly because it was his fault they were in this mess, and partly because she gazed up at him with such trust he didn't know what else to do.

He should have thought before he cupped her cheeks and stared into those steel-blue eyes. But one look into them, and he couldn't think clearly. She was too close, and he couldn't keep his eyes from drifting to her lips and imagining what it would have been like if he kissed her.

Instead, he ended up dropping his hands and stepping

away, putting as much distance as he could between them, and suggested they both get some rest before they left the cave and continued on their journey.

But Miles couldn't sleep, no matter how hard he tried. He just lay awake, listening to the sound of Renna's breathing and watching as she tossed and turned.

Finally, she was completely still. He hated to bother her. But they needed to get started. He gently shook her shoulder. "Renna, it's time to go."

She sat up, confusion on her face before she yawned and nodded.

He handed her a couple of pieces of jerky and a hunk of bread that he had taken from the dining hall. "Here. It's not much, but maybe we can try to catch some fish or something later."

"So, what's the plan? Keep heading towards the Outpost?"

"We had to veer off the path quite a bit to hide. We are going to have to double back some now."

She frowned. "Will ... they still be out there?"

"They ... aren't going to give up."

If his words bothered her, she didn't let on that they did. Instead, she finished the meager breakfast and took a drink from the canteen. Miles hoped she wouldn't continue her questioning. He couldn't give her an answer that would satisfy. Miles hadn't expected her to put together the clues so quickly, and he needed to keep it in mind. Because if she knew everything, she wouldn't stick around long enough to hear his explanation.

"You ready?"

"Ready as I'll ever be."

It didn't take long to remove the rock from the opening now that it had been moved from its resting place. Miles held it while Renna scrambled over the rocks and then rolled it back into its spot. He couldn't completely cover their tracks, but he would at least try. He arranged the hanging roots and scuffed their footprints out of the dirt.

Renna was quiet as they journeyed back the way they came. He could not blame her for the silence. He had certainly given her a lot to process. Every now and then, he glanced over his shoulder to make sure she was keeping up. She hobbled slightly but was able to maintain his pace.

"The forest is safe during the day?" Renna's voice broke the silence between them.

"The forest is never safe."

"I don't understand. You travel for your camp, right? To find stragglers in the woods."

He nodded, his stomach churning at her line of questioning. She dug for the deep questions. Ones that required answers he was not ready to spill. "I do, but it's always dangerous. There's always something out here."

"Then why risk it?" She stopped, holding a hand above her eyes, peering up at him. Bright sunlight filtered through the canopy of leaves, lighting up spots on her jacket.

No one had ever asked him that before. Keegan hated that he worked for Thomas, and Elaine never really questioned his desire to be out in the woods.

"Someone has to do it. It might as well be me."

"That's malarkey, and you know it." She shook her head and started walking again. "Does it have something to do with your dad and uncle?"

"I suppose it does."

"What happened to them?"

Miles squinted against the sun. "They're gone."

"What do you mean?" Her voice was soft, and the question sent his mind swirling back to his uncle abandoning them and the last time he saw his father, cold and unmoving. He banished the images from his mind. "It doesn't matter. It was a long time ago."

"Why doesn't it matter?"

Anger replaced the memories and threatened to overflow the carefully tight lid he kept on his feelings. Clenching his jaw, he shook his head. "Because it just doesn't, Renna. We need to focus on more important tasks, like keeping you alive long enough to get you home. Not trespassing down a memory lane that's been abandoned and left to decay."

"I'm sorry." Her voice was low and overflowing with concern. She reached out and touched his arm. "I shouldn't have pushed."

He shrugged her hand off and kept walking. They needed to keep moving. He wasn't as familiar with this section of the forest. Even though he deviated them off the path to escape their followers, they could not go back the way they came. Miles did not want to chance that their pursuers were hiding out where they started, so they had to travel through unfamiliar territory.

"Keep an eye out for traps."

Renna's face paled slightly, but she nodded and slowed her pace down to match his careful steps.

Where earlier they were tripping over roots and brush, now they were stepping easily through as if someone landscaped it. Before, the trees were so many and close together that a person couldn't see anything but forest. But with each step forward, the trees were spaced farther out, and Mile's uncertainty grew.

The forest continued to surround them, yet straight ahead, about fifty yards away, was a clearing. No trees, no buildings, or large rocks. Just knee-high grass and no way to know what was prowling inside the weeds.

He was in uncharted waters.

He would make for either side of the clearing, but this was not the woods surrounding the Outpost, and it wasn't the acres around his encampment. It was almost as risky as going straight through the meadow.

Sweat dripped down his neck, and he resisted the urge to reach up and wipe it off, wishing they would get a strong breeze to cool off. Stealing a glance, he looked over at Renna, her forehead wrinkled in concentration as he came to a halt on the edge of the covered woods.

"Miles, are we going the right way?"

He glanced down at his compass. "Yes."

"Then why do you look so worried?"

"Because I've never been here before."

She followed his gaze out in front of them, her eyes narrowing. "What do you suggest we do?"

"I need to get a better look at the surrounding area." He scanned the tree line beside them until he found a tree that would support his weight. He pointed to a maple tree on their right. "There. About thirty feet away."

"I've never climbed a tree before."

Miles led the way to the tree, grabbing the lowest branch. "Why doesn't that surprise me?"

"It's not like I had a ton of opportunity before, you know."

Movement behind them drew his attention away from Renna and towards the meadow. The grass began to weave back and forth.

Odd. The leaves weren't moving.

"Well, looks like you're going to learn on the job." He grabbed her from around the waist and hoisted her up on the branch.

"Miles! What are you doing?"

"Climb. Now!" He swung up beside her and then quickly climbed again. "Whatever is in the weeds is coming our way."

She gasped, turning back towards the middle of the meadow. "Miles, I don't see anything."

"Quit gawking and climb." He grunted, reaching down for her arm to help her to the next branch.

"Miles, is that a wild boar?"

"I hope not." Nevertheless, he searched the meadow and caught a glance of water. It wasn't a meadow at all but an over-grown pond. The reeds parted again, and brown leathery skin and razor-sharp tusks came into view. A wild boar stalked towards them.

And it wasn't alone.

"You were saying?"

Miles quickly counted five before he met Renna's worried eyes. "Climb faster."

She nodded and seized the branch, but her hand slipped.

"Renna, grab my hand."

She hesitated before finally reaching out. Miles guided her up to the next branch and then the next. They worked in silence, and now and then he would stop and help her reach a branch.

"Is this high enough?" She panted.

"Yeah, let's stop here." He climbed into a thick V in the tree and leaned back against the trunk, helping Renna sit down beside him. Miles had to be able to look around them, but for now, he needed to catch his breath. He took deep breaths and tried to wrap his mind around what he had just witnessed.

"I was right? They were boars?" She turned her head to look at him, her words coming out in short gasps.

Miles shook his head. "Yeah."

"What are they doing now? Circling, waiting for us to come down?" Her words were teasing, but her voice trembled.

"Probably."

Renna visibly shuddered and then wobbled.

19

Gabbi stared at the trapdoor, trying to get her feet to move. It was one thing to rescue her father, but it was quite another to openly flout the rules of the Outpost.

After Zeke helped her get her father to the bakery, he surprised her by coming back later that day to check on him, and he found her filling flour sacks full of food. He jumped at the chance to help her. She promised to meet him in the tunnel to work out some sort of plan to hand out the food bags. Gabbi doubted whether they could pull off such a feat, but Zeke was optimistic. Almost annoyingly positive they could do this. Gabbi wasn't so sure. Her stomach stayed in an ongoing state of anxiety since her mother dropped the latest secret on her lap. Her grandparents, along with Zeke's, were the ones who envisioned tunnels and started the construction. Both sets of their parents were responsible for keeping them running, but when their friendship fell apart at the seams, so did the tunnels.

She had to move quickly because Mother would be here any moment, ready to join her and Zeke in planning. She hadn't appreciated the note Gabbi left for her last time, but there wasn't another option. Gabbi wasn't going to let Mother put herself at risk. If the worst happened—getting caught—she wouldn't be able to live with herself knowing her mother would suffer the same fate.

Dust and mildew filled her nostrils as she descended the rickety stairs as fast as she dared. Her nose wrinkled, and she let out an onslaught of sneezes as her feet finally connected with the dirt floor.

"Bless you!" Zeke's voice called out from the distance as Gabbi rounded a corner to the left, following the tunnel in the direction of the smithy.

"I'd hoped I could have snuck up on you."

A smile lit up his face as he got to his feet, a rolled-up paper in his hands. "Well, I've never heard someone sneeze so loud. I heard you all the way back at your place."

"It's because of the echo down here."

An adorable grin lifted the corners of his lips, and Gabbi had to force her gaze anywhere but towards his teasing smile. "What's that?"

"Something you will like." He handed her one end of the parchment and carefully started to unroll it. "I know your grandparents had a sketch of the tunnels, but after I talked to my dad, I found out that it was his grandfather that was entrusted to actually draw up the blueprints."

A spark of hope ignited as she took in the thin, precise strokes of the map of their community. "Wow, this is amazing."

A glimmer of pride filled Zeke's eyes before he pointed to a spot on the lower right side. "This is where we are now." He trailed his finger up along the tunnel lines and towards the top of the map, where the residential houses were marked. "Here's the Blacksmith's shop and where each of the tunnels feeds to the other buildings on this path."

"And this will show us which businesses we can access?" Gabbi's stomach eased just a little at the news. It would make things so much easier if they weren't going through the tunnels blind, hoping that whatever trap door they stumbled upon would let them in.

"Yes." His finger trailed to a box on the opposite side of the map. "He also made us a key. A square is for the ones that have a direct path to a trap door, a shaded square for ones that have a trap door and should be sympathetic to our cause."

Their cause? Gabbi's stomach churned at the idea. Did Zeke think this was some attempt to get back at the Officials, some way to rebel against their way of life? Was he trying to carry out the misguided agenda their grandparents had when they built these tunnels?

Gabbi wanted to ask her parents for more information after getting her father home, but there wasn't a good time to bring it up. Father spent the night suffering from a high fever, and Mother never left his side. Gabbi brought fresh cool water and washcloths for his forehead, and even though she had so many questions, she couldn't bring herself to pull her mother away from him.

Gabbi shifted her thoughts back to the map. One step at a time. Answers would come, but for now, they needed a plan to get food out to the people.

"How are we going to do this?"

Zeke pulled a piece of paper out of his pocket and laid it on top of the map. Three columns filled the page in neat, lined rows. "The first row is all the businesses, the second is residential houses, and the third states if there is a direct trap door or if we have to go above ground for admittance."

Warning bells sounded in her mind. Go above ground? It was too much of a risk. Gabbi shook her head, her braid sliding back and forth across her back. "No. That's crazy." Zeke nodded, but his expression didn't change. "You can't be serious."

"We don't have a choice." He pointed to a large rectangle shape on the far left of the paper. "Does that look familiar?"

His words were sharp and Gabbi didn't have to glance at the shape for long. "Of course I know what that is." She rubbed sweaty palms on her jeans. "It's family housing."

"Yes, and you think you can live with yourself knowing that we aren't doing everything in our power to bring food to those children? Some of these families have infants."

Tears filled Gabbi's eyes, and she covered her face with her hands. "I know. I know."

Silence filled the space beside her. Gabbi wiped the tears away and tried to think of some way they could slip by unnoticed. "Do you have an idea on how to get to these houses? I just assumed there would be tunnels going everywhere."

"That's what we have to figure out. We need a plan, and we need it fast. It's already been five days since Renna disappeared."

Her sister's name sent a jab straight to her heart. Each day that passed, the more Gabbi suspected that something must have happened to her. There couldn't be any other explanation for her continued absence. "I know."

Zeke's hand found hers, and he squeezed. "Don't give up hope, Gabs. She's going to come back."

Somehow, a smile crept across her face. "Gabs?"

"I'm trying it out." He released her hand and leaned back. "I think I like it. It fits."

"You can't be serious."

"Everyone needs a nickname."

She laughed at his amused expression. "Gabbi is my nickname."

"Well, you need a fun nickname."

"And Gabbi isn't fun?"

"Come on, it's not as fun as Gabs." He laughed and gently bumped her with his shoulder. "And it did make you smile."

There was truth to his words. Zeke definitely had a way of

drawing her out of her shell and making her feel at ease. She rolled her eyes. "Fine. You can call me Gabs."

He beamed, his enthusiasm making her smile, but she held up a finger before he could say anything. "But I get to come up with a name for you."

"Fine. But it's kind of hard to find a nickname for Zeke."

"I'm up for the challenge."

Silence filled the space between them as the mood suddenly shifted and the reality of their situation set in. Her stomach knotted again. She glanced back at the symbol box. "What about the X symbol?"

"What?" Zeke asked, but it took a moment for his gaze to shift back to hers. What was bothering him? Creases on his brow showed deep thought. Were they similar to her own?

"The X on the key."

"Oh." His tone darkened, and Gabbi stiffened, bracing herself for whatever news he was about to drop on her.

"They are the ones who stopped helping when the tunnels passed to our father's care." His frowned. "They locked the trap doors and refused to open them again. They didn't want anything to do with the tunnels."

She lifted her gaze from the map to look at him, trying to process his words. What would suddenly make them stop helping? Did they not trust them? It seemed like such an absurdity. Renna's family had always been one of the pillars of the community. "Why would they want to stop helping?"

Zeke's shoulders drew up in a shrug. "What else? Fear."

"They were afraid of the Officials?" Gabbi focused back on the map, going over each of the businesses and trying to visualize it in person, putting a face to each business owner. These were essential businesses. The Outpost depended on them. She thought of some of them as friends. As her parent's friends.

"Aren't you?" Zeke's question weighed on her the longer she stared at the map. Didn't she say as much when her mother first started talking about feeding the people? Wasn't that her argument against doing something so crazy? Fear made people do crazy things. Could she blame them?

"Of course I am."

"But you're going to do it anyway."

It wasn't a question. Zeke's voice rang with certainty at his statement, a little bit of amusement mixed with something else she couldn't quite put her finger on. Admiration, maybe?

"And so are you." Gabbi's certainty matched his. There was no doubt that when she went to the first door and handed over the sack of food, Zeke would be right there beside her.

"There's no other place that I'd rather be." His emerald eyes spoke more than his words, and for the first time in a long time, Gabbi didn't feel so alone.

20

"Come on, Renna, you've got this."

Relief filled Renna as she managed to stay perched. Why did they need to come down so soon? They had already spent a few hours in the tree, what would it hurt to stay a little longer? She resisted the urge to look down, hoping to keep her small breakfast at bay. Miles had already started descending the massive tree, and all she could think about was tumbling out of it. "Please don't let me fall."

"You're not going to fall. Just take it nice and slow."

Panic overwhelmed her but she tried to focus on the task at hand instead of heaving her breakfast all over Miles and then falling to the ground. "Just a second ago, you said to hurry."

"Well, maybe hurry just a little." Miles's voice sounded assured, so she tried to let it give her the confidence to descend again. She would just have to ignore the waves of dizziness and the rushing in her ears long enough to climb down.

Sweaty palms and rough bark were not a good combination. Renna desperately wanted to wipe the moisture from her hands, but she was terrified to let go. She squeezed harder, sucking in a breath as the bark stabbed her skin. Maybe if she kept the conversation with Miles going, she could temporarily forget how high she was in the tree. "Did you at least get a good look while we were camped up there?"

"I did." His hesitation in answering distracted Renna, and her foot slipped. She clung to the limb above and tried to get her feet to stay on the branch under her.

"You okay?" Miles's worried tone didn't calm her in the least.

"I'm fine." She huffed, righting her balance and willing her body to relax. "Just got to wait for my heart to get the memo."

A low chuckle drifted up to her, and she squeezed her eyes shut to keep from glaring down at him. Miles Butler was going to be the death of her. Why couldn't he just give her details? "Well, what did you see up there?"

"If we go parallel to the pond and our wild friends, we should be able to avoid them and slip back into the cover of the woods."

"So we should intercept your usual path soon?"

"In theory."

Miles halted his descent, and she barely avoided stomping on his hand. "Why are we stopping?"

"We're almost at the bottom."

Relief flooded her. Finally. "I'll be glad to have my feet back on solid ground."

"You say that now, but as soon as we land, be prepared to run. We have to get deeper in the woods as quickly as we can."

"This must be where your 'in theory' comment comes into play."

"I noticed a building a couple of miles out. If it's the one that I'm thinking of, we can take a break there. We use it for overnight stays when we can't get back to the Forest Community in a day."

"And if it's not the same building?"

There was silence before he finally mumbled. "I'm not sure yet."

They started moving again, and Renna had to force herself to not think about anything else except placing her feet on the branches and then lowering herself down just to repeat the process all over again. At the last limb, she waited until she heard him drop and call up to her to do the same.

As soon as her feet hit the ground, he was already pulling her deeper into the tree line. She followed close behind him, trying to match her steps to his and place her feet where his went. Miles was much better at gauging where to run. Left to her own devices, she would inevitably find every sharp rock and noisy stick, alerting everyone and everything around them of their presence.

The deeper they ran, the more trees appeared; they were once again in the middle of the forest. Miles slowed to a jog before completely stopping, waiting for her to catch up. Taking deep breaths, she slid her backpack off and leaned against a tree, willing her heartbeat to return to normal.

"I'm not cut out to be a runner."

"Neither am I, if it makes you feel any better." He chugged some water and then pointed to her canteen, dangling from her bag. "You need to stay hydrated."

She nodded, reaching for the water. "Maybe we can just stay here? I'm so tired."

Miles laughed. "I don't think your family would like that very much."

"No, probably not." She sighed and reattached the canteen to her pack. "Can we at least sit for a minute?"

He dug around in his bag. "If we are taking a break, at least eat something." He said, passing her a biscuit.

Nodding, she lowered herself to the ground and took a bite, suddenly thankful that Miles thought of eating. If it weren't for him, she wouldn't have made it this far in her journey to get back home.

"Tell me about your family."

She jerked her head up, surprised by his sudden curiosity about her life. Usually, she was the one asking the questions. "Well, my parents run the bakery." Her heart ached. "They are probably the best people that I know. They are both so hard-working and kind. My dad would help anyone that needs it."

A look of sadness crossed Miles's face, but it was gone as quickly as it came. Renna sighed and continued. "The bakery is always warm, and everyone lingers over sandwiches, soups, and pastries. Even the ones who don't have as much money still visit the bakery. My parents would never let anyone go hungry."

"It sounds nice."

Renna nodded. "Yeah, it is. It's a family business for sure, though. I've helped my parents for as long as I can remember. I go there after I read the rules. Even my sister, Gabbi, helps at the bakery. She'll probably be the one who takes it over one day." A pang of guilt hit her again at the thought of her family waiting for her to return.

"You have a sister?"

"Yeah. She's two years older." A picture of Gabbi rolling her eyes flashed in her mind. "She thinks she always knows better than me." Renna gave him a smile. "Big sisters are oddly good at bossing you around."

"I wouldn't know anything about that."

"Well, when I get home, she probably won't speak to me for a few days. She's going to be so angry."

Miles took a bite of his biscuit. "I'm sure she will be happy to see you, though."

"Maybe. But she has every right to be mad at me. I should have never left."

"They are probably just worried about you. I can't imagine them hanging onto their anger when they see you."

"I hope so." Renna rubbed her eyes. "I have a lot to make up for. I mean, I may have messed everything up. If they haven't replaced me already. People stuck at home, businesses closed. It's been five days now." Her throat burned. "There are probably people hungry. All those kids at the orphanage. Miles, we feed them daily."

His face softened, and she had to look away from his pity. She did not deserve it. "There is a part of me that is scared to go back. How will I explain why I left in the first place?"

"They will forgive you."

She turned back to him, wiping the tears from her eyes. "Would you?"

He opened his mouth to respond but then closed it, and Renna didn't wait for him to reply. "I didn't think so. What I did was unforgivable."

He nodded. "Maybe. But isn't that the powerful thing about forgiveness? To mend what shouldn't be mendable?"

Renna leaned back against the tree, mulling over his words. Was that the way it worked? Or were there some things that couldn't be fixed no matter how hard you tried? No doubt her mother and father would welcome her back with open arms. But Gabbi always criticized her, and the people of the Outpost —she couldn't even think about it.

"I wasn't expecting this conversation to get so deep." She chuckled. "Do you think everything we do can be forgiven?"

"I hope so." His voice was wistful, and Renna wanted to ask what he'd done that he worried couldn't be forgiven. But something in his eyes told her he wouldn't answer. She took another drink of water and dusted the crumbs off her lap.

"Why did you leave? Weren't you happy?"

Renna looked away from Miles, working through the emotions his question stirred inside her. His tone wasn't spiteful, but it made her feel even more guilty.

Was she happy?

She should be content with her lot in life, but being content and happy were two vastly different things. She had two loving parents, a sister who didn't always drive her crazy. A respectable position in the community. But when she added them all up, something was lacking. No matter how she analyzed it, she always came back to the same feeling. Renna just couldn't put a name to it. "I wasn't unhappy."

Miles grew silent for a moment considering her words before he gave her an amused grin. "That's not the same thing."

Renna shrugged. "I know. But it's the best I've got right now."

Miles stared at her for a few seconds before he finally nodded and got to his feet. He walked over and reached out a hand to help her up. "Fair enough."

Miles tried to pull his hand from hers, but she held onto it for a few seconds longer. "For whatever it is worth, thank you for helping me get home. I know we haven't exactly seen eye to eye since we met, but I'm glad you're here."

Her stomach fluttered as Miles's fingers tightened against hers. Doubt, confusion, and other emotions she couldn't place raced across his face as he processed her words. For a brief few seconds it seemed like he wanted to respond, but as usual, he backpedaled and wiped his face void of emotion. Renna almost sighed out loud but caught herself in time. Miles's wall returned as it did every time she tried to be honest and real with him.

"We're losing daylight." He pulled his hand from hers, taking all their progress along with it.

21

With each step closer to the safe house, the meager ration of jerky knotted in Miles's stomach. When he brought Renna back to his camp, he convinced himself that he was doing the right thing. That Renna was just like all the others he had brought to Thomas. How many scouting trips had he successfully accomplished in the three years he had worked for Thomas?

Too many to count.

The hunting trip was just a ruse, and of course, Keegan saw right through him. But his demeanor changed when Miles slipped up and hinted about Renna's true identity. There was a look in Keegan's eyes when he ordered Miles to take Renna home, something he couldn't quite place or ignore. Keegan never hid his distaste for Thomas—but Miles had never questioned it before. Miles loved being out in the woods, and his job helped people, right? The weight of Keegan's pleading spread enough doubt that he listened.

And each mile they ran, each time they dodged a Guardian, each time they escaped the next danger, that doubt spread. Like a disease spreading through his veins, making him second guess his actions, instincts, and ability to do his job.

Because taking Renna home wasn't like his job at all. It wasn't like the others he had found and helped in the woods. It wasn't another mission accomplished to add to his list.

Renna James wasn't like the others. He didn't care about them.

Not like he cared for Renna.

And confound it all—it was messing with his head.

Miles paused, surveying the area, and tried to push away the uneasiness sweeping over him. What if this wasn't the safe house? He brushed back his hair from his forehead, sweat coating his fingers and no doubt leaving the ends to spike straight up. The day's heat had begun to wane, and he needed more time to figure out his next course of action. But he was out of time. By usual mission standards, he missed the drop-off time. Which meant Thomas was not the only one who learned he was AWOL.

When he promised to protect Renna, he put his job and his way of life in danger. Not to mention physically putting them both in jeopardy.

"Miles, are you all right?"

He jerked his head in the direction of her voice and noticed he had fallen several steps behind. "Of course. I just—" He paused, stopping the words from coming out of his mouth. Miles needed to come clean with her and tell her everything. But how was he supposed to explain? He stared at her while he debated back and forth.

She walked back to him and stopped in front of him, concern in her eyes. "You could have fooled me."

Renna was much too observant for her own good. He needed to make a decision, and fast.

"Miles—what's wrong?"

The way she gazed at him, with complete trust and understanding, punched him in the gut. He didn't deserve that level of confidence, but he wanted to earn it, and it had to start with the truth.

Movement in one of the safe house windows caught his eye. He turned just as the fabric fell back into place; was someone peering out from behind the curtain?

Instinctively, Miles grabbed Renna and pushed her behind the nearest tree. How could he be so stupid? His distraction disguised the real danger. Renna was counting on him, and he couldn't afford any mistakes. There would be no do-overs.

"What are you doing?" Shocked filled her voice and her cheeks flushed as he placed his hand above her head and stood in front of her, making sure neither of them was in view of the building.

She tried to peer around him, but he blocked her from leaning too far.

"Something's not right." He dropped his voice to a whisper, his face inches from hers.

"What do you mean?" She frowned and then lowered her voice to match his. "Is there someone there?"

He held up his finger for her to wait for a second and slowly bent as far as possible to sneak a peek toward the building. The curtains were completely still.

What was he doing? Jumping to conclusions and seeing the enemy where it wasn't? Miles dropped his arm and stepped away from Renna. This trip was making him paranoid. "Come on. There's nothing there after all."

"I don't think I've seen you so on edge since we left the camp."

"I'm sorry." He surveyed their surroundings, but nothing else appeared out of the ordinary.

"You don't have to be sorry." Renna gave him a small smile. "I'm really grateful for everything you're doing to get me home. Even though I know you don't agree with me going back."

This girl was tangling him up in knots. If only it were a matter of a simple disagreement. But it went far deeper. "I don't disagree with you, Renna."

A grin lit her face. "Miles Butler agrees with me on something for a change? Can I get that in writing?"

"Nah. No one would believe you."

"You're probably right." She stopped smiling and peered up at him, "But seriously, Miles—"

"You don't have to thank me. If anyone would understand the duty you feel for your people, it's me. How desperate you are to help them."

Silence filled the space between them, and Miles breathed a sigh of relief. She didn't push him for more information, even though he could tell she was curious.

He could trust Renna with the truth.

A lightness settled over him at the revelation. Who better to understand the duty one had to their people but Renna? He just had to open his mouth and tell her.

"Before we go in, I wanted to tell you—"

Fingers wrapped around his arm and stopped him. "Please tell me that's a friend of yours smiling at us."

Friend? Miles jerked his head from looking at Renna to the building and cursed. Another glance at the safe house confirmed his instincts. He was in the right place. So how in the world did Grant find them?

"Not a friend, then?" Her voice was shaky as her grip on his arm tightened.

"Definitely not a friend." Anger dripped over every word. What a mess he made, and he could do nothing to stop it. Not now, not ever.

It was too late.

He had hesitated to tell her the truth, and then in one second, everything changed. He was too late to stop it now. It was already in motion the moment the Guardian spotted them.

And Renna would hate him forever.

He put everything at risk—his job, his life, Renna's life—all to have it come crashing to the ground in an instant. He could tell her to go. To run as fast and as hard as she could. To never stop running. But that would only be a death sentence. Wild fright filled her eyes. She would not leave without him.

And the weight of that reality crushed him.

Miles covered her hand on his arm with his own. "I have to tell you something—before ... he gets closer."

"What's wrong?"

He turned to face her but didn't drop her hand, relishing the feel of it in his. He stared into her eyes, was that fear or trust? He couldn't do this.

He didn't have the heart to shatter hers.

"Miles, you're starting to scare me. What's wrong?"

"I should have told you this from the beginning, but my job doesn't let—" His words stopped as the Guardian's movement caught his attention.

"Miles?"

Renna's voice forced his gaze back down to her, and he gently grabbed both of her shoulders, filling his voice with as much sincerity and urgency as he could. "There's no time to explain, but whatever you hear in the next few minutes ... just know that I'm sorry, and I was about to explain it all. That I wasn't following through with it."

"I don't understand—"

"Renna, please. Say that you will let me explain."

"You know I will—but Miles ..."

He wrapped an arm around her waist, pulling her closer and bending down to place a quick kiss on her forehead. He didn't give her a chance to respond before he quickly moved her to stand behind him, blocking Grant's view of her.

"Miles, how nice of you to finally join me."

Miles turned to acknowledge the Guardian. "Official

Grant."

Amusement crossed over the Guardian's face. "Who did you bring to me this week?"

"I'm sure I don't know what you mean."

A short bark of laughter escaped the man's lips. "I will let that untruth go because I'm suddenly very interested in why you are lying to me. Who's the girl hiding behind you?"

Fingers gripped the back of his sleeve, but thankfully Renna didn't say anything. Miles scrambled to come up with something to give the man but shot down each new idea that sprang to his mind. Grant wouldn't believe him, no matter how good a story he could spin.

"I'm training her to scout. I decided I need a helper."

Official Grant snapped his fingers, and in seconds, Guardians filed out of the woods, surrounding the area and aiming weapons straight at them. Anger coursed through him as laser lights dotted and moved across his chest.

"Miles?" Renna's defeated tone pierced his heart. It was useless to lie, but he had to try. Now he would have to play along. No matter how much it killed him to do it. Boots crunched over the ground behind them. They were within arm's reach.

"Can't come up with a better story? I'm disappointed." Grant waved his hand towards the Guardians. "Take the Speaker inside," Grant's smile returned, "while Miles and I have a discussion."

"I'm sorry." He faced Renna, his tone pleading for her trust. The look of terror at the mention of her title shook his self-control.

"Miles?!" Her hand grabbed his in a desperate attempt to stop the Guardians from pulling her away.

It went against every fiber of his being to drop his hand from hers. Guardians capitalized on her moment of shock and dragged her away. Miles did nothing to stop them.

22

"Are you ready?"

Gabbi's gaze drifted up from the map clutched in her hands to Zeke's expectant look. His voice was calm and reassuring, but it did nothing to stop the flurry of worry and anxiety whirling around inside of her.

"Gabbi?"

Warm fingers gently nudged her arm, and she forced a brave smile. "Of course. Let's do this."

"Yes, ma'am." He picked up the wheelbarrow, filled to the brim with food, and started down the uneven tunnel floor to their first stop—the Orphanage.

"Miss Parker is not going to turn us away."

"I know."

"Do you? Because your face looks like you're going to high-tail it out of here and leave me standing all alone knocking on the tunnel door with a cart full of food."

"I can handle this, Zeke." Her words came out sharper than intended, but Zeke didn't tease her for the rest of the short journey to the tunnel beneath the Orphanage.

They still hadn't figured out how to get past these initial

tunnels. They could feed four, maybe five businesses, but after that? How were they going to get to the ones on the other side?

Were they going to have to go outside?

"Hey, one step at a time. Okay?"

Gabbi's thoughts had so consumed her that she hadn't realized Zeke had stopped the cart a few steps ahead. Concern filled his eyes, but there was also a slight tic in his jaw. Was he just as worried? No one asked him to help her. She didn't need him to tag along.

Except she couldn't imagine not having Zeke by her side. It didn't matter how often she reminded herself they were doing the right and honorable thing; doubt still had a foothold. There was just something about him that calmed her down and chased away her anxious thoughts.

"Yes, one step at a time." She joined him at the cart and pulled out the list from behind the map. "I can't wait to see Miss Parker's face when we bring this food. I haven't stopped worrying about the kids since Renna ... since the lockdown."

"Why don't we leave the cart here and only approach the doors with the bags?" He frowned. "I'm not saying someone would take advantage of us, but if you were starving, how far would you go to make sure that didn't happen again?"

Goosebumps rose on her arms, and she wiped sweaty palms on her pants. What would she do if she was a parent watching her children go hungry? While his words rang true, she didn't want to admit how much they frightened her. Desperate people did desperate things.

Like abandon their posts.

Ugh. No matter how hard she tried to stop punishing Renna, Gabbi couldn't help it. A part of her couldn't wait to let her sister have a piece of her mind, while the other part was jealous and hurt that Renna hadn't even thought to ask Gabbi to join her.

She folded the map and list and tucked them back into her

pocket before grabbing one of the flour sacks on the cart. The children had waited long enough.

Zeke grabbed another bag and matched her steps, staying right beside her the whole way up the stairs and to the trap door. He gave her an encouraging nod, and then she raised a trembling hand to knock on the knotted wood.

Gabbi stepped back and let out a shaky breath, but nothing happened. The door didn't open.

"Maybe they didn't hear you."

Gabbi gave him a quick nod and rapped again. This time she leaned closer to the door, hoping to hear footsteps.

Nothing.

"Can you open it from the outside?"

Zeke ran a hand over the wood, examining all of the edges. "There's not a knob on the outside—it only opens from the inside. A built-in safety feature."

Dread filled Gabbi. This was supposed to be their easiest drop-off. It was the one place where Gabbi had zero concern of being caught or someone turning them in.

What if there was something wrong with one of the little ones? "You try. Maybe I just wasn't loud enough." Her voice trembled. "You know, kids are noisy."

"True." He raised his fist and pounded on the door. He glanced over at her and then rapped on the door so hard that Gabbi feared it could be heard throughout the tunnel.

She held her breath as they waited, straining to hear any sounds coming from inside the Orphanage. Gabbi shifted the flour sack in her arms, already trying to develop a plan. They had to get inside. It was now more important than ever.

"We need to find something to knock down the door." Zeke was already setting his bag down to look for something when Gabbi heard it. Footsteps running toward the door.

She grabbed the back of Zeke's shirt. "Wait. Someone is coming."

Rusty hinges protested as the door slowly opened, and two wide blue eyes peered around the side of the wooden slab.

"Opal!"

"Gabbi?" The girl's eyes filled as she swung the door open and collapsed into Gabbi's arms. "Oh, Gabbi, what are you doing here?"

The teenage girl clung to Gabbi, her body shaking as she cried. Gabbi held her for a moment before gently pulling away. "We brought food."

"We?"

"Zeke." Gabbi took back the sack of food that Zeke had rescued from hitting the ground when Opal flung herself into her arms. "He's helping me."

"Miss Parker will be so glad to see you." She stepped through the door. "Come in."

"We can't stay, Opal. We have more food to deliver."

"You mean you're going to other places?" Opal's voice rose an octave, her eyes brightening at the news. "Can you get a message to the Healer?"

Gabbi's stomach lurched. Althea lived on the other side of the Outpost. "What's wrong? Who's sick?"

"It's one of the babies. We don't know what's wrong with him."

Gabbi looked over at Zeke, who nodded slightly. "We will come in and talk to Miss Parker for a moment."

Opal opened the door, and they climbed up into the orphanage. Gabbi's nose tickled at the smell of dust and musty air. This many bodies under one roof? Without fresh air, it would make anyone sick.

Miss Parker was in the upstairs nursery, rocking a sweet baby with curly blond hair. His cry was gut-wrenching, and it was all Gabbi could do not to reach out and try to soothe him.

"Gabbi? What are you doing here? How did you get here?"

"I found them, Ma'am. They were banging on the cellar

floor." Opal let out a nervous laugh. "That's what took so long. I didn't know where it was coming from. Finally, I moved the rug over and saw the door."

The woman glanced from Opal to Gabbi and then to Zeke. "You used the tunnels?" Her voice was quiet, but her eyes blinked back tears.

"We did. We brought food for you and the children."

"Truly?" Miss Parker patted the little boy's back, but he continued to wail. She stood up and paced. "My mother told me about the doors before she passed, but I never even thought about them again. There wasn't a reason to use them. Nothing like this has ever happened before—we've always had a Speaker." Her eyes darted back to Gabbi, and she frowned. "I'm sorry —I didn't mean to insinuate anything about your sister. Any news about Renna?"

"No. Not yet."

Miss Parker nodded and dabbed her cheek. "Well, I will be forever grateful you are here."

The little boy stiffened his legs and let out a high-pitched wail. But it was Zeke who reached for the baby. "Here, let me." He scooped up the little boy and took a seat in the rocker. He gently laid the baby on his stomach and rubbed his back. "My younger brother used to cry like this, and Mama always said colic was just as miserable for them as it was for us."

Gabbi watched in amazement as the fussy baby finally quieted. "You are full of surprises, Zeke."

He gave her a big goofy grin. "I can handle them when they are this young. It's when they start talking and walking that it gets scary."

Miss Parker sighed, and the worry etched on her face starting to fade. "You're right about that. Thank you both so much for coming. I was starting to worry about what we would do. Our emergency rations ran out yesterday."

"Well, you don't have to worry anymore. We brought you enough for a few days and then we will bring more."

"I don't even know what to say."

"You don't have to say anything. We are glad to help." She followed Miss Parker to the kitchen as Zeke laid the now sleeping baby in the crib.

"Opal said something about needing a healer?"

"For the baby. We didn't know what was going on with him. He would just cry and cry. I thought it might be colic, but nothing that I tried worked. Maybe Althea would have some medicine or suggestions on what I should do?"

"Althea is all the way across the Outpost. I'm not sure how we would get to her." Gabbi finished unloading the food sack and helped Opal assemble lunch for the twenty children.

"Surely, the tunnels connect to every house. Right?"

"I don't see how." Zeke answered, joining them in the kitchen. "I think the little guy is going to stay asleep."

The relief on Miss Parker's face broke Gabbi's heart. They had to do something to help her. She must be exhausted from staying up with a fussy baby and trying to take care of twenty other orphans.

"Wait—did you say your mom told you about the doors? You mean there's more than one door?"

Miss Parker's eyes widened in surprise. "Yeah, there's the door in the cellar and the one in my closet floor."

Gabbi reached out and gripped Zeke's arm. "Is your bedroom on the other side of the house?"

"Yes, why?"

Zeke grinned. "It sounds like you have a second tunnel."

23

R enna stumbled on the rocky path surrounding the supposed safe house as the Guardians pushed her forward. Hurt, confusion, and doubt filled her mind jumbling everything together. Miles asked her to trust him—and she would—but that man referred to her as Speaker. Her hope vanished.

Renna looked back at Miles in one last-ditch effort to bolster her spirits. To let her know whatever was going on would work out. That it didn't matter that the man knew who she was. She just never expected to see such anguish in his eyes.

What was she going to do now?

She was shoved through the doorway of the small, concrete building. Dirt and dust coated the floor, and it took a few minutes for her eyes to adjust to the dimly lit room.

"Take a seat." One of the Guardians ordered, his voice echoing throughout the sparse room. "Official Grant will be in to talk to you soon."

"What's going on? What does he want with me?"

"Take a seat, please." The phrase was nicer than his tone.

Turning around, she found two wooden chairs and a small table pushed up against the wall. She sat, cringing as the legs wobbled underneath her. Several of the Guardians filed out of the room, but the one who had spoken stayed, guarding the door.

She wanted to laugh at his rigid and alert posture. He held his gun in ready response like she would overpower him at any minute. Even if she could, where would she go? There were at least a dozen armed guards waiting outside.

The man stared in her general direction and, now and then, turned his neutral gaze on her. She opened her mouth to say something snarky but chickened out each time his cold stare met hers.

She rubbed her palms on her jeans, trying to calm her nerves. The desire to peel back the curtains and look out nearly overwhelmed her. What were Grant and Miles talking about? The man obviously had a connection with Miles, but she couldn't help but fixate on the how and why. Why would Miles bring people to the Guardians? It didn't make any sense to her.

Had Miles intended to bring her here instead of home? She nearly shook her head in response to the crazy thought. Miles was helping her. He wasn't trying to turn her over to the Guardians.

Never one for having patience, Renna wanted to jump up from the seat and pace. She considered it, but another look from her guard made her shrink back in the chair.

"Do you know how long they will be out there?"

The man's eyes narrowed at her, but he finally responded. "No."

She took that as a good sign. At least, he wasn't telling her to be quiet. "How can you stand there so still?"

There was a slight twitch of his upper lip, but it stopped just as suddenly as it came. "It's not that hard. Why don't you try it?"

"You try being held at gunpoint and see how still you are."

"I can aim it directly at you if that would help." Annoyance seeped into the man's voice.

She clamped her lips shut and tried to focus on anything other than the guard. Or the dirty room. Or the fact that Miles was outside talking to a Guardian.

About her.

"I'm so stupid." She mumbled, covering her face with her hands. None of this would have happened if she hadn't left the Outpost—all for the sake of curiosity.

A hard tap on the door jerked her thoughts back to the present in time to see the Guardian move as Grant entered, followed closely by Miles.

Miles met her eyes and slightly shook his head. Her heart sank. So much for wishing he could smooth everything over for her, and this was all just a huge misunderstanding.

"Miss James, I'm Official Grant." He swept the cap off his head and tucked it under his arm. "I'm sure you have several questions."

She nodded but couldn't find the words to answer. She shifted her gaze to Miles, hoping to find some sort of reassurance or hidden message in his expression, anything to let her know that everything would be all right. Except his face was expressionless. Hardness replaced the anguish in his eyes from earlier.

Grant turned to the guard. "If you will excuse us."

The Guardian nodded, taking one more glance at her before sliding quietly out of the door, a hint of amusement on his face.

Official Grant waited for the door to slam shut before sitting opposite Renna. He crossed his legs, placing his cap on his knee rather than on the dirty surface.

"You seem like the type who would appreciate jumping straight to the point."

Renna met his gaze, raised her chin slightly, and cleared her throat. "Isn't that best for everyone?"

The man chuckled, and Renna squared her shoulders, trying not to show the trembling that had overwhelmed her insides. He knew she was a Speaker. What kind of horrific penalty was she going to suffer?

"Well, the simple fact is, I work for the government you disregarded and left so abruptly. The very one who feeds you, clothes you, takes care of you."

Ouch. Straight to the point.

Grant sighed but continued. "No reason to try to deny it. I know all about you. Renna James, age seventeen. Born June 2nd. Your parents, Oscar and Grace, own and operate the bakery, along with your older sister, Gabriella." His eyes narrowed, his voice growing louder with each syllable. "Speaker. Respected. Loved. Honored. And you abandoned all of it. For what? To join some rag-tag group of rejects in the forest?"

"No! I didn't leave to join them." Renna matched his glare. "I didn't even know anything about them. Or that people could survive outside of the Gates." She caught Miles stiffening out of the corner of her eye, but she continued. "I thought the forest was forbidden and dangerous."

"Risky. Provoking the very one who holds your life in his hands." He chuckled. "Not smart at all."

No response she could think of would keep her from digging her hole more, so she leaned back in her chair, waiting for him to continue.

"I think I like you, Renna James." His eyes lit up. "It's smart. Not giving in to my angry banter, sitting tall in your seat, meeting my stare." His lips curved into a sly smile. "Not giving up your opinion."

"I don't see the point in trying to appease you. You already decided my future."

Grant's smile yielded to a full-fledged toothy grin. "True. We have protocols we must follow in this situation. But never have we had a Speaker abandon their post."

The calm Renna clung to vanished in an instant. Replaced with a fury that bubbled inside and erupted. "I did not abandon my people!"

"Well, Miles brought you to me today."

Renna longed to argue with the infuriating man—tell him Miles was taking her home, not handing her over to the likes of him. But the urgency in Miles's warning before the guards took her sprang back to her mind. She couldn't break her promise to him.

"Your government is not your enemy, Renna."

The Guardians chasing them in the forest proved otherwise, but she bit the inside of her cheek to keep from blurting out that nugget of truth.

Grant grinned again. Mistaking her silence for agreement. "In fact, that's why we made our deal with the Forest Community. They bring us the people they find in the forest, and we give them a choice. A simple test, really."

Renna's eyes moved to Miles automatically, trying to read his expression. It was blank, but his jaw was clenched. Perhaps he was having a hard time keeping silent as well.

She turned back to Grant. "What kind of test?"

"I'm so glad you asked." He leaned forward, taking his hat off his lap, and resting both elbows on his knees. "Each person has two choices. Go and live in peace with the Forest Community or go back to the Outpost."

Warning bells went off in her head at his words. She could return to her people, but at what cost? Life at the Outpost thrived on what the people did for the government and what they gave in return. Her family kept the people fed, but the supplies came from the Guardians.

Nothing was free.

Renna leaned forward, placing her arm on the table. She

narrowed her eyes at Grant. "You're not telling me everything. What happens if I choose to go back?"

Official Grant mirrored her posture, leaning down to meet her at eye level. "We hunt you down. Like the traitor you are."

The insult hurt, but she steeled her face, remaining neutral. She needed time to think. "What happens to my people if I go to the Forest Community?"

"We would replace you. Eventually."

Death or death?

Two choices before her, and each one carried the same sentence. Keep her life at the cost of how many deaths at the Outpost before they finally replaced her? Or risk her life to hopefully save as many people as she could?

Grant banged twice on the steel door, and it swung open, revealing the same guard as before. "Nighttime is approaching. I'm going to ask Stuart to bring in some food and a blanket. At dawn, this door will be unlocked. If you're here when I arrive, we will escort you back to the Forest Community. If you are not —well, we will know the Hunt is on."

Renna couldn't move even if she wanted to. Fear, hope, guilt, and anger waged war inside, all demanding her attention. She didn't even notice at first when Stuart reached out and grabbed Miles, forcing him out the door.

"Official Grant, may I have a moment to speak with Renna?"

Grant glanced down at the watch on his wrist. "Fine. When Stuart brings back the food, you're leaving."

"Thank you, sir."

"Don't thank me, son." He shook his head. "She looks like the kind to run."

24

G abbi's cheeks grew taut as a smile spread across her face. For the first time in five days, hope filled her.

"I take it this is good news?" Miss Parker asked, looking between both of them.

"Do you know where the tunnel leads?" Gabbi's mind raced with the possibilities. This could be the answer they had been looking for all along. They wouldn't have to go outside and risk exposure, and with Zeke's help, they could feed the entire Outpost. The news that the orphanage had a second door refueled her eagerness to fulfill her mother's mission.

Now they just had to figure out which places had these new tunnels and create a new map. But at least they were on the way to filling in the missing dots.

The young woman shook her head. "No, I've never gone far enough to find out." She let out a small laugh. "I guess that sounds silly, doesn't it?"

"No, not silly at all. It was smart." Zeke offered her a sympathetic smile. "I wouldn't have wanted to try either. But given our current circumstances ..."

Miss Parker gestured to the door. "So, where do you think it leads? More businesses and houses?"

Gabbi spoke up before Zeke could reply. "We don't know. But would you mind if we take a look?"

"Of course not. I mean, you helped us." Her eyes filled as she held the flour sack of food. "If it will help someone else, well then, we have to try."

"Thank you." Zeke cleared his throat. "We need to deliver the rest of the food, but we will come back. Will that be all right?"

"Of course. Thank you both so much."

"You're welcome. If you need anything at all, send Opal, and we'll do what we can to help." Gabbi followed Zeke back through the trap door and into the tunnel. Gabbi waited until the trap door clicked back into place before turning to Zeke. "Okay, what was that?"

"What do you mean?"

"Oh, come on. When Miss Parker said we could take a look, you said we would come back?"

Zeke gestured to the wheelbarrow. "We need to deliver this food, don't you think?"

"Of course." She pulled out the map and opened it. "But if we could take a look at the tunnel and figure out where it leads, it might just be the very thing that we've been looking for."

"Or it could be the very thing that gets us in trouble."

"Zeke, we've been worried about how to branch out among the rest of the Outpost, and now we have a real shot."

He picked up the wheelbarrow and started walking ahead. "Yeah, and it just opens up more risk for someone shutting the door in our faces."

"Hasn't that been a risk all along?"

"Yes, but our parents built this tunnel. They operated it at one time. Why didn't they mention there were more tunnels? Doesn't that seem odd to you?"

"I don't know. Maybe they forgot to mention it?" Even after the question left her lips, she realized how silly it sounded.

"I don't think they would forget something that important."

"No, I guess not." Gabbi stuck out her hand to stop a sack from tumbling out of the cart. "You think they are hiding something from us?"

"I don't know what to think, Gabbi." He stopped and turned to face her. "I just know we have to be careful. Promise me you won't go off by yourself, okay?"

Gabbi sighed, knowing he was right. They needed to be careful and pick their next step cautiously. It was hard for her to walk away from the tunnel when they were so close. Patience was never one of her strengths.

"Gabbi." Zeke's voice interrupted her thoughts.

"What?"

"Promise me."

"All right, fine." She averted her eyes under his scrutiny. "I won't go alone."

After a few moments, he sighed and picked up the cart. "What's our next stop?"

"The Trading House."

"That's going to be a toss-up." Zeke rolled his eyes. "Mr. Marlin is nothing but a cranky old man. He may not even let us in."

"Do you really think he will turn away food?"

"I have no doubt he's well-stocked in the food department."

"Are you insinuating that Mr. Marlin skims off his customers, Zeke?"

"Why do you think it's so hard to get a decent trade there? Or why sometimes you can't find an item that should be easier to come by?"

It was true. The Trading House started a way for the people to use their natural skills to trade jobs and items. Especially items the Officials didn't provide that month. While they gave the bare essentials, the citizens never knew what would be included. Over time, people crafted more luxury items, and Mr. Marlin inherited the Trading House from his ancestors.

"He does like to make it difficult to trade, even though the value doesn't match the trade sometimes."

"Nope." Zeke grunted. "So, I have no doubt that Mr. Marlin is sitting pretty right now."

"Well, at one point, his family helped with these tunnels, so surely he won't turn us over." It was more of a statement to assure herself, but Zeke's silence didn't help alleviate the worry.

Zeke parked the wheelbarrow out of sight of the trap door and then grabbed the assigned flour sack. "Let's just get his stop over with."

"Sure."

Zeke took the lead this time, rapping hard on the wooden door. Gabbi hung a little back behind Zeke, trying to calm her nerves as the hinges on a lock slid, and a metal flap opened. Two eyes surrounded by wrinkles flashed into view briefly before going away.

"Who's there?"

"It's Zeke and Gabbi, Mr. Marlin."

A huff came from the old man. "Do your parents know you are down here?"

Zeke raised his eyebrows at Gabbi. "Yes. They sent us."

This time, the man snorted. "That's a fine tale you're spinning. Everyone knows they loathe each other."

Gabbi had to cover her mouth to keep from laughing out loud. Leave it to Mr. Marlin to not sugarcoat their family's history or the fact the entire Outpost knew about it. She cleared her throat, "My mother sent me to find my father, and part of a tunnel had collapsed. I had to ask Zeke and his father for help."

"I bet that was interesting." The man's tone changed to interest. "Now, what are you two doing here? On our closed tunnel, I might add."

"We wanted to make sure you were okay and offer some food." Gabbi held up a flour sack.

"Oh." His voice faltered for a moment. "I'm ... fine. You wasted your time."

Gabbi took a step forward beside Zeke. "Come on, Mr. Marlin, we made enough to share."

The flap slammed closed, and Zeke mouthed, "I told you so."

"Wait." She reached for his arm to stop him from leaving.

The door swung open, and he held out his arms for the sack. "Fine. I'll take it, but I'm not doing any trades right now, so don't expect anything in return."

"Not a problem, Mr. Marlin."

"You say that now, but everyone always wants something. Everything ends up having a price. Even if it comes in the guise of free."

Gabbi's heart softened just a tad at the man's statement, and she tried to put herself in his situation. Could she handle the endless haggling over items and the pressure of deciding an item's value?

Perhaps he wasn't so bad after all, but just misunderstood? She glimpsed at Zeke, but by his expression, he wasn't thinking the same thoughts.

"I promise, we don't expect anything in return." She gave the man a smile. "We are just making sure that our neighbors have food."

"No one would be needing food if it weren't for your sister." The old man sneered. "She's the reason we are all in this mess to begin with. She's a traitor to the Outpost."

Gabbi sucked in a breath at the words, and opened her mouth with a comeback, but Zeke beat her to it.

"Well, Mr. Marlin, enjoy your food, we need to be going."

Gabbi glared at Zeke, but he tugged her along, and the old

man went back inside his house, mumbling something about people needing to stay in their assigned jobs.

"Don't say a word, just keep walking." Zeke gently led her down the stairs and around the corner, where they'd left the wheelbarrow.

"The nerve of that man!"

"You see why I was dreading that encounter?"

Gabbi rambled on, completely ignoring him. "And to think for a moment, I felt sorry for him. I actually thought maybe we misunderstood him."

"I can't even come up with an excuse for him." Zeke sighed. "I'm sorry he insulted your sister, though."

"Well, I'm sure he won't be the last." Gabbi kicked at a small stone embedded in the dirt. "Everyone's going to have something to say, and if—I mean *when* Renna comes back, it could get really bad."

"Then we will weather that storm when it happens, and we will get through it. Until then, we just keep doing what we can to help."

"Thank you, Zeke. You've been a good friend to me."

A teasing smile lifted the corner of his mouth. "Well, I figured you were going to need one."

"Zeke!" She playfully punched him in the arm and set off down the tunnel.

"Too soon?" He asked, catching up to her.

"Way too soon."

25

As soon as the metal door closed, Miles opened up his arms, and Renna collapsed into them, relishing how they enveloped her. For a moment, she forgot all about the Outpost, the Forest Community, Official Grant, and his impossible choice. She cast away all the times Miles had pushed her buttons. Renna even forgot how he stopped her outside of the Gates.

Because at that moment, nothing else mattered but the thud of his racing heart that echoed her own. Or the warmth of his cheek pressed to the top of her head. Or the way the simple act of his embrace calmed the fear running rampant inside.

It was perfect. How she wished she could freeze time. To stay with him. It was an impossible wish. Instead, she banished that dream from her thoughts and clung to the image in her mind, memorizing every detail. Tears threatened to expose the misery that kept trying to crack open her happiness.

Miles must have sensed her unease because he suddenly pushed her from him, his eyes displaying his own agony. "Renna, you have to come back with me."

How simple it would be to nod her agreement and go. To

give in to the moment of terror and pick the easy choice. To save herself and stay with Miles. To find some sort of fulfillment in the Forest Community. Her throat went dry. "I can't— Miles, you know I can't."

He gripped her shoulders harder. "You must. This is a game to them, Renna. A cruel and exciting hunt. This is what they train for, and you will lose."

If he expected his words to paralyze her—to scare her— well, he succeeded. Tears slipped down her face. "I know." She barely got the words out. "I'm just now figuring that out."

He let go and walked away from her, pacing the small room. "Okay. Give me a second. We will figure something out."

Miles kept rambling, but Renna didn't hear any of his ideas. They wouldn't work, no matter how much she wished they could.

She reached out to Miles, trying to get him to stop and listen. "There's nothing you can do. I can't go back with you. I can't leave my people."

"You can. You just won't."

There it was. The ugly truth, fissuring a gap between them, and she didn't know if it could ever be mended. Miles finally voiced what they were both avoiding. Renna cleared her throat. "Would you? Would you leave Keegan and Elaine and everyone else at your camp just to save yourself?"

Miles's face hardened. "They would want me to live." He crossed the distance between them and threaded his fingers through hers. "Your parents would want you to live."

"I can't live with myself if anyone dies because of me." Her voice caught in her throat. Could her heart shatter any more? Renna didn't know how much more she could take.

"Then I will go with you."

She ripped her hand from his. "No!" She shook her head, rejecting the idea before it had the chance to take root. "I will not let you risk your life like that."

"I already risked my life, Renna. Don't you see?" Miles rubbed his face. "The moment I went back and helped you in the forest, I gambled my life. I knew I would have to bring you back to Thomas—to Grant. I knew who you were, and I brought you back anyway."

"You helped me, Miles. I was bleeding and hurt."

"Yes, I did. Even though I knew I would have to turn you over. I didn't know what Grant would do, to you, to me. I took a Speaker away from the Outpost. I jeopardized the entire Forest Community."

"So, you understand more than anyone else the guilt." Renna let out a shaky breath. "Miles, I did the same when I left the Outpost. I endangered everyone, and I can't walk off into the sunset—with my life intact—for the sacrifice of theirs."

"Going alone is not an option." He crossed his arms, lost in the thought. "Maybe if you had help ... if we could come up with a plan to evade them."

"You know Grant won't let you come—even if I agreed to it."

"Which means the only option is for you to come back with me." Miles's voice took on a whole new level of pleading. "You're not going to make it back before the Gates lock again."

He was right—heaven help her—he was right. The odds of her making it through the forest, on her own, were slim. But to have to wait out another three days? It was laughable.

Renna knew they only made it this long because of Miles. He was the reason she was still alive. Or were they? Something Grant said earlier sprang back to her mind. "Wait a minute." It was her turn to pace. "We only made it through so far because you work for Grant. It was all a ruse."

His eyebrows shot up. "No, it wasn't a ruse—"

"He said he gives you safe passage in exchange for bringing people to him." Did that mean that it was all some sick joke? Did Miles plan on bringing her to Grant all along?

"He does." Miles reached for her hand, his eyes swarming

with an intensity that made it impossible to look away—not that she wanted to. Because the way he looked at her, with such sincerity and warmth, held her captive. "But Renna, I swear to you I wasn't ever going to take you to him."

Her stomach roiled at her suspicion. How could she doubt him now? Miles had proved himself to be trustworthy over and over. "I believe you." Tears blurred her vision. "But Miles, you still bring people to Grant for this very purpose, and you'll keep doing it."

He took a step backward, her words landing on their intended mark, though she didn't feel any better for saying them.

Disbelief and hurt crossed his face. "Wait. Are you saying you won't come back with me because Thomas has a deal with the Guardians?"

"I won't go back with you because I can't live with the knowledge I'm hurting people."

"But you think I can?"

"That's not what I'm saying—"

"I don't get to decide who I bring to Grant, Renna. I have no say in the matter." He narrowed his eyes. "Have I looked the other way when one or two people a month are asked to make this decision? Okay, sure. But Renna—those people had already made the decision to walk away from the Outposts. And they always choose to stay at the Forest Community."

"I never wanted to leave the Outpost. You made that choice for me." As soon as the words were out, she wished she could take them back.

He nodded. "You'll get your wish this time. Because this decision—no, this death wish—I won't be a part of it."

Tears pooled in her eyes as his declaration settled over her. How did this conversation go sideways so quickly? How, in a matter of moments, did she feel so alone? Renna wanted to take back everything she said, to start over and not spend their last few moments together arguing.

The door swung open, and Stuart was there with a tray in one hand and a blue wool blanket in the other. He glanced back and forth between the two of them and whistled. "Tough room."

Stuart tossed her the blanket before placing the tray on the table. "Time to go. If you haven't persuaded her now, you never will."

"Hang on." Renna let the blanket fall and stepped toward Miles for one last hug. He hesitated before finally pulling her towards him. With his other hand, he tucked a stray strand of hair behind her ear, then traced her jaw with his finger. His eyes lowered to her lips, and before he could move another inch, she rose on her tiptoes and kissed him.

The perfect moment minutes before could not compare with now. There was the Renna before meeting Miles and the one after. How could she walk away from him? Tears threatened to spill, but she closed her eyes tighter, ignoring them completely. Before she was ready, Miles pulled away, resting his forehead on hers.

Stuart cleared his throat. "Time's up."

Miles kissed her forehead, and she didn't want him to leave with so much left unsaid between them. What if she never made it home? What if she couldn't ever tell him how she really felt about him? "Miles, I—"

"Please be here in the morning." He lowered his voice and whispered into her ear. "But if you can't, stay alive long enough for me to find you."

26

Day Six

Every muscle in Miles's body tensed—waiting for the moment he would be released and could bust out of his temporary cage. Who would be waiting for him on the other side of the door? Official Grant? Stuart? Or some other nameless robot doing the dirty work of the Guardians?

It didn't matter, because he would get out of here and find some way to catch up to Renna. Miles didn't even pretend to hold onto some fantasy that she would still be waiting for him this morning. The look in her eyes as the Guardian dragged him away confirmed what he already knew in his gut.

Renna would do everything in her power to get back to the Outpost, and he would do everything in his power to make sure she made it there alive.

He didn't even know why he wasted his breath trying to convince her of some other future. A future with him at the Forest Community. As if that alone was enough to get her to save herself and forget about her family. Her people.

For a few brief seconds, he entertained the idea he just might be enough to get her to change her mind.

A click of the bolt on the door of Miles's cell jarred his thoughts back to the present as the metal panel on his door slid open, revealing a tall figure standing on the other side. The man bent slightly to peer into the panel.

"I figured you would refuse to eat breakfast before we go to check what Renna decided." Grant's voice filtered in through the bars of the opening.

Miles got to his feet, joining Grant at the bars, and simply nodded.

Grant let out a long sigh before placing a small round plate on the steel ledge of the window sill. "That's what I thought. Maybe just eat this on the way then."

Miles eyed the wrapping but didn't say anything.

"Come on, Miles. You can't tell me you don't like bacon biscuits."

Bacon? And a biscuit? Miles's stomach rumbled in anticipation. Guiltily, he reached for the biscuit. Would Renna have anything to eat this morning? Miles's pack carried most of their food rations. "Thanks."

"You won't be thanking me when we find out that your girlfriend is gone."

The buttery, flaky crust turned to stone in his mouth. "She's not my girlfriend." It would be better not to show Grant any of his feelings for Renna. It would only complicate matters even more and give the Guardian more leverage.

"You don't sound very convincing." Grant slammed the window shut, and a few seconds later, the latches and bolts clicked one after another before the metal door slid open. "My goodness, boy. Didn't Thomas tell you that you can't get involved with those people?"

Those people? Miles forced the remaining bite of biscuit

down, ignoring the question. He wouldn't give Grant the satisfaction of answering.

Thomas ordered him not to get involved with the people he found in the woods. To separate it from his personal life. Show them just enough to be kind and welcoming, listen to their stories, but don't get invested in their lives.

Miles broke every one of those rules with Renna. He stayed up all night, going over in his head what he could have done differently.

No matter how many times he ran the scenario in his mind, the problem didn't lie with Renna or the fact he helped her. It was with Thomas and Grant. Miles had been so blind.

He never questioned Thomas on why the Guardians let them live in peace or why they granted them safe passage through the woods. Was he so bitter against the Outpost, about living on the run with his father and uncle, that he hadn't even taken a moment to stop and think?

If it wasn't for Renna, would he ever have questioned this entire process? Miles wasn't so sure he would have, and that little piece of information made him sick.

Grant led him out of the holding cell, and Miles tossed his empty plate to the guard standing at the entrance. The Guardian fumbled with the plate but managed to keep it from falling to the ground and shattering into pieces. Miles thought he heard a curse thrown his way but simply continued following Grant to the other part of the building.

Maybe, just maybe, Renna would surprise him. He waited at the bottom of the stairs as Grant pushed open the door.

"She didn't take the bait." Grant's voice held a notch of admiration as Miles marched past him and into the room to see for himself.

Deep down, Miles knew Renna wouldn't be waiting for him on the other side of the door. But as Grant turned the knob and pushed the door back, a tiny spark of hope still lingered.

So much for hope. Miles anxiously searched around for a note, her plans, or just a few short sentences to show that she hadn't given up. His eyes trailed over the small room, but nothing appeared out of place. An empty plate on the small table was the only evidence someone had been in the space at all.

"I'm sorry, Miles."

"Are you?"

Grant's face appeared momentarily shocked at Miles's bold question before he composed his face. "Of course. I'd hoped she would go back to the Forest Community."

"I wish I could say I believe you."

"Careful, boy. You are already walking a very thin line."

Miles glanced around the room once more. A blanket sat on the opposite side of the room, neatly folded into a square. Renna didn't have much in the way of supplies, so why leave the blanket? He would have stuffed it into the bag before downing the food and running.

He knelt beside it, running his hand over the tattered yet neatly folded fabric. A hard object was underneath the first layer, and he grasped the cool metal, already knowing what it was before his fingers traced the familiar letter S.

She had a few hours' head start on him. It shouldn't be too hard to pick up her trail. A grin slid across his face as an image of her stomping through the forest filled his mind. But just as quickly as it came, it faded, and worry filled its place. Renna would no doubt leave every trace of her trail. If he could track her—so could the Guardians.

But the question was, who would find her first?

27

P ain shot through Renna's side and reverberated down her leg to her injured foot. She had long ago given up on tracking how far she ran or even glancing back toward what she left behind. Who she left behind.

Miles.

A low overhanging branch slapped her across the cheek, momentarily distracting her from her thoughts as she quickly darted past it. The break was just enough time to clear her mind once more from the stabbing pain in her ribs.

All Renna was doing was tormenting herself. She had to stop thinking about Miles. Thoughts of Miles would only lead to more hurt. As much as she hated to admit it, he didn't matter anymore. The only thing that mattered now was her family and people. Getting back to the Outpost—alive—was the most important thing.

Everything else, in contrast, was a distraction. One Renna couldn't afford to indulge.

Another wave of pain washed over her and sucked the breath from her lungs, forcing her to stop. Leaning against a tree, she clutched her side, trying to even out her breathing.

A surge of panic threatened to overtake her, and she struggled to squash it back. She searched the forest floor and counted rocks larger than her hand. It was a silly game, but it kept her focus on anything else but how little control she had over this whole situation.

How did the Runners race through the woods every day? This wasn't for the faint of heart. Although—to be fair—they probably had a well-traveled path and didn't have to run through the forest, tripping over old roots and rocks and dodging Guardians.

And they certainly didn't have a week-old injury to slow them down with each step.

The urge to rest overtook all of her judgment, and she started scanning the area for a stopping point. Could she take a moment to slow down? Her foot throbbed, and she could swear there was something sticky in the bottom of her sock. If Miles were here, she wouldn't hear the end of it if she'd ripped out one of her stitches.

But he wasn't here. She made that decision for both of them. She peered up at the pink sky and sighed. By now, Grant and the others would have found her empty cell. They would already have begun hunting her. If she wanted to stay alive, she had to keep moving, stay off her foot, and somehow get back to the Gates. A feat that was utterly unmanageable since she was stuck in the middle of the woods all alone.

She had no time to check her foot. She must keep moving.

Gulping in one more deep breath, she took a step forward, then another, and another. Each step brought her closer to the Outpost, but it also took her farther away from who she left behind.

By noon, the sun beat down with such ferocity she couldn't keep the sweat out of her eyes or her limbs from shaking with exhaustion. She had to find a place to cool off, rest, and drink some water. As if in reminder, her stomach growled. The last thing she ate was the pitiful dinner the Guardian brought the night before. She forced down whatever watery soup they gave her, wrapped the loaf of bread in her napkin, and took a few small sips of the water.

But none of that would matter if she didn't find a place to cool off. The humidity was thick and coated her lungs, bogging down her air and making her cough. Her face, neck, forearms, and even her scalp burned. She didn't need a mirror to tell her fair, freckled skin was lobster red.

She lowered the backpack she'd found in the building and pulled out the canteen, taking a couple sips. The last thing she needed to do was give into her thirst and down the entire supply of water now.

Where would Miles look for shelter? She instantly recalled the cave they'd escaped in when the Officials were first chasing them. What she wouldn't give to be back there with Miles. She would have to find somewhere that could easily be hidden in plain sight. A huge fallen log or large rocks. Not exactly the easiest thing to find in this massive forest that never ended.

Renna tossed the canteen back in her bag and zipped it. Now wasn't the time to wish for things that couldn't happen. And she couldn't afford to think about him right now, either. Shelter and water were her top two priorities. Without either, the Guardians wouldn't have to kill her. She would just waste away.

Pressing on, she ventured deeper into the forest, trying to keep an eye out for a water source, shelter, and anything that might alert her to a Guardian's presence. Difficult with the sun beating down on her head and her foot throbbing.

But as the heat finally started to subside, she came across a familiar outcropping of rocks. No. This wasn't happening.

She spun around in a circle, her eyes sweeping the area. But her heart already understood what her mind didn't want to accept.

She'd somehow come back to where she paused earlier in the day for a break. Tears welled up in her eyes, blurring the rocks in front of her. How could this happen? She ran for hours, then walked for several more, only to end up circling back around.

Some hero she'd turned out to be. How would she help her people if she couldn't even navigate her way back to the Outpost?

"Keep looking. She couldn't have made it that far yet." Voices carried to her from her left and she didn't waste any time sprinting for the large boulders that had frustrated her moments before.

If she could climb over the rocks and down the other side, surely, she could find some kind of crevice or ledge to hide while the Guardians passed. She stepped on a smaller rock to her left and hoisted herself up to the top of the nearest boulder. Jagged stone scrapped her palms, but she kept pulling. She climbed up and over the next rock, and then down to a thin ledge where she could squeeze behind an opening.

"Why didn't we go searching for her farther out?"

Renna strained to make out the other guards' words. Lights flickered above her head, and she slid down the last rock, scrapping her arms in the process.

"They all make the same mistake and never learn from it. Why do you think we use this area? It all eventually loops back to this zone unless you know what you're looking for."

"Sneaky."

So that's why she ended up back here. It was a dead end. She leaned against the cool stone and tried to slow down her racing heart.

"You think she's foolish enough to be out here?" One of the men asked, confusion in his tone.

"She would have to be crazy to attempt something so dangerous." The other man's voice sounded wistful. As if he would enjoy finding her hurt—or worse. "If she's crazy enough to hide in there, the scorpions will drive her out soon enough."

Scorpions? Out here? Sweat broke out across her forehead and down her neck. How long could she hide before they found her? A beam of light stopped inches above her foot, and she pulled it back, praying she'd moved it in time.

Heart racing, she froze, every muscle in her body tight and alert. Her forearm burned where it had scraped against the rocks, and sweat stung her eyes. She forced them closed and tried to resist the urge to wipe them.

"We know you're there, girly." Was that the voice who asked all the questions? She couldn't tell. Every joint in her body ached and trembled. She didn't know how much longer she would be able to stand still.

"Come on, let's go. She'll show herself eventually."

Was that sympathy in the other man's voice? Renna couldn't tell, and she didn't care as long as they backed away from the rocks so she could collapse in a heap on the hard stone.

Finally, footsteps retreated from the edge, and she used the inside of her collar to wipe away the sweat. She slipped out of the crevice, taking a moment to gather her thoughts and settle her nerves. That was close.

Too close.

She touched her neck, where her silver S usually rested. It was more difficult than she thought to leave it behind. Renna had never taken the necklace off before. It was as much a part of her as her position in the community. She just hoped Miles was the one who found it.

She just spent half a day going around in circles. A tiny nugget of doubt settled in her stomach. No matter if she somehow found Miles—it didn't change the fact she chose this. It was her decision to walk away. To escape into the forest and become ...

Hunted.

Wiping her hands on her jeans, blood on her fingertips snagged her attention. Several nails were torn, the delicate skin around her nailbeds split. She reached for her backpack but stopped when she grabbed the canteen. She couldn't waste the precious resource to clean her hands.

Please find me, Miles. I don't think I can do this alone.

28

"How about we get you home?" Official Grant waved over a small group of Guardians.

"Sir." The tallest of the three spoke for the group as he approached. There was something familiar about his voice, but Miles couldn't place why.

"I need you to take Miles back to his community, please." Grant turned to the two other men. "As for you two, form a team. We are going hunting."

"Yes, sir!" With quick but firm salutes, they ran off barking orders to the grunts under their rank.

Red hot anger blurred Miles's vision. They were talking about hunting Renna right in front of him. Grant just flung it out like it was a sport, and the Guardians were excited.

Grant walked away from them, giving orders to a nearby group of guards. The one left standing beside Miles removed his gun from its holster and raised it toward him.

"Move."

Somehow, Miles got his feet to cooperate and walked toward the nearest vehicle. He had only seen these large machines once or twice in his lifetime. It made sense they would provide the Guardians with them.

The man pushed him to the right-side door and pulled it open. "You're riding in the back."

Miles nodded but took a second to look around them. There had to be some way to ditch the Guardian. He had to just wait for the right time to ambush the man. But Renna's life depended on him, and Miles would do whatever it cost to save her.

The chances of escaping narrowed significantly if he got in the vehicle. Guardians were stationed all around the compound. They were fewer in numbers since the green light was issued on Renna, but there were enough of them that even if he overtook the Guardian standing behind him, he wouldn't make it far.

Metal pressed into his back, and Miles stiffened. If he was going to escape, now would be the chance.

"Don't even think about it." The Guardian's voice was low and stern. "Get in the jeep, son."

The guard's lilt of the word *son* made Miles pause long enough to think through the consequences of trying to escape.

The man took advantage of Miles's hesitation and practically shoved him into the vehicle. His shin banged on the side of the jeep as he tried to right himself. The door slammed behind him, and Miles searched the panel for some way to open it, but there wasn't a handle on the inside. The Guard climbed in behind the wheel but didn't immediately start the vehicle. Miles began to ask what was going on when a figure approached his window.

The Guardian turned on the jeep and pushed a button to lower his window just enough that Miles could hear. Official Grant peered down at him, a smug smile on his face.

"Have a safe trip back to the Forest Community, Miles."

Miles ignored the man's words and instead just stared at him, doing his best to make sure his face appeared neutral.

"Oh, and Miles," Grant slapped the door. "Don't forget to tell Thomas you owe me double the number of people from now on, for your protection." A smile lit up Grant's face. "I'm sure he will be so thrilled at the news."

The jeep rumbled to life, and the driver glanced over his shoulder at him as Grant walked away. "Put on your seatbelt, kid."

"How long will it take to get back to my community?"

"A few hours."

That didn't make him feel better. He missed his opportunity to surprise the Guardian and escape. How was he supposed to develop a new plan and execute it and not drive so far that it would be impossible to find Renna again?

"I know it doesn't seem like it right now, but Official Grant is a good guy."

"Whatever you need to tell yourself, pal." Miles was not in the mood for small talk with someone who would do whatever he thought was necessary to fulfill his orders. The Guardian was a walking, talking puppet.

If he couldn't get his door open and jump out, could he somehow overpower the Guardian and grab the wheel? Too many things that could go wrong with that plan. The Guardian could crash while trying to fight him off, or Miles might not be able to control the jeep long enough to stop the vehicle. Even though they were on a path, trees and rocks thickly lined the edges of the makeshift road.

"Listen, kid. It's not like you are innocent here. You willingly left the Outpost and joined the Forest Community. Then you went a step more and started bringing people to Official Grant, who is a leader in the government you abandoned." The Guardian watched him through the mirror on the windshield. "You're the one who led people to their deaths."

"They always came to the Community. I didn't know Grant was hunting down people. If I had, I'd—"

"You'd what, exactly?" The guard's voice grew cynical. "You'd stand up to Grant? There's nothing you can do, kid, and the quicker you figure that out, the better it will be for you."

Miles rubbed his face. "I don't know, but I wouldn't have let Grant have them."

The guard sighed. "You really shouldn't be telling me all of this."

"What are you going to do? Arrest me? I'm already in trouble with Grant."

The man let out a loud laugh, and an old memory resurfaced. Miles stared at the Guardian as if that would somehow make the memory clearer. Except he couldn't get a good look at his face with the shiny helmet blocking his features.

Miles needed to focus on getting back to Renna. He continued his examination of the vehicle. The doors were a no-go, and there were bars and netting running from the ceiling to the floor, acting as a barrier to keep him in the back. If he had his supplies, he could easily cut the netting. He searched the back of the jeep. There had to be something he could use to saw away the cord.

"Are you nervous, kid?"

Miles paused in his search so he wouldn't draw more attention to himself. "It's not me that I'm worried about."

The corner of the man's mouth turned down. "How well did you know the girl?"

Why the sudden curiosity about the Speaker? Miles leaned forward, grabbing ahold of the netting. "Why do you care?" He pulled while he spoke, testing for weakness. "You're a Guardian. Are you supposed to care about such things?"

The guard stared Miles down in the mirror for a few seconds before looking back at the rough trail, every few feet avoiding large ruts that would no doubt do some serious damage to the vehicle. "Because I need to know what I'm about to do is worth it."

Another warning went off in his head. What was the guard talking about? Was he going to try to hurt Renna somehow? No. The look in the guard's eyes didn't show any sort of malice— just the opposite. Was that concern? Miles couldn't tell, but it was like the Guardian wanted to help him.

"I don't understand." Miles narrowed his eyes at the man. "If I didn't know better, it would sound like you were going to help me."

The man swerved away from another deep rut in the path, going off the trail as he whipped around it. "Against all reason, I am." The guard slammed on the brakes, the force propelling Miles forward, his face mashing against the rough cord. "I told you to wear your seatbelt for a reason."

The guard pulled off his helmet and placed it on the seat beside him before turning around. "It's good to see you again, Miles."

Miles's breath caught in his throat, and he shook his head, not believing the sight before him. There wasn't any way this was possible, but there he was, sitting a few feet away. "Uncle Mack?"

"In the flesh."

Gripping the net in front of him, Miles tried to get his mind to stop swarming with questions. It didn't make any sense. Miles was a kid the last time that he saw his uncle. He went to sleep in the cave, and the next morning, his father told him his uncle was gone. No explanation from his father, and his uncle didn't leave behind a note. Any time that Miles tried to bring up the subject, his father shrugged him off and told him some things were better left in the past.

"You became one of them." He couldn't hold back the bitterness that welled up inside and spewed from his lips. "How could you do that?"

Pain flickered across his uncle's face. "Didn't you do the same?"

Anger burned away the bitterness in an instant. "I didn't abandon my family for the likes of them!"

Hurt flashed across his uncle's face. "You think I just up and walked away from you? From my brother?"

"I don't know what to believe anymore." A smidgen of doubt worked its way into his brain. What if his uncle didn't just up and leave? What if he didn't have a choice?

"I know you don't have any reason to trust me anymore. But I am trying to help you." His uncle sighed and then rubbed a hand across his face. "You're going after the Speaker, aren't you?"

"Are you going to stop me?"

A few seconds of silence went by before his uncle finally said, "No."

Miles wasn't expecting that. "Why not?"

"Because I promised your father I would always look after you." He shifted the jeep back into drive. "I can't keep that promise if you're dead."

29

"Can I see the map?" Gabbi's father asked, his hand outstretched from the bed. He seemed to be in better spirits today and stayed awake for longer, but he was still weak.

"Miss Parker said she has a second door at the orphanage." She dug the parchment out of her bag and passed it over. "Did you know anything about this tunnel, Dad?"

Father scooted up in the bed, leaning against the headboard for support. He unrolled the map, spreading it across his lap, and then sighed. "No, we didn't know about it."

"I don't understand. Why would Grammy and Grandaddy keep this a secret? If they helped build the tunnels that connect ours to the rest of the businesses on this block, why not leave that information for us?"

"Those are the right questions to ask." Wrinkles formed in between his eyebrows as he studied the map. "Unfortunately, I don't have the answer for them. I have no idea why they wouldn't have told me."

Gabbi pulled up a chair to the side of the bed. "But wouldn't it make sense for them to want to expand? To connect all the houses and businesses?"

"Yes—" A coughing fit disrupted her father's words, and Gabbi reached for the glass of water on the nightstand. He took a few sips before handing it back to her. "Thank you."

Gabbi placed the back of her hand on his forehead. "It's almost time for more fever medicine. Can you wait for a little while longer?"

"You worry too much, Gabbi-girl." He gave her a weak smile. "I'm going to be just fine."

"You better be, old man."

Gabbi looked up as Mother entered the room carrying a tray of soup. "Ready for lunch?"

"You two fuss over me too much." But he accepted the food and grinned. "What's this? I finally have dessert?"

"Don't get too excited. It's not too sweet. You don't need a lot of sugar on your stomach."

"What's the point of dessert if it's not sweet?"

"Would you like me to take it away?" She grabbed the plate, but Father pulled it back.

"I didn't say that."

Gabbi laughed at her parents' banter. Worry and anxiety constantly plagued her, and for those brief few minutes, it was nice to watch them be themselves. The comebacks were a daily occurrence with those two, and it reminded Gabbi of normalcy, even if only for a few minutes. It was a comfort she hadn't realized she needed.

"How did the deliveries go yesterday?" Father asked, lifting his spoon.

"They were grateful." Gabbi tucked a loose strand of hair behind her ear. "But no one knew anything about another trap door."

Which meant the orphanage was the only one.

Gabbi wanted to go immediately back to Miss Parker and see for herself just where the mysterious tunnel led, but Zeke refused, insisting they should speak to their parents first. Gabbi obliged, not sure what good it would do. Hopefully Zeke had better success with his family.

"Gabbi? Are you all right?"

Jumping at Mother's question, Gabbi cleared her throat and forced a reassuring smile. "Yes, I'm fine. Trying to figure out this tunnel. I'll admit it has me rather stumped."

Father tore a piece from his roll and dunked it in his soup. "You're not the only one. My parents never mentioned it to me, and your mother didn't know about the tunnel system at all until after we married."

"Did Grandaddy and Grammy leave any information about this whole project? You just called it a system, and you couldn't tell Mom until after you were married, so maybe they had some sort of documents about it somewhere."

"I suppose it's possible." Father exchanged a skeptical glance with her mother. "But all of those records would be at home."

Hope deflated in an instant. Of course it wouldn't be that easy. Why would it be? "You don't have it here?"

"No. I wouldn't want anything of that nature here in the bakery office." He frowned. "It's at home—safely hidden away."

It was understandable that her parents would go to great lengths to hide something of such importance—and incriminating. Businesses were subject to random searches if the Officials ever got the urge to go snooping.

If the documents weren't here, then Gabbi would have to go and get them. She sat up a little straighter, the decision made. "Then I will go and look."

"Absolutely not!" Mother's voice rose in surprise.

"Just the other day, you were going to send me to go get Father. So what's the difference?"

"I was desperate, Gabbi. He was sick, and I couldn't leave him there all alone." She narrowed her eyes. "And then you decided to go and leave me behind."

Softening her gaze, Gabbi continued but kept her tone serious. "But you can leave the rest of the Outpost to fend for themselves?"

Hurt filled her mother's face as Gabbi's words hit their mark. "It's not the same thing, and you know it."

Gabbi leaned back in her chair slightly. "Then I can go down the new tunnel at Miss Parker's and see who answers on the other side."

Her father tried to sit up straighter in bed and provoked a coughing fit. "You are not going into this blind." His voice hardened when he finally caught his breath. "We don't know who we can trust outside of our tunnel. The fact there's another tunnel is proof there's too much we don't know about."

"Unless something in Grammy's journal tells us otherwise." Gabbi waved her hand in annoyance. "You took a chance and came to the tunnel."

Father narrowed his eyes. "We have special permission to leave our house early to get to the bakery before the reading. But now—with the lockdown—it's too risky."

"So I will go to Zeke's. It's only a house or two away from ours."

"I don't like this." Mother stood and started pacing. "And Zeke said his parents didn't know anything either?"

"We talked to both of them. They were as clueless as you."

"I'm not sure—"

"I will go out the back of the Blacksmith's shop. There's nothing behind their house or the neighbors'."

Her father pushed back his tray and picked up the map. "But you will have to go around the corner and up the street."

"So, I will go in the middle of the night, when everyone is asleep."

"You won't be able to take any light."

"No. I wouldn't." Her stomach flip-flopped at the idea of sneaking around the Outpost at night without any light.

"What does Zeke say about all of this?" Father met her gaze, his eyes a mixture of concern and curiosity.

"I haven't brought it up yet. But he can't stop me."

He frowned. "That's not what I'm worried about. I know he won't say anything. I just would feel better if you weren't alone."

"She won't be."

Gabbi gasped at the voice coming from the doorway. Zeke leaned against the door jamb, a grim smile on his lips.

"Zeke! What are you doing here?"

"Did you forget we planned to meet and discuss our next steps? I got worried when you didn't meet me in the tunnel."

Gabbi turned her gaze from him to the clock on the dresser. "I'm sorry. I was talking to my parents about the new tunnel and completely lost track of time."

"It's okay." He pulled away from the doorway. "How are you feeling, sir?"

"Much better, son." He sighed, looking back and forth between them. "If I agree to this crazy little adventure, you will go with Gabbi?"

It was a question, but also bordered on stating that Zeke didn't have much of a choice. She did her best not to roll her eyes at her father's words. She was more than capable of going out alone but couldn't deny having someone else with her would be comforting.

Zeke met Gabbi's eyes, his stare intense, sending her stomach into a flurry of nerves. He didn't miss a beat when he replied, "Of course, sir, you have my word. She'll be safe with me."

30

Hours passed before the Guardians finally gave up and left. Renna had already lost most of the day's travel, and the longer she hid in the rocks, the more anxious she grew. Her legs ached from the tight space, and she desperately wanted to stand, but fear held her to her hiding spot. What if they were waiting to catch her as soon as she crawled out of the rocks?

Cover of darkness seemed like the best choice, but even that didn't seem to go in her favor. A full moon illuminated the night sky, casting stark shadows all around.

Had she waited too long and missed a better opportunity to flee? Renna was too exposed, and her stiff legs kept her mind focused on just how much they hurt. The urge to jump up and run nearly made her bolt from the tight crevice. Common sense was the only thing holding her back.

There wasn't anything she could do but try to peer over the rocks, scope out the area, and then make a plan.

She took a deep breath and stood. Her knees protested as she stretched. Climbing up the rocks proved a much harder task than falling down them. Somehow, she managed to get to the top and pull herself up to take a quick peek over the edge.

Not a single vehicle or light in sight. The lack of Guardian presence didn't mean they weren't there—hiding—just waiting to pounce.

The forest was quiet. Almost too quiet. Renna let go of the rock and dropped back down to the small ledge. She couldn't stay in the rocks. She hadn't seen a scorpion yet, but she didn't want to stay to find out if the Guardian had been simply trying to scare her out of hiding or if he had told the truth.

Water and food were her two top priorities, but she didn't know where she should go. Recalling the area in her mind should not be hard since she managed to walk in a giant circle today—for hours. Except the forest was so vast that it all blurred together.

When she left Official Grant, she headed in what she hoped was north, toward the Outpost. Since she made a loop, there had to be something she missed. A trail, passage, or something the Guardians used to move to a different location.

But where was it?

Think, Renna, think.

She retraced her steps in her mind, but her memory was hazy.

The forest was thick and the brush nearly impossible to sprint through. At the top of a steep incline, a small break in the trees had intrigued her enough to pause. She'd briefly debated taking it but kept running straight, not wanting to veer away from her heading.

Renna could kick herself now. What if that was the trail? A way around a large hill or some sort of natural barrier?

Just move. No more stalling.

She pulled herself back up, and instead of hovering at the top, she placed her foot in a crevice and hoisted herself over and down to the other side. Her lungs burned, exhausted from the second climb, but she couldn't afford to be exposed for long. She rolled over to her stomach, pushed herself up, and ran into the forest.

Ignoring everything around her, she focused on the trees, where she could disappear more into the darkness. Pain stabbed her sides, and her breath came out in short puffs of air. Renna pressed on, ignoring the buzzing in her ears until she was well hidden under the thick branches.

Collapsing at the base of a oak tree, Renna leaned against the trunk, and concentrated on getting her breathing back under control. She had made it. No idea how, but she had. There was a long way to go, but she crossed the first hurdle.

As she waited for the ringing in her ears to go away, she took a few small sips of her remaining water. The cool liquid soothed the dry patches of her throat. She allowed one more gulp before she put the canteen away.

You can do this, Renna. Move your feet. She could almost hear Miles's voice in her head, urging her forward, telling her not to give up. She pushed off from the tree and crept deeper into the forest.

.

31

"What promise?" Miles asked, taking a seat close to the fire. His uncle finished warming up food in some type of container he'd never seen before and passed it to him.

"It's good. Eat up." His uncle held out the food and a spoon. "Come on, you have to be hungry."

Nodding, Miles accepted the food and took a bite. Uncle Mack was right. The food was surprisingly good. He took a few more bites before attempting to redirect him back to his earlier question. "What promise were you referring to?"

"The one I made your father before I left." His uncle cleared his throat. "The promise I made to help you if you ever needed it. No matter what it would do to me." He looked away for a moment before meeting Miles's gaze. "So, when I saw you today, I volunteered to drive you back."

Miles stared at his soup. The words tumbled over him as he tried to make sense of the whole situation. Why would his father let Miles believe his uncle was dead?

"Your dad would have been content to stay in the forest forever." He took a bite and then smiled. "Not me. I got tired of being on the run, of living in that tiny cave."

"That's why you left?"

His uncle shook his head. "No, I left because I got caught."

Miles's stomach churned at the thought. "What happened?"

"You were out foraging with your father, and I was supposed to stay at the cave to keep watch. But I really wanted to finish mending the fishing net. It had a tear we were taking turns repairing, and I thought I could finish it and then slip down to the pond to surprise you both with a whole bunch of fish by the time you got back."

"Except you never made it back." Miles filled in the missing blanks, and his uncle nodded.

"The Officials found me at the pond. They demanded to know who I was with and didn't like it when I refused to tell them."

"What did they do?"

"They offered me a deal." He snorted. "I think you're all too familiar with how much they love their deals."

Miles set his soup aside, no longer hungry. "Unfortunately, yes."

"Well, I had to choose between becoming a Guardian or letting them torture the information out of me." His eyes narrowed. "There was no way I would freely lead them to you and your father. Becoming a Guardian was the only choice."

"I always assumed you left willingly, and Dad didn't try to persuade me otherwise."

"Don't be angry with him. It was part of our promise."

"It's kind of hard not to be angry." Miles rubbed a hand over his face. "This whole time, I thought you abandoned us."

"Look, we agreed if anything should ever happen to your father and it was in my power to protect you, I would." His eyes glistened. "Since you are by yourself, I take it my brother is gone."

His uncle's question launched him straight back to the last time he saw his father. Throat tightening, Miles finally met his uncle's eyes and nodded. "He died when I was fourteen."

"I'm sorry." His uncle paused. "You must be around eighteen now?"

"It's not your fault." Miles averted his gaze, his mind going back to those few months when he was on his own before joining the Forest Community. "And yes, I'm eighteen."

"Maybe, maybe not." He sighed. "I often wonder where I would be if I had stayed at the cave that day. What your father must have thought of me."

"You were his brother, of course he loved you." Miles finished off the remaining soup in his container. "He never said one unkind word against you. Even when I thought you abandoned us."

It was a moment before his uncle finally nodded. "You had no way of knowing, and you were just a kid. Don't sweat it." Mack took a drink from his canteen. "So, how did you get mixed up with the Forest Community? Your dad was against settling with them."

"Yeah, he preferred to be out on his own—"

"Where he could take care of himself." His uncle finished the phrase for him, and Miles laughed.

"That was his favorite comeback." His laughter faded when Keegan and Elaine flashed in his mind. What would they think if they knew he was reminiscing with his believed-to-be-dead uncle? Keegan was aware of what Miles was up to, but what about Elaine? How much did she know? Miles couldn't stand the thought of Elaine feeling about him as he once felt about his uncle.

"After he passed away, I tried to go it alone. I really did, but I was just a kid. I couldn't stand the loneliness, and I needed to be with other people."

"So, you went to the Forest community?"

Miles smiled, remembering how he had hidden along the

outer edges of the Forest Community to see what the place was like. "I did. It took me a few days of watching them before I decided. I wanted to make sure everything was on the up and up before I walked in. Elaine, the community's healer, took me in."

"And now you're a tracker."

"It seemed like a good idea at the time. You know, help people see that the Outpost isn't what it's cracked up to be. That we can live out in the forest and don't need the Officials."

The fire crackled and Miles tossed his empty food container in it. "I just didn't realize maybe the Forest Community isn't what it's supposed to be either." He shook his head. "I should have questioned Thomas. But I didn't want to think that anything bad happened to the people when I took them to Grant."

"How would you have known something bad was going on?"

Mack might be right, but it didn't alleviate his guilt. "I don't know. I only had to do it twice a year, and the people always came back with me to the Forest Community."

"No one wants to believe the worst of someone else." Mack sighed. "You did what you thought you had to do to survive, kid. No one is going to blame you for that."

"You didn't see the way that Renna looked at me when she found out. She was disgusted."

"She surprised me with her choice."

Miles laughed. "Not me. She's stubborn. It was always her plan to make it back to the Outpost—with or without my help." He pulled her necklace out of his pocket and gripped it in his hand. "I have to find her."

"We will. But you can't dressed like that." He stood and motioned for Miles to follow him to the back of the jeep. "You may have to roll them up some, but it should work." He pulled out a stack of neatly folded purple uniform pants and shirt and held them toward Miles. "Congratulations, you're now a Guardian."

Miles accepted the clothes and helmet. "If Dad could see me now."

"You'd probably be disowned." He slapped him on the back. "Get some rest. You're going to need it out there."

"We've been resting. She's already got several hours on us."

"If she'd been caught already, believe me, we would know. I've been getting updates all afternoon."

"What—how? Why didn't you tell me?"

"What good would it have done? I needed to make sure you weren't going to bolt and do something stupid to get us both caught. Remember, I'm putting my neck on the line by helping you."

Miles nodded and unfolded the clothes, slipping the new shirt over his head. The simple truth was Miles wouldn't have made it without his uncle's help, and he definitely wouldn't have been able to stop the jeep early enough to be anywhere in the same vicinity as Renna. But the thought of resting while Renna was alone in the forest, hunted like an animal, made his skin crawl.

"The only thing I'm going to do is get Renna back, and make every one of them pay for what they've done."

His uncle sighed. "If you go into this with your anger and rage leading the way, you're only going to either get hurt or get Renna hurt."

"They need to pay for what they've done."

"I never said they didn't." His uncle leaned against the jeep, his arms crossed in front of him.

"Are you going to be able to do this?" Miles watched his uncle's expression as he continued. "You've spent a lot of years with these people. Are you going to be able to help me?"

"I told you I would."

"That's not the same thing, and you know it." Miles

narrowed his eyes. "If it comes down to it, will you be able to fight them?"

"I'm hoping it doesn't come down to it."

Miles wanted to laugh, but for his uncle's sake, he didn't. While he appreciated the help, it would come at a cost. Fighting was inevitable. The last thing Miles wanted was to put his uncle in a situation that would require him to choose. Mack said it himself earlier—the Guardians weren't all bad. How many others had joined for the same reasons as his uncle?

Before finding out the truth about this sick little game Grant played, Miles didn't have a reason to wonder how people became Guardians. He always imagined they were born to the role, just like all the trade jobs at the Outpost. Those passed from generation to generation.

But what if they didn't have a choice? What if, just like his uncle, they had to choose to save their families?

This new revelation didn't sit well with Miles. Just how many people were Guardians who didn't want to be in the first place? Did they use people from the Outposts and refugees to form their army?

"Maybe it would be better if I go alone," Miles said, not meeting his uncle's gaze.

"Not happening. I'm going with you."

"I could take the jeep, and you could say that I crashed it." He gestured to the communication device hanging from his uncle's belt. "You have a radio. You could ask for help later."

"What makes you think I would ever let you go off on your own?" His uncle stepped forward and placed his hand on Miles's shoulder. "I've watched after you since the day you were born. What kind of uncle would I be if I abandoned you now and let you have all the fun?"

"It's not going to be fun, Uncle Mack."

He nodded, shutting the back of the jeep. "You're right, it's not. It's a game, but I know how to play it. You don't."

32

Renna didn't know how much longer she could keep going. Every part of her body protested in agony, and exhaustion threatened to take over. It became increasingly difficult to hold her eyes open. With each step, the lids begged to close. Each time she managed to find a place to rest and shut her eyes, every creaking branch and animal call had her looking over her shoulder.

Her mind wouldn't let her sleep anyway, so instead, she kept walking. One foot in front of the other. The cool night air sent goosebumps up and down her arms, but she had long since rolled her sleeves down as far as they would go and untied the leather jacket from her waist to slip it on.

Every so often, she tried to speed up, but she no longer had the energy to sprint. Instead, she settled for glancing over her shoulder more often. The forest floor proved to be another battle all of its own, slowing her down even more.

She had no clue what time it was when she found the hidden trail. It was a short-lived victory because the path kept ascending, higher, and higher. It would tease her with a brief span of flat land, and when she thought she would be over the ridgeline, another incline awaited.

The trail was well worn, but she opted for walking in the forest instead. The path was used for vehicles, which meant even though it was her way out, the Guardians were also traveling, and they wouldn't be in the forest. They had jeeps and would be out in the open. So, she kept to the dense trees, ensuring the road always stayed in her peripheral.

As she crested the next hill, Renna paused, placed her hands on top of her head, and took deep breaths.

She could do this. She would do this. She had to do this.

Stopping wasn't an option, and neither was giving up. One more inhale and exhale, and then she would keep going. She checked her surroundings and noticed three jeeps parked along the tree line. She darted behind the largest tree beside her to hide while surveying the vehicles. They weren't on, and their lights were off.

What if they were in the woods searching? If they were, then that meant there wouldn't be anyone in the jeeps. Could she sneak over and steal one of the vehicles? She had never driven before, but it couldn't be that hard, could it?

Renna crept closer for a better look. Her heart raced, just thinking about the possibility. How wonderful would it be not to have to run anymore? She let herself imagine how delightful it would feel to be off her feet, and the temptation was more than she could bear. She was about to step out into the road when she jerked to her senses. Just because the vehicles appeared empty, it didn't mean the Guardians weren't sitting inside them—waiting for her to show herself. She shook her head and sighed, turning to head back deeper into the trees again.

Renna needed sleep. How deprived she must be if the idea of stealing a Guardian's vehicle—one she had no clue how to drive—sounded like a good idea.

She didn't make it three steps before bright lights passed over the tree line in front her.

No!

Renna ran toward the right, farther away from the trail than before. Her hazy mind now raced as she tried to find a place to hide, but all she could see were trees—none of them wide enough to hide behind.

Where were the rocks and hillsides now when she needed them? Risking a glance behind her, she nearly stumbled when she glimpsed the outline of the vehicle maneuvering through the trees.

Shocked, Renna doubled her efforts to run, but her body was too exhausted. She had already pushed herself to the breaking point. Pressing on, Renna tried not to think about anything but finding a place to hide.

Beams of light swept in a circle, and it took her a moment to realize they were shining a bright spotlight from the truck in all directions.

They were catching up to her, and the light would come back around in her direction in a few seconds. What could she do? She had to find something. Anything.

She kept running to the right, and out of the corner of her eye, a shadow along the ground caught her attention.

A fallen log?

Renna couldn't tell, but she was out of options, and there wasn't time to debate or second-guess herself again. She sprinted to the spot, praying the whole way it would indeed be wide enough for her to hide behind.

Yes!

Finally, something was going in her favor. She managed to half jump, half fall over the log and drop to the ground. Scooting as close to it as she could, she froze as sticky fibers engulfed her hands and face. This couldn't be happening. Not now. Anything but spiders. She sputtered, trying her best to wipe off the cobwebs without raising her arms higher than the log.

Her skin crawled at the thought of tiny, velvety legs touching her face and arms. The light went over her hiding spot and moved ahead, but she forced herself to wait a few seconds longer. Finally, she couldn't take it any longer and sprang to her feet, dancing around and flicking the webs from her neck and hair.

Renna shuddered and kept walking, her nerves more on edge than before. What if they turned around and came back this way? Or what if another vehicle wasn't far behind? How many Guardians were after her?

The adrenaline faded as she walked, and fatigue nearly knocked her to the ground. If she didn't rest soon, she would fall asleep walking. Was that even physically possible? Her eyes blurred and drooped, and she could no longer keep them open. She found a tree with low-hanging branches and crawled underneath them, leaning against the trunk. She sighed, letting her body relax, and darkness overtook her.

Lights flashed across her face, and instantly her eyes flew open. How long had she been asleep? She had no idea. Minutes? Hours? It couldn't have been hours because her brain was still foggy, and exhaustion still weighed her down. She couldn't keep doing this.

Jumping to her feet, she took off, trying to stay ahead of or beside the beams. She dodged them as much as she did the broken limbs, vines, and rocks beneath her. Car doors slammed in the distance, and four sets of lights appeared.

"Spread out and search." A man's voice echoed through the trees, and Renna shivered at the coldness of his tone. "You have permission to shoot on sight."

Bile rose in her throat, and Renna doubled over, throwing up whatever was left in her stomach from the morning's meal. This was it. They were going through with it. Grant told her this would happen, but somewhere in the back of her mind, she hadn't thought it would. Perhaps she simply convinced herself everything would work out.

Renna should have known better. This wasn't something she could will to go her way. This was life and death, and death tipped the scales at the moment.

Except Renna wouldn't go down without a fight. She looked around the woods, forcing herself to concentrate. This time the adrenaline kicked into overdrive, overcoming her exhaustion.

Endless trees and brush. No buildings or caves. Nowhere she could hole up in and hide. She peered up at the treetops, but even in the darkness, she could tell they were too skinny to hold or cover her enough to wait out the Guardians.

She kept running anyway. Constantly sweeping her eyes across the area, continually looking for anything that appeared promising. In the distance, about fifty yards away, she finally found it. A hollowed-out tree somehow still standing. It appeared as though a chunk of the tree was missing on the side, and she might be able to fit through the opening.

She bolted for the tree as men catcalled and cried her name all around her. In one fluid motion, she swung her backpack off her back and looped her arm through it. She stopped right in front of the tree and took a deep breath before ducking under the opening. Holding her breath, she squeezed through the tight space and then brought her bag in last. It caught on a jagged piece of bark, and Renna tugged on the strap before she thought better of it, snapping the brittle wood.

The voices stopped, and the lights paused wherever they were shining. Even the animals seemed to cease their shrieking. The only thing Renna could hear was her heart thudding violently inside her chest. Her mind whirled in a rush, imagining scenarios of the Guardian's finding and dragging her from her hiding place.

Then, a voice rang out through the trees. "Renna ..." The

tone was melodic, but every inflection rang nothing but evil intent. "Come out and play."

Another voice from her left parroted the first. "Ren ... na."

And another behind her.

Each voice echoed the one prior until it was an endless round of voices taunting her.

They had her surrounded.

She shrank back into the tree, as far from the opening as she could manage, terror taking over.

"Renna, where are you?"

Her breath escaped in jagged spurts, and she couldn't ignore the rushing sound of wind in her ears.

"Ren ... na ..." The voices stacked on top of each other, dragging her name out into a chilling chorus.

Tears poured down her cheeks as she pressed her hands over her ears.

"Ren ... na ..."

33

Miles doused the campfire while his uncle packed up their utensils and canteens. Mack finally gave in and agreed to cut their rest break short. There wasn't a doubt in Miles's mind that his uncle thought they needed to stay a little longer, but Miles couldn't sit still—not when he learned that Mack could overhear what the other Guardians were saying.

It was a surprise Miles would call a win, and wins seemed few and far between. But it sparked the tiniest flicker of hope.

If they could pinpoint the current search area, they could join the Guardians and slip into the ranks undetected. All he would have to do would be to find her and get out without being seen.

"What are they saying?" Miles finished buttoning up the guard uniform. The scratchy fabric made his skin crawl, but he was thankful his uncle had an extra set for him to wear. Even if the pants were a few inches too long.

"Get in." His uncle gestured to the jeep. "They are in the Dark Woods."

"That doesn't sound good." Miles pulled open the passenger side door and climbed in.

His uncle frowned. "I'm not going to lie to you, Miles. That place is nothing but trees. There's no creeks, ponds, or buildings for her to hide in."

"Don't hold back. I need to hear it all."

"There's a reason why it's called the Dark Woods." He cranked the ignition and pulled out onto the small one-vehicle path. "It's nothing but miles and miles of woods and brush. There are not even any rock formations to hide in. Grant intentionally holds The Hunt here. Most players never make it out of this section of the forest."

Miles bit his tongue, resisting a smart-aleck comment about his uncle's term for Renna, and focused on another key word— most. "But it's been done before?"

Silence filled the space between them, and Miles cursed under his breath. Why would he say that if it wasn't true? Just to get his hopes up and then crush them again?

"Don't give up. We're going to find her."

Miles didn't reply, pulling Renna's necklace out of his pocket instead. She strategically left it for him to find, hidden inside the folded blanket; she was counting on him. Depending on him. Miles squeezed the pendant and then slid the necklace over his head and tucked it under his uniform shirt. Leaving the necklace meant she wasn't going to give up either.

"We hike it from here."

Miles hadn't realized his uncle had pulled the jeep off the path. He slid his helmet on and climbed down out of the vehicle. Bright stars and a full moon lit the night sky. "She's in this area?"

Mack opened his intercom and turned the volume up. There was silence, then a burst of static.

"Squadron Five, state your position and status. Over."

"Headquarters, this is Squadron Five. We are in the Dark Woods. We lost sight of The Hunted and suspect she is hiding.

We are pursuing on foot and closing in. There's nowhere else to run. Over."

"Affirmative Squadron Five. Radio when The Hunted is eliminated. Over and out."

Red hot anger shot through him as he listened to other squadrons still on the airwaves talking back and forth. Miles could hear them calling out her name. Taunting her. Stalking her.

He couldn't stand to listen to it anymore. Miles jerked the radio from his uncle and twisted the knob to silence. His hands shook. Clenching and unclenching his fists, he wanted nothing more than to charge into the forest and take out every one of the Guardians. To make them feel just a tenth of the fear they were undoubtedly making Renna feel.

His uncle sighed. "I know you're upset, but the last thing we need is for you to lose control and go barreling in there." He sighed. "This is tough. But if we are going to save Renna, you will have to act the part. Do you think you can handle that?"

Miles considered his uncle's words before nodding. "Of course."

Mack stared at him a moment longer. "Good. The plan is to blend in and act like the other Guardians."

"They won't be suspicious of us?"

"Not as long as you do what they do. Search the way they are searching. Stay far enough away from them that you do not get pulled into their conversations. With any luck, they will think we've been assigned a different Squadron."

Search the way they were searching? Could he do that? Could he sneer her name and act like one of the Guardians? His stomach roiled at the thought of playing such a cruel role. That's what the Guardians, Grant, and this stupid Hunt were —cruel.

"And when we find her?"

"If we have to hide, we will. If we need to run, we will. And if we need to fight, so be it."

"Thank you. I know this can't be easy for you. As much as I loathe the Guardians, I'm sure you've made some friendships over the years."

His uncle hooked the intercom onto his belt and pulled out a pistol. "Some of them are good people, but remember they are trained soldiers with a job to do."

Miles nodded and followed his uncle away from the jeep and into the trees. Beams of light shined in all directions from miles away. "How are we going to find her?" Miles hissed, falling into step beside his uncle.

"Call her name and hope she recognizes your voice." He pointed to Miles's belt. "Look the part and get your gun ready."

The slick, cool metal wasn't foreign in his hands. He had shot plenty of weapons when he'd been out hunting with some of the others in the Forest Community, but he felt more himself without it.

"Stay within earshot, but spread out a little, like the others."

Nodding, he took the right, and Mack took the left. Miles called Renna's name, but he couldn't bring himself to use the creepy tones like the rest of the Guardians. He wouldn't stoop to their theatrics, and he wanted her to hear his voice—not hide from him.

He yelled her name, all the while searching for places she might use to hide. But each time he thought he might find her, it ended up a dead end.

Where are you, Renna?

Pressing on, he shook away the doubts. After a mile or so, he started walking back toward Mack. "We are getting too far from the vehicle."

"I know. If we need to run, we won't make it back to the jeep."

Despite the cool air, sweat dripped down his neck, and

Miles wished he could take the bulky helmet off to wipe it. "What do you suggest then?"

"We go back and drive it a few miles up and then search some more."

Miles shook his head, afraid of what could happen in the meantime. "We will lose too much time going back for it."

"Well, I could go back for it, and you keep on."

"Wouldn't that be suspicious? Don't they work in pairs?"

"Yeah, but do you have any other suggestions? It's not like we are going to stumble upon any building to hide in around here if we have to make a run for it. We are going to need the jeep."

"No, I don't." Miles swept his flashlight around, and something reflected in the beam. He held his finger to his lips before whispering, "I think I've found something."

Mack nodded for him to go first, and Miles took the lead. Two figures stopped in front of them. Miles raised his gun out of instinct.

"Woah there. It's just us." One of the Guardians lifted his hands, his gun hanging on a strap across his chest.

His uncle stepped in front of him and put a hand on his arm, pushing it down. "You'll have to pardon my partner here." He let out a chuckle. "He's new and still a little jumpy."

"No problem." The second guard spoke up, glancing over in Miles's direction and looking him up and down. "Fresh meat, huh?"

Miles lowered his weapon and tried to laugh it off with the other two Guardians. But inside, he wanted nothing more than to put them flat on their backs.

"Any updates on the girl?" His uncle's tone was flat and uncaring. As much as Miles was glad he was alive and willing to help him find Renna, it wasn't easy to hear his uncle switch over to play the role of a Guardian. But it wasn't a role, was it?

His uncle had become the enemy. He donned the uniform and joined their ranks.

"We got called back to base. They think they found her."

Mack nodded. "I was hoping to be the one who found her."

Miles sucked in a breath and held it. They wanted to blend in, not bring more attention to themselves. He tightened his grip on the gun to be ready if everything went south.

The Guardians froze, their jaws tense as silence filled the space between them. Finally, they relaxed, wide grins spreading across their faces. "Well, there's always the next Hunt."

Bile rose in Miles's throat. How could they be so excited about something so horrible? Miles tuned out the rest of their conversation, only picking up on a couple of words here and there. He couldn't stand standing idly by making small talk when it wasted precious time for finding Renna.

When the two Guardians saluted, Miles forced himself to return the gesture. They waited as the pair walked away and out of earshot before continuing in the direction where Miles had seen the reflection.

The only question: how deep was Mack's loyalty to Miles's father? To him?

They hadn't made it ten steps before more headlights flooded the path behind them.

34

"Are you sure about this?"

A wave of fear washed over Gabbi as she stood in Zeke's house, staring at their back door. As custom dictated, the windows were covered, and the bolt firmly in place. No one went out, and no one came in.

They would do both. Twice. "No, but when have we been certain about anything lately?"

"True enough." He sighed and shifted his backpack. He insisted on carrying their supplies. They had what basic first aid items they could find and emergency rations in case—well, Gabbi couldn't even let her mind go there. They were going to be fine. It would be a quick run from his parent's place to her house. In and out.

Piece of cake.

"Gabbi? Are you okay?"

Zeke's voice broke through her thoughts, and she glanced up at him. "Sorry." She looked behind her. "We should probably go."

"Yeah. My dad is out in the shop, and my mom is already asleep. But if either one of them finds us right here—"

He didn't have to finish his statement. Gabbi knew what they would say. That they were being careless and stupid.

She reached out and gripped the doorknob, and her heart instantly started pounding. What would happen when they opened the door? What if someone saw them?

"You remember the story of *Old Man Hector*?"

"Who doesn't?" Zeke lowered his voice. "But it's just a tale to scare little kids, to keep them inside."

"No, it's not. My Grandparents were our age when it happened." Gabbi's heart pounded at the thought. "Someone alerted the Officials when he tried to leave, and they took him away. No one ever laid eyes on him again!"

Zeke reached out to touch her arm. "It's just a silly story."

"I thought so too when I first heard it. But someone turned him in for breaking the rules." She gestured to the door. "And that's exactly what we are about to do."

"No one is going to turn us in."

"You don't know that."

"No, I don't." He nodded. "But I know that we have to do this, and I have to believe that people would want us to help rather than rat us out."

"People do illogical things out of fear."

"True." Zeke gave her a small smile. "They also do brave things."

Her heart racing, hands shaking, and knees trembling screamed the opposite. She drew in a deep breath and let it out. "We are going out there ..."

"Yes."

"In the dark."

"Yep."

"Where everyone can see us." Silence, and then Zeke finally responded. "Correct, again."

It's not too late to turn back.

"Gabbi?" Zeke's voice was soft but calm and held more than just a question in it. It was now or never.

She took a deep breath and slid the bolt.

"Wait!" Zeke grabbed her arm, making her cry out in fright. "The lights."

She nodded, reached for the lamp on the counter, and flipped the switch. Darkness enveloped them, and Gabbi inhaled to calm her nerves. As she fumbled to find the doorknob, her arm smacked against something propped up by the door. It started to fall, and she grabbed it, slowly setting it back against the wall. A broom, maybe?

Stiffening, she waited, praying the sound hadn't been loud enough to wake Zeke's mom. Thankfully, no footsteps sounded overhead.

"Go." Zeke's whispered breath tickled her ear, and she nearly missed the doorknob again. At this rate, they would never get the door open.

She grabbed the cool metal and gently pulled it open. The sky was inky black, with dim stars, but the moon was full. She slowly descended the stairs, careful not to stomp, and waited at the corner of the house for Zeke to close the door and join her.

So far, so good.

The Outpost was eerily quiet. Nothing moved. No curtains blowing in the breeze, no light spilling from the porches. No sounds coming from the inside of the houses. It was like she'd been transported to a completely different time and place.

She hesitated, waiting for her eyes to adjust to the new surroundings, but the walkway between the Blacksmith's shop and the row of houses was pitch black. Gabbi wouldn't have known Zeke was behind her except for the sound of his breathing.

Inching along, she kept her left hand on the building. She tried to maintain an even pace but had no idea if Zeke was close behind. She kept going. The last thing she needed was to stop and have him run into her.

The ground was hard and uneven, difficult enough to manage even in the light of day.

What little security kept her calm vanished the second she rounded the corner. She couldn't hesitate now. She had to take the turn at a sprint and run. She couldn't stop. The longer she was out in the open, the more risk of someone seeing her.

Gabbi picked up her pace, but when she broke into a sprint and her foot connected with the ground, she realized she had messed up. She slid in the rocks, her leg stopping but momentum propelling the rest of her body. She windmilled, trying to keep from falling, when Zeke grabbed her around the waist and pulled her upright.

She followed him toward her house and nearly tripped up the stairs in her haste to get to the door. Zeke already had the spare key in the latch and pushed the door open for her. He closed it and she bent over, gasping for breath.

A grin split across his face. "We did it."

She couldn't help but smile back. "We still have to make it back."

He sobered. "You couldn't let us have just one small victory?"

His arched eyebrow and lopsided grin made her want to reach over and ruffle his hair or slap him playfully on the arm. Anything to get close to him.

Zeke caught her staring, and his expression changed as he leaned forward. She cleared her throat. "Come on. The office is this way." She led him through the sitting room and down the hall, passing doors on the right and left until they came to the end of the hall.

"Dad said the journal is in his desk." Walking over to the oak desk, she sat down in the chair and pulled the bottom drawer open, feeling for the hidden latch Father told her about.

She pushed the button, and a smaller drawer popped open, with a thick, brown leather journal tucked inside.

"The curtains seem thick. We should be able to turn on the light." Zeke slid the fabric back into place, and Gabbi flipped the switch. She started thumbing through the pages, skimming the lines to find out whatever she could about the tunnels.

Two-thirds through the book, she finally found it. Halfway down the page was a note written on the side of the entry. "Not everyone is happy with our ideas about the tunnels. I told Arthur not to trust Lee. But my husband insists that we can count on him. If we can connect a portion of the tunnel and go south, then we will be able to come and go at will."

Gabbi stopped reading and glanced up at Zeke. His eyes were narrowed in concentration. "Come and go at will? What is she talking about?"

"I'm not sure." Zeke took the journal and flipped through the next few pages. "Here's another entry. We've ceased the tunnel work. It was a dream I will probably never see to fruition in my lifetime. Our tunnel is complete, though, and I can only hope that Lee finishes his end of the deal."

"So, my grandparents and your grandparents had the tunnel built, but they never made it farther than our tunnel and the one going from the orphanage to where?" Gabbi swung her bag around and dug out the map, laying it on her father's desk. "Let's say we go to the orphanage, through her tunnel, and go south. Where do we go? Who lives over in that direction?"

Zeke stood slightly behind her, his breath tickling the back of her neck as he studied the map from over her shoulder.

"Isn't that the largest area of residential homes?" She asked, trying not to think about the hundreds of tiny butterflies that suddenly fluttered in her stomach.

Gabbi closed her eyes and tried to picture the layout of the Outpost in her mind. If this tunnel indeed took them to the complete opposite side of the Outpost, they would be in the most populated residential area. But it wasn't all houses. Some were cabins. Reserved for single or married couples with no families. And the Runners.

The Runners. Her grandmother told her grandfather the man couldn't be trusted.

"I think you're right. But the farthest buildings are the cabins. Where the Runners live."

Gabbi's mind whirled around with the possibilities. For the first time in a while, she felt the tiniest burst of hope. "Zeke, my Grammy said they would be able to come and go at will. If that passage leads outside the Gates, I can go find Renna!"

"Wait just a minute—"

"We can use this new tunnel to reach the rest of the Outpost, and then I can go look for my sister."

"You can't be serious."

"What if she's hurt out there? Or nearby but too scared to come back?"

Zeke grabbed her shoulders and turned her around to face him. "Gabbi, you're not thinking straight. We don't know where this tunnel goes or *if* it's actually built."

"That's a chance that I'm willing to take."

He stared down at her, his eyes wide and fearful, before finally dropping his hands. "And what if it is a Runner's house?"

"Then hopefully, they've built the tunnel like their family promised my grandparents."

Zeke cursed in frustration. "You're not thinking clearly. There's a reason they shut down the whole operation. It's not safe. You're talking about walking in blind to a Runner's house. A Runner, the second-highest-ranking position in the Outpost, after ... your sister."

The mention of Renna's position brought a fresh wave of sadness followed by guilt. In the last few days, her mind had been consumed with mapping the tunnels and feeding the people. She worried about her sister, but Renna hadn't been at the forefront of her mind. Now there was a chance she could go, could leave behind these walls and do something. To find her sister and bring her home. She had to at least try.

"So what are you going to do if I go? Turn me in?"

Zeke let out a deep sigh but didn't say anything to contradict her words. Tears welled in her eyes as she stuffed the journal back into its hiding spot.

She stood and whirled around to face him, anger bubbling in her chest. "Really? You would turn on me just like that?"

"You know that's not what I want to do."

"If there's even the slightest chance that I can find Renna, bring her home, and help the people of the Outpost, I have to take it."

He reached for her hand. "It's too dangerous. Renna made her choice. Please don't make her mistakes."

Gabbi pulled her hand from his. "I think my only mistake was trusting you to do the right thing."

35

The Guardians' voices continued to sing her name in rounds. Each building off the one prior until it was so loud Renna could no longer try to tune them out. It filled the space all around her to the point where she couldn't tell which direction they were coming from. All she could picture was the Guardians closing in on her, surrounding the pathetic hollow tree where she hid.

How long would she be able to hide before they finally discovered her? Her legs already burned from standing in the confined space, and forcing her sobs to stay quiet had taken its toll. The wood dug into her back and side, where she tried to lean over to the left as far as she could so the Guardians couldn't see her through the opening.

Maybe it would be better for her to run. To escape the tree and go as fast and as long as she could. What would it matter if they caught up to her? At least this part would be over. The crippling anxiety mixed with adrenaline would disappear. This messed-up game they were playing would end. She wouldn't have to look over her shoulder every few seconds.

But Renna couldn't step out of the tree with the Guardians so close. She'd already abandoned her people and her family. She wouldn't do it again voluntarily. And if she failed—well, she would go down fighting. Every step of the way.

Renna needed to outlast their mind games. Surely, they would tire of calling her name, of combing the woods, searching for her amongst the trees.

She could wait it out.

And just like that, everything stopped. The animal calls, the wind, the voices. The overwhelming buzzing of noise suddenly ceased. Nothing but silence filled the space of the trunk and it took her breath away.

Renna lowered her hands from her ears, halfway expecting to raise them again. Instead, she pressed them against the trunk and leaned forward, moving as slowly as possible so she could peer out of the opening.

Her lips trembled as short gasps of air escaped, her body trying to keep up with the changes in heart rate and panic. Her fingers slid down the bark, and splinters jabbed her sweaty palms. She fell forward but caught herself before tumbling out of the opening.

Lights flickered in front of her, and she flung herself backward, banging the back of her head. She should have run when she had the chance. Now, everything was too quiet, and there wasn't anything she could do but wait.

Five seconds.

Ten.

Fifteen.

She quietly counted, staring at the opening. Weighing her options and not liking the odds one bit.

Twenty.

It was now or never. Should she go? Just make a wild run for it.

Thirty.

Renna leaned forward, and a hand clamped down on her ankle and pulled, yanking her so hard from the opening that a sliver of bark caught her shirt and ripped a hole in the bottom corner.

She let out a scream and kicked her attacker as he dragged her out of the tree and onto the ground. Leaves, sticks, and small rocks dug into her back, and she cried out in pain. Tears stung her eyes as she tried to keep the panic at bay. She couldn't make it if she gave in to the terror.

"Well, well, well. Look at what I found." A pair of boots came into view and the Guardian—much taller than herself—grabbed her arm. He yanked her around and then pushed her back to the ground in front of a second Guardian.

"So, this is the Speaker." The second guard knelt and grabbed her chin, forcing her eyes up to his. His eyes were cold. Cruel with a hint of pleasure lurking in their depths.

She spit in his face.

"She's a feisty one, I'll give you that." He raised his hand to smack her, but the tall guard grabbed his hand.

"Official Grant said to shoot on sight, not torture her first."

The grip on her chin tightened, and the cruel Guardian hesitated, his hand raised for a few more moments before he finally nodded. "Fine. Tie her up."

"No!" She screamed as loud as she could and got to her feet, pushing past the guard who almost hit her.

"Not so fast, girly." One of the guards, she couldn't tell which one, grabbed her arm and yanked her back. He gripped her around the waist, and she screamed and kicked as hard as she could.

"Leave me alone!"

"We can't do that. We have our orders, you know." He forced her arms behind her back as the other Guardian tied her hands together. The more she fought, the more the coarse material dug into her wrists.

"Hold still, Speaker." One of the men sneered—had to be the harsher guard—his anger dripping off every syllable. "This is delaying the inevitable."

"Let me go!" Renna jerked her elbow back and up, hoping to connect with the man's nose. She wasn't disappointed. He let go of her, sputtering and cursing as she lunged forward.

Except it wasn't enough time. The other Guardian who held her still recovered from her escape attempt and secured his hold.

"You stupid girl." Blood trickled from the Guardian's nose, and she couldn't help a bit of satisfaction at the sight. He reared back and slapped her across her cheek. Her eyes watered, and she fell to the ground again, pain welling up on the side of her face.

"I told you not to hit her!" The taller guard reached down to examine her cheek. "She's just a child."

"Well, she got what she deserved."

A metallic click came from behind the guards.

"Let her go. Put your hands up, and step away from the girl."

"Hey, what are you doing? We found her, fair and square." The nicer of the two Guardians stepped forward and aimed his weapon at the new arrivals. "*We* get to claim the reward. Now go away before you get hurt."

"Oh, I don't think I'm going to get hurt."

The man's eyes narrowed in confusion as a fourth Guardian came out of the shadows behind them and conked the man in the back of the head with a tree limb.

He slumped to the ground in a heap. His partner cursed, grabbed her, his hands slick from the nose bleed, and lifted her to her feet. "What are you doing? We're on the same side!"

Renna gasped as her would-be rescuer lifted off his helmet. "I'm not one of you."

"Miles!" She lunged forward, but the man tightened his grip on her arm and yanked her back to him. Tears filled her eyes and she blinked them away. Miles had found her! Somehow, someway, he had found her.

Miles pulled a gun from his side and aimed it at the Guardian. The other man with him did the same. "Let go of Renna and back away. Slowly."

Her captor squeezed tighter. "Wait. I know you. You're that Scout. The one who works for Grant." The man sneered. "You're a traitor."

Miles's eyes hardened, and Renna had never seen anyone so angry before. "I told you to let her go."

"No, that is certainly not happening." The Guardian took a step back, and Renna wiggled, trying to squirm out of his grasp. But he held on tighter.

She leaned against him and raised her legs in the air to try to throw him off balance. He scrambled to get both arms around her again. Out of the corner of her eye, Miles's partner walked around them.

"Oh, I think it is." The partner said, raising his gun at the Guardian's chest. "Let her go. I'll only ask this once."

The Guardian released Renna, pushing her forward, but Miles caught her before she fell on her face. He gently wrapped his arm around her and led her away from the Guardians. "Come on, let's go."

Shouts and angry cries echoed behind Renna. She peeked over her shoulder to see Miles's partner fighting the Guardian, knocking him to the ground. He walked beside the unconscious man and picked up a large stone. Renna turned away, but it didn't mute the sound of the man's skull cracking.

Once they were a safe distance away, Miles untied her bound hands.

"I can't believe you found me."

"I told you I would." He grinned, pulling her toward him to

caress her face. Renna rose on her tiptoes and didn't hesitate as his lips found hers. She sank into his kiss as his hands dropped from her cheeks to draw her closer. He leaned back, but she followed him, kissing him again. She wasn't ready to let him go.

"You think you can save that for later? We need to go. Now."

Miles pulled away and gently kissed her forehead before turning towards the newcomer. He threaded his fingers through hers and pointed to the man with his free hand. "Renna, this is my Uncle Mack."

She gawked at Miles in surprise, running over their conversations about his family in her head. "But I thought ..."

"So did I."

She looked back and forth between them. "I don't understand."

"I'll explain everything later, but my uncle's right; we have to get out of here before the other Guardians find out what happened." Miles gently grabbed both of her shoulders and gave her a once over. "I'm sorry I didn't get here in time to stop them." He inhaled as he tilted her face to the side, getting a better view of her cheek. "Are you hurt anywhere else? How's your foot?"

She followed his gaze to the hole in her shirt and then her foot. "I'm okay. Just bruises and scratches. My foot throbs and I may have re-opened the wound. But I can walk."

"I think we may have to do more than just walk." Mack sighed. "It's a long way to the jeep and it won't be long before someone investigates the shouts."

Renna jerked up in surprise, excitement filling her at the news. Maybe she could actually rest for a few moments, close her eyes, and get off her injured foot. "You're joking. You have a jeep?"

"Yes, but it's three miles back." Mack holstered his gun. "When we took the Guardians out, we forfeited our one advantage—surprise. I don't have another uniform for Renna."

"We'll make it work." Miles reached for her hand, threaded his fingers through hers, and grinned. "We've made it this far. What're another three miles?"

36

Day Seven

"Don't stop. Keep going!" Miles urged Renna as he kept pace with her, but she was spent. He could see the fatigue etched on her face, and every few seconds, her stride faltered. He couldn't imagine what she was feeling, how exhausted she must be, but there would be plenty of time to talk once they got out of these dangerous woods and had her back home.

"I can't—" Her voice came out in short gasps, and she stopped, nearly dropping to her knees.

"Miles, we can't stop." His uncle called out as he passed them both.

"I'll get her, you keep going." He bent down and pulled her up, wrapping one arm around her waist and her arm around his neck. "I've got you. Come on."

She grunted but didn't say anything else as he supported her weight, giving her some stability. If Elaine saw Renna now, she would no doubt give him an earful for allowing her to get in this condition.

But nothing he could do would change what happened or how they got to this point. Now, he could only keep her safe going forward. And he would hold up his promise. He would get her home. No matter how much it would hurt him to leave her at the Outpost.

He couldn't go there. Not right now. Miles couldn't allow himself to think about what would happen after he got her back to her family.

"You can make it." He whispered to himself as much as her. He needed the reminder just as much as she did.

"Miles ... I can't ... breathe."

He slowed his pace but didn't stop. They were too exposed. That was the problem with this terrible forest. Endless trees left nowhere to hide.

"We have to keep going, Renna."

"How much longer?" She barely got the words out, and he slowed down a little more. His uncle was now a good distance ahead of them.

"A few more steps."

A hint of a smile touched her lips. "You've said that before."

"I remember."

He walked her over to the nearest tree and leaned her against it. He bent down to look at her leg, feeling for any swelling around her ankle. "I can't risk taking off your boot." He glanced up at her. "I doubt I could get it back on."

"Can you still see your uncle?" She whispered, her words coming out in short gasps.

"Yeah, he's still running towards the jeep."

"I can't believe you found him."

"It's more like he found me, but yeah. My dad and I thought he was dead all these years." Miles surveyed the area around them. "Okay, break's over. We can't stand still for too long."

"Miles—if I don't make it back—"

He shook his head. "Nope. Not even an option."

"We have to look at this from a logical standpoint."

He nodded. "I am. And the only outcome I'm allowing is that you make it back."

She gave him a sad smile. "Grant told me no one has ever survived The Hunt."

A wave of anger welled up in his chest. "I don't care. Grant's wrong." He pulled her away from the tree and started walking again. "We are not giving up, okay?"

Nothing but silence and then finally she answered. "Okay, Miles." He didn't want to dwell on how weak her agreement sounded. They needed to get her somewhere safe before she completely collapsed from exhaustion.

Miles kept pushing her forward. Their chitchat ceased, except for him encouraging her, urging her on when she needed it and carrying her when the ground became to rough for her to navigate.

Uncle Mack slowly started to come back into view, and Miles breathed a little easier. At least he was still on the right course. It was increasingly hard to tell where they were and what direction he was heading. The thick forest was identical in every direction—just an endless course of trees.

Sunrise was upon them. Miles scanned the sky as it slowly started growing brighter. The last thing they needed was to be out in the open come daylight. They needed to be long gone before the forest lit up.

"What's that?" Renna's voice alerted him to the danger before he even sensed it.

Up ahead, about thirty yards away. A Guardian raised his hand in greeting to Mack but instead of returning the gesture, his uncle shot the Guardian square in the chest. He didn't even stop to look at the man but kept running toward the jeep, now visible in the distance.

"Don't they work in pairs?" Renna asked as they skirted the body.

"Yes." He picked up the pace and flinched as Renna yelped. "I'm sorry, Ren. Just a little bit more."

Mack was already in the jeep and turning it around to drive toward them when the dead Guardian's partner crashed into Miles, knocking him to the ground. Renna collapsed as he lost his grip on her.

"Renna!" He bent over to pull her up, but a boot connected with his stomach and propelled him backward. As pain exploded through his body, he did his best to ignore it. Lunging for the Guardian, he grabbed him around the waist and rammed him to the ground. The man's head hit first, his helmet taking the brunt of the force, causing his helmet to fly off.

Anger overtook Miles, and he quickly pinned the Guardian, punching him before he could counter.

The Guardian groaned, so Miles hit him again.

"Miles, stop!" Renna grabbed his arm and pulled him back. "Your uncle's here."

He rose, pulling Renna along as he sprinted for the jeep. She cried out in pain, her steps faltering.

"Miles, just go." All the fight was gone from her statement.

"No way." He stopped, readjusted his hold, and tossed her over his shoulder. It wouldn't be a comfortable way to be carried, but he could run a little faster.

As he neared the jeep, the door flung open, and Mack helped him haul Renna into the seat. Miles climbed in beside her, his uncle already moving before he could close the door. He glanced back to see the Guardian sitting up and reaching for his intercom. Dread filled him at the sight. It wouldn't be long before all the Guardians would be following them. "Now what?" Miles asked, leaning back against the seat, panting to catch his breath.

"We get as far as we can before we have to ditch the jeep."

Miles noted Renna's pale face. Sweat dripped from her forehead, but her skin felt clammy to the touch. "I don't know how much more she can take."

Mack's stoic features spoke volumes as the speedometer needle rose higher.

37

"Are you here to turn me in?" Gabbi stopped in front of Zeke, who sat on the ground before the tunnel leading to the orphanage.

"Very funny." He stood and dusted off his jeans. "I'm going with you to the Runner's house—or whoever may happen to live there."

"I can make it on my own just fine."

"I never said you couldn't."

She folded her arms across her chest. "Why the sudden change of heart?"

"I've already let you talk me into going out there once. What's one more time?"

A small part of her wanted to go to the Runner's house alone. She had no idea why other than to prove herself capable. Her entire life had been decided for her—every aspect of it. It didn't matter if she wanted to do something else with her life; it was already chosen for her by birthright. She would inherit the bakery as the oldest child.

Except she didn't even have the luxury of choosing what

she wanted to do in the bakery. Her jobs were given to her by her parents.

Gabbi shook her head to clear her thoughts. It would be stupid to go without help. What if she ran into trouble? What if the Runner wasn't hospitable? What if there was something amiss with the tunnel itself? Numerous scenarios could go wrong.

Sighing, she nodded. "Fine. Let's go." Marching past him, Gabbi knocked on the trap door and smiled when Miss Parker ushered them in.

"What are you guys doing back so soon?"

Gabbi cast Zeke a glance before answering. "We need to access your second door."

The woman's face drained of color. "Are you sure that's a good idea?"

"We have to be able to reach the other half of the Outpost, and this will put us on the other side." Gabbi didn't want to let on anything else about why she wanted to use the tunnel.

"Then you'll be close to the Healer." Miss Parker's eyes brightened. "You could check with her and see if she has anything that might help baby Oliver."

A lump of guilt settled in Gabbi's stomach. She'd been so focused on getting her answers that she forgot about the baby. For the first time, she took in Miss Parker's appearance. Her eyes had black circles under them, and her hair was stuffed into a haphazard bun with strands hanging down. "He's not doing any better?"

A toddler ran up to Miss Parker and wrapped his arms around her leg, trying to pull her toward the playroom. She bent and swept the boy's curls out of his eyes. "I will come play as soon as I finish talking with Miss Gabbi and Mr. Zeke." She sighed and rubbed her eyes as the boy ran off to join the others. "He's still fussy off and on. I don't have anything here that might help soothe him."

"We aren't sure where the tunnel leads exactly, but we will do our best to get to the Healer." Zeke's voice was calm and assured, and Gabbi wished she felt the same confidence, but they didn't know what they would be walking into today.

"Thank you both." Miss Parker wiped away a tear and motioned for them to follow her. "My room is back here."

They followed the young woman through the open spaces of the main floor— divided into play and school rooms— and toward the back of the house. Tiny, sticky hands reached out to hug Gabbi as she passed, and Zeke chuckled behind her.

"They like you."

"They've missed you, Gabbi." Miss Parker added as she opened what must be the door to her bedroom. "They talk about you all the time."

"And I've missed them. I'm sorry I haven't had more time to visit before all this." Gabbi sighed and looked around the room at the children playing. She couldn't imagine having the responsibility of so many little lives in her hands and no one to help shoulder the tasks. As soon as they figured out how to get food to the rest of the people, she would come back and take a shift so Miss Parker could get some much-needed rest.

"There's no reason to apologize. I know Opal is so grateful for you and your family. She has missed being at the bakery the past few days."

"Hopefully, she will be back very soon." Gabbi's voice teetered on the edge of breaking. How much longer until Renna came home?

Miss Parker removed her glasses and wiped off the lenses. "The closet is to the left." She gestured to the back corner of her room, and Gabbi's palms started itching. She let the sleeves of her shirt fall over her fingers and gripped the cuffs.

"Gabbi. Are you all right?"

Her attention snapped back to Zeke and Miss Parker, who already had the door open, revealing an extra-large closet.

Pushing her sleeves back up, she did her best to drive away her anxiety. "Yes. Of course."

She gave Miss Parker's arm a gentle squeeze as she slipped through the passage door.

"I will leave it open until you return."

"Thank you."

She pushed the button on the end of her flashlight, and a yellow beam dimly lit the tunnel. Wooden stairs led down into darkness, but she couldn't tell how far down they went. She swept her light around the walls. "Do these stairs look like they go deeper than our tunnel?"

Zeke clicked on his flashlight. "There's only one way to find out."

Nodding, she started the descent on the wooden steps. Groans and creaks echoed in the tiny stairwell, and a steady stream of dust and grime coated her hand on the railing. She kept going, placing one foot down in front of the other as the stairs slowly curved around. Perhaps she should be grateful, because the idea of having to climb straight up on the way back already had her exhausted.

"Are we there yet?" Zeke's voice called out from behind her, and she couldn't help but smile.

"I take it you liked that selection from one of the Books of The Past?"

"You didn't?"

"I didn't say that." Gabbi sighed in relief as her foot finally found the floor. She moved over to allow Zeke room. "It's kind of neat to read about sayings that were once popular."

"Have you ever thought about what it would be like to take a—what did they call it? A road trip?"

"We aren't supposed to think about such things." Gabbi adjusted her backpack and swept the beam of light around the new tunnel. It looked similar to theirs, except there was only one passageway. From here, it didn't look like there were any other side tunnels.

"Come on, Gabbi. You can't tell me you never wondered what life would be like if we were from a different time."

"I guess." She bit her lip and started walking through the tunnel, leaving Zeke to catch up with her. Admitting out loud her desire for somewhere else—the freedom to travel—felt wrong. If the world outside the Gates was safe, they wouldn't be kept in, would they?

He must have got the hint because he let the conversation drop. She wanted to confide in him that she wished she had escaped out of the Gates instead of Renna. But every time she got close to opening her mouth, the words died on her tongue.

"I think we are almost there." Zeke picked up the pace, and this time, Gabbi had to keep up with him. When she finally reached him, he had his flashlight pointing up a rickety-looking set of stairs that had either been built in a hurry or by someone who didn't quite know what they were doing.

"Umm. We have to climb up this?"

"I don't know." Zeke reached out and gripped one of the railings, and Gabbi took in a deep breath as the entire foundation wobbled. "I don't like the looks of this."

"Surely this isn't it." Gabbi swept her light around them. "Maybe this one wasn't finished."

"I'm afraid to say it, but I believe that is complete." Zeke pointed his light toward the top of the stairs, and above them was a door similar to the others.

"Great."

"Ladies first?"

She whipped her head around to face Zeke.

"I'm only thinking of your safety. If it collapses, I will be there to break your fall."

"True. You'll be the one most likely to get hurt."

"Does that make you feel better?"

Gabbi gripped the railing and climbed up the first couple of stairs. "Oddly, it does."

He gave her an exaggerated bow. "Then I'm glad to be of service."

A step creaked as if to remind her what she was doing, and she froze.

"Everything okay up there?"

She waited a few more seconds before continuing the climb. "Yeah, found a creaky stair."

"Wonderful. Any other news?"

She glanced down at him and grinned, even though he probably couldn't even see her. "Don't look down."

"You are full of wisdom, Gabbi James."

"Don't you forget it." She reached the platform and took in a breath. "Maybe I should go ahead and knock, so we both aren't up here at the same time?"

After a moment of silence, Zeke called up, "Good idea."

She shook out her hands, and then before she could think about it anymore, knocked on the door.

The door swung open before Gabbi could even raise her hand to knock for a second time.

"Well, well, well." A lanky and muscular man leaned on the door. "Gabriella James. It's about time you showed up."

38

R enna pulled a blanket up to her face, the scratchy material tickling her cheek. She groaned, not wanting to fully wake, still exhausted from her time in the forest.

The Hunt!

Her eyes flew open, a scream ready to burst from her throat. A calloused hand clamped over her lips, and Miles hovered over her, a concerned look on his face.

"You're okay!" Miles's calm voice reassured her, and everything flooded back into her mind. The Guardians finding her, Miles and his uncle saving her, and the horrible run back to the jeep.

Sitting up, she brushed back her hair from her face, finding Miles and his uncle sitting beside her on a splintered wooden floor. Dust and mold tickled her nose, and she sneezed. "Where are we?" She balled the blanket up in her fists and looked around to see a dilapidated building. There were four walls and a roof, except pieces were missing in various spots.

"It's an old hunter's shack outside the Dark Woods," Mack replied, taking a package out of his bag and opening it. He passed it over to her along with a canteen. Steam rose from the container, and her stomach growled in anticipation at the familiar smell of rice and beans and maybe some sort of meat? She couldn't remember the last time she had a hot meal.

"How did you find it?" She greedily took a bite and sighed. "This is amazing. Thank you."

Mack chuckled, his eyes crinkling in the corners. "I don't think I've ever heard anyone compliment those rations before, but you're welcome."

"What's the Dark Woods?" She downed the stew in a few bites and then turned the canteen all the way up to drink it.

"Woah there, slow down before you make yourself sick." Miles reached for her arm and pulled the canteen away. "Small sips. You're dehydrated."

Renna had no doubt that was true. The water didn't seem to quench her dry throat, but she did as he instructed and took slower swallows. His face was dirty, with smudges across his forehead and a bruise forming under his eye. But his face showed more than just filth and injuries. Worry etched between his eyebrows. His shoulders were pulled back, tense, and his whole body was alert, as if he would attack whoever came through the door.

"How long have I been out?" The last thing she remembered was being pushed inside the vehicle and feeling a huge wave of relief. She must have passed out on him.

"All night." Miles frowned. "I was going to wake you up in a few minutes. We have to keep moving, although I hate to leave these four walls. I would feel better if you could rest a little longer."

"She might be able to." Mack gestured to their surroundings. "Since this is an old hunting cabin, we might be able to find some traps." His face lit up at the possibility. "If we could hide a few traps between here and the Gates, then we just might be able to make it back in one piece."

Hope welled up inside at Mack's enthusiasm. From what

little she witnessed of Miles's uncle earlier, he seemed like he wasn't sure about their chances. "How far are we from the Outpost?"

"Probably a day's walk. Maybe a little more."

Renna mentally did the math in her head. She leaned foward in excitement, but every muscle in her body protested and she stopped, waiting for the spasms to ease. She focused on Mack's announcement instead. "I can get home before the Gates lock down again. Otherwise ... it's another seventy-two hours out here."

"That's the plan." Miles's warm smile didn't quite reach his eyes. An ache filled her chest as she realized the truth behind her statement. She could go home, but what about Miles? How was she going to leave him ... again? Joy and sadness whirled around in her mind until she had to force the thoughts away. It was too painful to think about. She reached up and quickly wiped a few stray tears pooling in the corner of her eyes. Now wouldn't be the time to fall apart.

Mack cleared his throat and got to his feet. "Well, I'm going to go look for the traps and walk them back to the jeep."

"Where's the jeep?" Renna asked when it was just the two of them.

"A few minutes away. We couldn't drive it up to the house. It was too risky."

It made sense, of course. They wouldn't want to alert any of the Guardians to their presence. But that meant—her face heated. "You had to carry me—all the way here."

Miles's smiled for the first time since she woke up in the cabin. "I don't think I could have woken you up, even if I wanted to."

"You're kidding?"

"Nope, not at all." He shook his head. "You were out cold, snoring and everything."

"Oh, come on."

"Yeah, I thought the Guardians would hear you with that snore. I had to run."

"All right, all right. Enough about my snoring." She rolled her eyes at his absurdity and then laughed. "How many times have you had to carry me today?"

"I didn't mind." His voice turned serious as his eyes drifted to her lips and then back up. She leaned forward, pausing, her pulse skyrocketing at the thought of kissing him again. She didn't have to wait long because his mouth found hers a second later.

Her heart was definitely going to shatter into a million pieces in less than twenty-four hours. She pulled away, tears filling her eyes.

"Hey." He brushed her hair back from her cheek and tucked it behind her ear. "Everything's going to work out."

She nodded and pretended she believed him, but inside she was a mess. There wasn't any way it could work out. They were only lying to themselves. Renna would get to the Outpost, and Miles would have to return to the Forest Community.

Pulling away, she changed the subject. "Have you surveyed the damage yet?" She pointed down to her foot.

"No, I didn't want to wake you." He stood and grabbed his backpack. "But we should take a look."

She untied her laces and gently pulled the boot off. Her sock was soaked, but there wasn't as much blood as she feared. She tugged the sock off as well. "What's the verdict, doctor?"

He placed her foot on his leg and unwrapped the old cloth. "Amazingly enough, it's not too bad."

"Don't lie." She could tell by his expression that it wasn't as good as he let on. His jaw tensed, but he kept his face neutral as he reached for the medical kit in his bag. He dabbed her foot with antiseptic liquid, and she nearly punched him on the other side of his cheek. She settled for his shoulder instead.

He gaped at her dumbfounded. "Hey! What was that for?"

"That hurt!" She took in a deep breath. "You could have warned me it would sting."

"It couldn't have been that bad."

She stiffened as he held up the dropper for her to see before he applied more of the medicine. "See. Not so bad."

"For you."

He returned the bottle to the kit and grabbed the ointment Elaine had given her that first day at the Infirmary. "Are you ready this time?"

"Ha-ha." She rolled her eyes. "That one actually is soothing." As soon as the cream hit her foot, she pulled her leg away. "And cold!"

"Really?" He raised an eyebrow and reached for her foot to bring back to rest on his knee.

"Are all the stitches still there?"

"There's one, maybe two spots that I think have worked themselves out, but it hasn't reopened." He grabbed a clean cloth and started re-wrapping. "I think it will be okay. We will pad your boot too."

"Thanks, Miles." She sucked in a breath as he tied off the cloth into a knot on the side of her foot. "For everything. I wouldn't have made it this far without you."

"Well, you also wouldn't have been in this mess without me either."

His words were full of guilt, but she couldn't help but laugh. "I'm sorry. I just can't stop remembering the look on your face when you realized you were going to be stuck with me."

His mouth opened to give a rebuttal but then started laughing as well. "Oh, man." He wiped his face. "That seems like forever ago, instead of what, almost a week?"

Almost a week.

Pain clenched her stomach at the sobering thought. Almost a week since she left. She put her boot back on her foot and laced it up. The humor in the memory was already fading.

Two cycles of the Gates being opened and closed, and she hadn't made it back yet. What was going on at home? Was everyone okay? What would she find when she returned?

Renna didn't know if she could handle the answers to those questions. What if she got home and they rejected her? She was pulled from her reverie as the shack's door burst open.

"We got to go. Now!" Mack stumbled in, out of breath. "The jeep is gone."

39

Gabbi forced herself to concentrate on what the man had said. Her brain whirled through so many scenarios. Did he know what happened to Renna?

"You know where Renna is?"

"Why don't you guys come in where it's more comfortable? I'm sure your friend doesn't want to wait on that old heap of wood."

Nodding, she followed the Runner through the trap door and into—well—Gabbi had no idea what this room was. A gasp escaped her lips as she took in the floor-to-ceiling bookcases and luxurious furniture.

"Ah, you like my treasures?" The man gestured to one of the shelves. Instead of books—like the other three walls—this shelf held trinkets, knickknacks, unfamiliar items she had only seen in the pages of a Books of the Past.

Zeke let out a long whistle as he stopped beside her, his eyes widening as he took it all in. "Is that a globe?"

"Good eye." The man walked over to the shelf, found the item, and handed it to Zeke. "I found it on one of my runs."

"This is amazing." Zeke gestured to the shelf. "May I?"

"Have fun." The young man grinned and turned to Gabbi and held out his hand. "I'm Porter."

She grasped his hand and smiled. "It's nice to meet you, officially."

"I kind of feel like I already know you. Your sister talks about you all the time."

"How did you know I would show up here?"

Porter frowned for the first time since she'd entered his house. "Are you telling me you didn't know about the outdoor passage?"

"Not until just now." Gabbi sighed. "Did you help Renna leave?"

"Look, I didn't tell her about the passage." He glanced between her and Zeke. "I haven't told anyone about the outside tunnel."

Gabbi wanted to believe him, but at least blaming him would give her some explanation for what had happened. Someone to hold responsible for all this happening in the first place. But that wasn't fair.

Renna made her own decisions, and she would follow her lead. Her stomach roiled at the directions her thoughts turned. But if Renna could do it, then she could too. For her sister's sake. If there was an outside passage, then Gabbi would use it.

"I believe you." Another yelp of excitement came from Zeke as he examined the last row of gadgets. She turned back to Porter. "You never said why you assumed I would show up here."

"Well, I figured your family would have conveyed the secret as mine did." He folded his arms across his chest. "I was giving it another day before I came to see you myself."

That got Zeke's attention, but with how quickly he drifted to Gabbi's side, she realized he had always been listening, even if he was also enjoying the treasures. "What do you mean?"

"Well, I was going back in through the Gates when I noticed her."

Hope ignited in her chest. "You saw Renna?"

"Yes." His face fell. "She was talking to someone. She was upset. I was going to yell for her, but the sirens wailed, and well —you know."

"You knew she was out there, and you didn't go check on her?" The hope she had seconds ago crashed into a thousand angry pieces. "You had the passage. You could have found her. Saved her."

"I risk my life every day for this Outpost." He took a step towards Gabbi, his eyes flashing. Zeke stepped in front of her, but the Runner continued. "And just so you know, I did go to the passage and ran all the way to the door. I opened it and saw her running—no—chasing some guy into the forest!"

Gabbi's legs were gelatin. It was worse than she feared. Tears pricked her eyes, and she moved to the nearest chair to sit down. Renna chose to leave. She willingly went into the forest after some guy? It didn't make any sense.

A figure knelt in front of her, and she looked down to see concern in Zeke's eyes. "Gabbi?"

"She left us ..." Gabbi swiped a tear from her cheek.

He nodded. "What can I do, Gabbi?"

"You can't do anything. Just give me a moment." She stood, turning away from both of them, and closed her eyes. Even as she said the words aloud to Zeke, they didn't feel true. A nagging piece of unease settled in her stomach and wouldn't go away, no matter how many times she ran through the scenario in her head. Each time she came back to the same thought.

Renna would never willingly leave the Outpost or their family.

Which meant there had to be another explanation. She scrubbed her face free of tears and walked over to her backpack. She didn't even remember taking it off.

"Gabbi, what are you doing?" Zeke's voice was full of alarm. "There's no way Renna willingly left us."

"Okay, but you heard Porter. She ran into the forest."

Gabbi shook her head and grabbed a strap of the bag, threading her hand through it. "I know what he said, but it's not true." She looped her other arm through the remaining strap. "It can't be true."

Zeke reached out to gently take her hand as if she were a fragile piece of glass. And well, maybe she was. Her emotions and brain warred with each other for control, and she just wanted to let her emotions win at the moment. To scream, and cry, and fall apart.

"Gabbi, please. You can't do this."

She closed her eyes, taking in a deep breath. How did he know? When had Zeke slipped under her walls and gotten to know the real her? And more importantly, why had she let him? She'd been so careful over the years to make sure she was who her parents expected her to be. Who the Outpost told her she was. Not even her sister knew the real Gabbi. But just one statement from Zeke was all it took for her to confirm what she was too afraid to put together in her mind and voice out loud.

She was going to find Renna.

"You can't stop me."

"Why do you always say that?" Zeke let out a frustrated groan and turned away from her.

"Are you guys hungry? I'm going to go get a snack." Porter interrupted before walking out of the room. "I'll let you two work this out. When you're ready to go, I'll show you the passage, Gabbi."

Gabbi ignored Porter and reached for Zeke, turning him to face her again. "Look, I have to go out there. Renna didn't just walk away; I know that in my gut. Something happened for her to have to go into the forest."

Zeke searched her face, his eyes flashing between anger and annoyance. "But you don't know that for sure. It's too risky."

"Yeah—well—everything is a risk right now."

"But that doesn't mean you need to put yourself in the middle of it. You might as well just go out there and surrender."

"She's my sister, Zeke!"

"You don't think that I understand that? You're not the only one who has lost family to the forest." Grief flooded his voice, and Gabbi instantly wanted to comfort him.

"I'm sorry. I didn't know."

"Why would you?" His voice lowered to a whisper. "Who wants to be associated with someone who has a traitor for a family member?"

"What happened?"

"My parents won't talk about it." He cleared his throat and looked down at the floor. "My brother left when I was a kid. Just like your sister. That's why my mom and I moved to the Outpost. To have a fresh start. It was a miracle they even approved the transfer. When she married the Blacksmith, and after they had my little brother, they told me not to mention my oldest brother again. I don't know, he was so much older than me that it was easier to not think about it."

"He was a Speaker?"

Zeke met her gaze and nodded. "Oh, Zeke." She slipped her arms around him and squeezed. "I'm so sorry."

"But not enough to stay."

She let go and took a step back, her eyes filling with tears all over again. "I can't go another day without trying to save my sister."

"So, who cares what happens to the people you leave behind. The ones who care about you?"

"That's not fair, Zeke. I'm doing this *because* I care."

"What happens to your parents when you leave? When

they realize that you're not coming back home? You going to put them through that pain?"

"They would understand I'm trying to fix our family. To bring Renna home."

"What about me? You going to just walk away and know I'm going to be worried sick about you?"

Gabbi took a step back, processing the meaning behind his words. How did they go from friends to this? She didn't realize how much he cared for her, and now she'd gone and messed everything up. Because there wasn't any way either of them would concede, and now it was too late. She had to go after her sister, and her heart would pay the price.

She took a step forward and grabbed his hands, willing him to understand. "Zeke—I—I have to do this."

"No, you don't."

"Come with me." The words were out of her mouth before she thought about them. Zeke clenched his jaw, the worry line between his eyebrows etched deeper.

"Don't make me choose between my family and you." Pain lined every word. "I can't put my mom through losing another son."

"I'm sorry. I shouldn't have asked." Gabbi shifted from one foot to the other, her mind a whirl of what needed to happen next. "You will have Porter help you get to the Healer, right? Baby Oliver needs that medicine."

"Gabbi—"

"And then, you can continue to make our deliveries."

"Will you stop—"

"Oh! You should be able to get deliveries to the rest of the Outpost now. I'm sure my father will help you when he's better." Her voice cracked when she mentioned her father. "Or you could try Opal."

"Gabriella James." He reached out and took her hand. "It's killing me thinking about you leaving. Don't do this."

Their silly argument the night before came back to her mind. She grinned. "Are you going to turn me in for real this time?"

"That might be the only way I can get you to see reason."

She sobered. The time for joking and convincing Zeke was over. Gabbi would survive going out in the forest. Her friendship—relationship—whatever had gone on between the two of them—there was no way it would survive.

"At least be a gentleman and give me a head start."

40

"What do you mean the jeep is gone?" Miles rose from his spot on the floor beside Renna and moved toward his uncle.

"The jeep's not there. My guess is the Guardians found it."

"So there goes our cover."

His uncle walked over and set his traps down on a nearby table. "Yes. We're back to square one."

Just when Miles believed they could breathe, something sent them backward, scrambling to get a few steps ahead again. He glanced over his shoulder at Renna, still sitting on the floor. Fatigue shadowed her eyes.

Miles stepped closer to his uncle and lowered his voice. "Renna can't make it far on foot. She's exhausted."

"I know, son. But we don't have any other choice. If she's hoping to make it back to her Outpost, we have to go now. They found our vehicle, so they can't be very far away. If they find us in this shack ..."

Miles nodded. "I know. I know." Miles rubbed the back of his neck, longing to rub away the tension. "I just wish we had more time to prepare and let her rest."

Mack gave him a thin smile. "It's now or never."

"Okay." Miles turned away and picked up his bag, then Renna's. "You get the traps, and I'll help Renna."

Leaning down to Renna, Miles said. "I'm sorry, but it looks like rest time is over."

"I figured it couldn't last long." She pushed herself up from the floor, and Miles gingerly helped her stand.

"How's it feel?"

"Stings a little."

"I figured." Miles raised his arm. "Ready?"

"As I'll ever be." She wrapped her arm around his waist and leaned into him after a couple of steps. "Sorry. Maybe it hurts a little more than I wanted to admit."

"I wish I had some pain medicine for you."

"Then I would be knocked out, and we wouldn't get anywhere."

"Quit talking and move faster, you two." Mack ushered them both forward. "I will set the traps as we go. With any luck, it'll slow them down some."

Renna didn't say much as Miles helped her navigate the rocky terrain, but after an hour, her breath started getting shallow. He slowed his pace, hoping it would help, but nothing worked. They continued on every time his uncle went to hide a trap, and Mack still caught up with them. With each trap, Miles's worry grew. Renna couldn't move fast enough. There was no way around it.

A guttural scream rang out from the hunting shack. Miles halted, looking behind, waiting to see movement in the woods. He couldn't see anything, but the cries and screams from the person injured echoed through the trees, and Miles flinched. The amount of pain the Guardian must be in to scream like that—he couldn't imagine.

"Was that a trap?" Renna's voice broke through his shock.

"It sounds like it." He turned to look at her. "Which means

it won't be long before these woods are crawling with more people."

Renna shuddered, and Miles pulled her tighter against his side. "Are you ready? We need to try to speed up."

Renna's eyes filled, but she nodded. "I can do it."

They started sprinting as best they could with Renna leaning on him for support. Minutes passed, and they continued to run. Where was Mack? He should have been done setting the last trap. He hoped the man was being smart and getting out of harm's way as soon as possible. There was no way they gained such a big lead on him.

"Miles, stop!" Renna cried out in anguish.

"What's wrong?"

"My ... foot ... I can't put any weight on it."

Where in the world was Mack? He quickly scanned the area for him, but he was nowhere to be found. He groaned, trying to think what to do. He was afraid that he'd pushed Renna too far with all the sprinting. Miles took one glance around before he moved into action. "Here, climb on my back."

"Wait—what?"

"Come on, we don't have time to argue." He bent down so it would be easier. "Just don't choke me."

"No promises."

The pace was slower than if they both ran but faster than Renna tripping and falling every few seconds, and she wasn't gasping in pain. Miles hurried over the rough terrain putting as much distance between them and the Guardians.

As they crested a hill, Renna's gasp filled his ear. "Is that what I think it is?"

"I'm afraid so." Miles stopped, taking in deep breaths. Two steps forward and three steps back. It was a never-ending nightmare of obstacles. Stretched out in front of them lay a massive body of water. He walked over to the nearest tree and gently helped Renna down off his back. "A lake."

"Is there a way around?"

They were high enough on the hill he could get a decent view and, judging by this side, the forest surrounded it. "Not one that won't add another half a day or more to our trip."

Renna took in deep gulps of air. "Is there anything else?"

"I can't tell. I need to get a closer look." About twenty-five yards away, there was a cluster of thick trees and large boulders, with a few old trees that appeared to have fallen over. "Let's get to that section of downed trees."

She followed his gaze to the logs. "It's a little out in the open, though."

"Yeah, the path is exposed, but the trees should shield us from view." He gestured around them. "It's better than here."

Renna sighed and then hobbled over to him. "If you say so."

Miles positioned himself to carry her once more. "Come on." He hoped by the time they got to the fallen trees and figured out the next course of action, his uncle would catch up with them. Now that Miles had his uncle back, he didn't want to leave him behind.

He helped Renna to the log and unhooked her canteen from her pack. "Do you need something to eat?"

She accepted the canteen and sighed. "No. I don't think I have the energy to eat."

Miles frowned but didn't push the issue at the moment. She needed to build up her strength, but they would focus on that as soon he figured out where they were and what they were up against. He gently raised her leg and slid the pack under her calf. Hopefully, that would take some of the pressure off her foot.

"Thanks."

He gave her a smile and then dug in his bag for his binoculars. Having the Guardian outfit came in handy, and when they ditched the uniforms, he took all the gadgets. He scanned the shoreline of the lake.

"What do you see?"

"Well, it's not much of a beach." He teased. Hard to imagine what it would look like to see the massive ocean and white sandy beaches from the Books of the Past.

"Funny."

"It's just a lot of rocks. The trees are thick around the border ..." His voice trailed off as he caught sight of something bobbing in the water. It couldn't be.

"Is something wrong?"

"There's a boat." He lowered the binoculars and gave her a smile.

"Can I see? I've never seen one in person."

He passed them to her and watched as her face lit up. "That's amazing. Do you think we could take it across the water?"

"It's too easy." A nagging feeling of doubt made him hesitate, and he took a seat beside her on the log. "They want us to take the boat."

Renna's smile faded. "You're probably right. But what else can we do? Walking around the lake is out of the question."

"I'm not sure."

"So, what happens if we don't take the boat?"

"We go around, but it's rough terrain for your foot, and it'll take us a lot longer."

Renna nodded. "Especially if you have to carry me." She lowered her voice. "What do you think might happen if we do take the boat?"

Miles glanced back at the water. It was peaceful and calm, but there wouldn't be any cover. A whole range of things could happen, and at this point, he wouldn't put anything past the Guardians. "We'd be sitting ducks."

She covered her face with her hands. "So, we are doomed either way."

Miles wished he could offer better news—he would take just one glimmer of hope at this point.

Gunfire broke out behind them, and Miles didn't even hesitate. He reached for Renna, knocking her to the ground behind the log. He gave her a push. "Get as close to the log as you can and stay down." He withdrew the gun he'd taken off the Guardian's uniform and peered over the top of the log.

"Miles!" Renna hissed. "What are you doing? Get down!"

He took one more glance around and then ducked back down. "I can't get a good look."

"So, what do we do?" Her voice wavered as she leaned against him.

He held her trembling hands, forcing himself to ignore his own panic. It wasn't like this was a part of his job training. He learned how to track, how to talk to strangers, but nothing on surviving a gunfight.

"Suggestions?"

Renna's grip tightened on his shirt sleeve. "Your uncle."

"At this point, we can only hope he's still alive."

"Wow. Thanks for your vote of confidence, kid."

"Mack!"

His uncle's hand reached out and pulled Miles up from the ground and into a hug. "I'm glad you two are okay. As I made my way back, I came up behind a pair of Guardians ..." His voice trailed off, and it didn't take much for Miles to fill in the blanks.

"We found a boat down there, but I don't think it's the wisest of decisions." Miles helped Renna to a sitting position. "We would be way too out in the open and for far too long."

"I agree."

"Do you have any suggestions?" Renna asked, dusting off her jeans.

"As a matter of fact, I do." A slow grin spread across Mack's face. "Are either one of you claustrophobic?"

41

"Are we sure this is a good idea?" Renna looked down at the round metal grate, her stomach churning at the thought of descending the rusty ladder to the unknown. She tried to peer inside, but it was pitch black.

How in the world would she maneuver down the ladder anyway? Were they just going to ignore the fact that Miles had to carry her most of the day? She hated to add another worry to Miles's plate, but her ankle had started swelling, and her sock dug into her skin. How would she descend the small metal ladder if she couldn't bear to put direct weight on her foot?

Mack gave her an encouraging nod. "Well, I don't think the Guardians know I'm helping you yet, so with any luck, they won't even consider the fact that you could find the maintenance shaft."

"And what if they do know?"

He pulled back the handle on the hatch and opened it. "Then we better hurry."

"I'll go down first to help Renna. I doubt her foot can handle the rungs." Miles took a piece of string from his pack and tied his flashlight to a button on his jacket.

"I don't know how this is going to work." She peered over the opening as Miles climbed down a few spots. "I can't even stand without help."

"It's not far down, if I remember right. Miles, I can probably even lower Renna down to you."

"Why does that not make me feel better?" With trembling fingers, Renna tied a flashlight to a loop on her jeans and took a deep breath. Sitting on the ground facing the tunnel, she lifted both of her arms above her head. "Please don't drop me."

"I wouldn't dare." Mack gripped both of her wrists and started to lower her down in the tunnel. Her body swayed, throwing her back into the metal ladder.

"Hey, be careful!" Renna glanced up just in time to see the night sky above Mack light up in a brilliant white light, followed by a thundering boom that shook the ground.

"Well, kids—that was the last trap that I set." He quickly lowered her, catching her off guard. She gasped, looking away from Mack, her legs flying.

"Renna, be still. I can't grab you." Miles called below her. His voice had taken on an edge that wasn't there earlier.

"I'm trying!" She hissed back at him through clenched teeth. "This isn't exactly easy, you know."

"We have about three minutes before the Guardians deploy to this area. The explosion will most likely bring all the Squadrons, which puts us at a huge disadvantage since we had to backtrack some to get to this shaft."

"Not helping." Renna willed her body to be still, but everything in her told her to flee. To get out of this situation. Hands gripped her ankles, and she nearly let go of Mack's hands as pain flooded her. She bit her lip, trying to relax as Miles adjusted his arms around her knees and helped guide her the rest of the way down the ladder.

"See? It wasn't as hard as we originally thought." Miles

helped her move out of the way to give Mack room to climb down the ladder.

She untied her flashlight and held it up for Mack as he closed the hatch and scrambled down.

"Let's move." Mack took the lead, and Renna decided to try walking with the help of Miles. She didn't know how long she would last, but it was nice to not have to depend on him to carry her at the moment.

"At least the ground is flat."

"I just wish we could see our feet." She shuddered at the idea of four-legged creatures in the tunnel, darting over her toes.

Miles chuckled. "You never know what might be scurrying around."

"I'll just add it to the list of things that I have to push out of my mind."

"Less talking, more hurrying," Mack called over his shoulder, his tone and scowl hinting now wasn't the time to have a conversation.

Renna bit the inside of her cheek as Miles tried to increase their pace. Each step on her bad foot sent pain shooting all the way to her hip. Talking kept her mind off it, but silence brought it right back to the forefront. Instead, she tried to concentrate on the tunnel.

The passageway's walls were narrow, and while the floor was fairly even, it was still bare ground. It was like the builders dug their way down to their desired depth and then proceeded in a straight line.

Metal pipes and black wires ran along the ceiling, weaving in and out of wooden rafters. Every so often, metal boxes lined the sides of the walls with more wires and cables. Whether this was remnants of the past or the handiwork of the Officials, Renna didn't know.

Finally, her curiosity got the better of her, and she couldn't keep quiet any longer. "Where does this tunnel end, Mack?"

"We should come out within a few hours of walking time to the Outpost."

Renna took a moment to let that information wash over her. She was so close. A few hours once they got past the lake? It didn't seem possible.

"Miles, why didn't we go this way when you found me?"

"I didn't know this section of the forest existed until Uncle Mack took me to find you."

"I have a feeling the forest is much larger than we've ever known."

"True enough, Renna," Mack said. "Why do you think the Outposts are scattered so far away from each other? They are strategically placed so you could travel for days and never see another one, but all in between, there's lots of land and plenty of room to get turned around."

She blew a stray strand of hair that fell from her braid away from her face. "They don't want us to know each other."

Mack snapped his finger. "Bingo."

A buzzing sound filled the shaft and Renna nearly fell over when Miles stopped walking, looking up toward the ceiling.

What is it?" She asked, trying to calm her racing heart, when red lights filled the tunnel, illuminating the path in front of them.

"They're here."

Renna didn't have time to process Mack's words before Miles was nearly running, forcing her to try to match his speed.

Voices and footsteps filled the tiny space behind them, and Miles called Mack to help. He nodded and fell into step beside her placing her free arm around his neck. Between the two of them, Renna was practically carried as they sprinted the best they could in the narrow passageway.

"What's on the topside when we get out of the tunnel?" Miles asked, his breath coming out in quick gasps.

"The same as before. Trees."

"Trees." Miles practically sighed the response, and Renna couldn't blame him. After this, if she made it home, she wasn't sure if she'd ever want to see another tree in her life. In fact, she didn't know if she'd ever want to step outside at all.

Her toes caught a large stone embedded into the ground, pitching her forward. Renna cried out as Miles and Mack stopped her, throwing her even more off balance. She bit back a yelp as her sore foot smacked another stone.

Her knee buckled, and she nearly dropped to the ground.

"Renna!" Miles pulled her up. "Come on, we have to keep going."

The voices and shouts grew closer, echoing down the corridor.

Mack urged them to pass him. "Go as fast as you can, and don't stop. I will hold them off as long as I can."

"No, you can't." Renna shook her head, ignoring the meaning of his words. "We're not going to leave you here."

"You need all the extra time I can buy."

"I can make it just fine." Renna tried to make her voice cheerful and encouraging, but it sounded weak to her own ears.

"The longer you argue, the more time you're wasting. Now, GO!"

"Uncle Mack—" Miles's voice broke, and his uncle simply nodded in response.

"Go. I'll catch up."

Miles tugged on her arm again, and this time, Renna let him drag her away. Tears poured down her face as they went farther down the tunnel. Gunshots assaulted her ears, and she screamed.

"Renna, hurry." Desperation filled Miles's voice as they reached a small section of stairs leading to a silvery metal door.

Miles had to drag her up them, begging her to move faster, but each step crushed her a little more. Mack stayed behind to try to buy them more time, and for what? Chances were, they wouldn't ever make it out of the forest. She was utterly exhausted and shattered.

"Come on, Renna, don't give up."

"You can read my thoughts now?"

He frowned. "I can see it in your eyes. But I'm not going to let you."

"Mack—"

"Is going to be fine, and so are we."

She wanted to believe him. Desperately. Except everything kept stacking up against them. Tears filled her eyes and poured down her cheeks. She wasn't worthy of this kind of loyalty.

"We are almost there—just two more steps."

Taking in a deep breath, she pushed ahead, ignoring the pain and the negative thoughts. She owed it Miles and Mack not to give up now. At the top, Miles threw open the door and burst through—right into a swarm of bright lights.

42

Day Eight

Gabbi couldn't blame Renna for running headfirst into the enticing forest. Everything invited her in and made her want to stay. She'd seen the outer edges of the trees in the brief hours the Gates were opened, but it hadn't prepared her for the breathtaking view before her.

Tree trunks wider than her arms could span were scattered all around her. Thick underbrush, plants, and rocks filled in the gaps between the massive trees. Birds called to each other in the canopies, and the leaves swayed in the gentle wind, sending loose tendrils of hair around her face.

It was beautiful and not at all like the scary stories she'd listened to growing up. The forest held an almost majestic and tranquil atmosphere, and she wished she could sit and listen to the leaves dance in the breeze.

Content, Gabbi had to force her gaze away from the picturesque view and focus on the task at hand. From the safety of the hidden passage, Porter pointed her in the direction he'd seen Renna run. She couldn't blame him for wanting to stay inside the Gates after the siren went off. By all accounts, it was what she should be doing, but Gabbi couldn't let another day go by without trying to find Renna.

Zeke's face filled her mind, but she closed her eyes and tried to think about something—anything else. Because when she thought about him, her chest ached and tears filled her eyes. She had hurt him by leaving, but how could he expect her to stay when she had the opportunity to find her sister? She chose to go, just like he chose his family, instead of risking his mother losing another son.

Following the compass Porter gave her, she headed off in the direction he witnessed Renna go. She walked for hours before finally deciding to stop and rest, thankful for the supplies she already had in her pack and the ones Porter gave her. She should be able to make it for a few days in the woods —if she could find her way to Renna.

Except that was the problem. Where was Renna? Would she be safe with the boy she chased after?

It stood to reason that if this guy was out in the woods, he had to come from somewhere. Perhaps some sort of camp or living quarters. What if there was a whole settlement of people?

She shook her head, laughing at herself. No one lived in the forest. It was hard to imagine it even being a possibility. The forest was too big and too empty.

She'd been out here for hours already, and there wasn't anyone around. No Guardians near the Gates like she'd always feared. No monsters hiding in the shadows, ready to pounce on the disobedient human who dared to enter the forest.

So what did it mean since she hadn't found any of these things? She took another sip from her water skin and then placed it back in her bag. Gabbi would continue to head sorth, and if she didn't find some sort of sign of human life, then she would alter her course and start all over.

But first, she pulled out the small notebook Zeke had

convinced her to take. Every time she stopped, she recorded which direction she went, what she saw, and how long it took her to get back there. It wasn't perfect by any means, but maybe it would help get her and Renna back home.

There wasn't anything out of the ordinary this time to mark as a waypoint, so she grabbed the bottom of her shirt and cut a piece of the blue cotton to tie around the tree. A gust of wind knocked the fabric from her fingers and carried the cloth away. She chased after it, stopping when she spotted a well-worn patch of dirt. Gabbi followed the smooth dirt, and it continued, winding its way through the underbrush.

She tied the piece of cloth around the nearest branch and took the path, following it until she nearly fell onto a log a few miles later. Sweat dripped from her forehead, and she wiped it away before it could drip into her eyes.

"Who are you?"

A gruff voice called out from behind her and gripped the straps of her backpack.

"Who's there?" She whirled around in every direction seeing nothing but more undergrowth and trees.

"Who I am doesn't matter." An older man stepped out from behind a wide tree. He was tall, taller than both Father and Zeke, with broad shoulders and thick arms. "Who are you, and what are you doing here?"

A flicker of fear went through her, but she pushed it away and got to her feet, raising her chin. No matter how much he intimidated her, she wouldn't look weak to this burly man. "My name is Gabbi."

"And what are you doing out here, Gabbi?"

His words were still sharp, so she matched his tone. "Looking for my sister."

Recognition crossed his face briefly but then he returned to glaring at her. "Is that so? What's her name?"

Should she give him Renna's name? Could she trust him?

An anxious laugh almost escaped her lips. Of course she couldn't trust him. He was in the forest!

He must have sensed her hesitation because he relaxed his stance. "I'm not going to hurt you, girl." Annoyance dripped from his words. "I'm trying to figure out why you are out here at the checkpoint. Did Miles send you?"

Miles? Checkpoint?

"No one sent me." She sighed. "I'm just trying to find my sister."

"You're from the Outpost?"

"Yes. And you're from …"

The man grunted. "You look harmless enough. Although I might regret this later. I'm from a community not too far from here."

Another spark of hope ignited. "A community? That's amazing! Is my sister there? She's a seventeen-year-old, a little shorter than me, long wavy brown hair, and brown eyes. Her name is Renna." The words tumbled out in a rush, and she took a quick breath. "Please tell me she's there."

The man held up his hands. "Woah, woah. Take a breath. I didn't understand any of that." He slowly made his way over to the log and took a seat, gesturing for her to do the same. "Please, sit."

He wanted her to calm down? To sit when Renna could be minutes away? She wanted to tell him they didn't have time for a conversation, but no doubt that would take longer.

"I just need to find my sister." She sat down.

"I can understand that." The man sighed. "Did you say her name was Renna?"

"Yes, sir."

The man's eyes lit up, and then he frowned. "I know Renna. But she's not at the camp right now."

"What?" Gabbi's voice escalated. "Where is she?"

The man looked around before he continued, motioning

for her to be quiet. "Look, I'm sorry, but she left several days ago. She was going back home."

Tears filled her eyes, and she shook her head, refusing to believe him. "No, it can't be true. You must be mistaken. She has to be there."

"She hasn't made it back home?"

His eyes filled with worry, and Renna's hope sank. "No. I snuck out so I could try to find her."

"I'm sorry." He cleared his throat, his expression changing. She couldn't quite explain it, but it was similar to the haunted look her mother had worn since Renna left. "I'm really sorry."

"There's something you're not telling me."

The man's eyes were full of regret. "Aye." He took his hat off and rubbed his head. "I thought maybe he decided to stay with Renna."

He? Oh, the man must have meant the boy he mentioned earlier. Was that his son? "So Miles hasn't made it home either?"

The man shook his head.

Gabbi got to her feet and picked up her bag. "All right. Well, let's find them."

A smile split across his face. "Yep. You're Renna's sister all right. You have her spunk."

She gave the man a big smile. "Or maybe she has mine."

The man got to his feet. "Maybe so." He extended his hand towards her. "My name is Keegan. I have a couple horses and supplies nearby. Let's go find Renna and Miles."

43

"Look, men, they made it too easy for us."

"Renna, did you not hear us calling for you in the forest?"

"I thought we would play the game a little longer."

Miles shielded his eyes against the bright light the Guardians held up and tried to count the pairs of feet before him. He needed to know exactly what they were up against.

"And look, boys, Renna brought a friend with her."

Laughter and snide comments continued and Miles could feel Renna tense under his arm. One, two, three, four ... His eyes trailed up as far as the beam of light allowed and checked each of the men standing in front of them. Weapons drawn, and more hanging from their waists. How were they going to get out of this one?

"What? You don't have anything to say about this, Miles?" One of the guards on his left asked. "Official Grant will be so interested to hear that you aren't at the Forest Community."

A man in the center of the group stepped forward, his words angry and cold. "I'm more interested in the fact that he escaped. Where's your driver? What did you do to him?"

"Back off, Miller." Another called out. "He's not worth it."

Renna leaned close to him. "What are we going to do?"

"Why don't you lower the lights, and we can talk." He slowly shifted his weight back, hoping she would get the hint and move with him. He still had his arm wrapped around her, supporting her bad leg as they exited the tunnel. If they could get back through the door, they could find something to secure it, buy them time to come up with some sort of plan and get away.

"I don't think you really want to talk. If you did, you wouldn't be considering going back through the door." The Guardian who first talked to him spoke up, and Miles suspected he was the leader of the group. "Which is a bad idea, by the way. There's more of us inside."

Renna's grip tightened around his shoulder. They were trapped. Guardians in front of them, and Guardians behind them.

"Just tie them up already, Miller." The impatient Guardian took another step closer. "You're just toying with them."

"But that is what makes this all fun." Miller pulled some type of plastic out of his pocket and motioned for the others to follow him. "Don't forget to take their backpacks."

"No!" Renna screamed as hands grabbed and dragged her away from him.

"Be careful, she's hurt!" Fury lit up inside like a fuse ready to explode. He swept one of the Guardian's legs causing him to fall to the ground, and punched the other man in the face. The Guardians recovered quickly, though, advancing on him at the same time. One man grabbed his arms and forced them behind his back while the other one landed a punch to Mile's stomach. Bright lights blurred his vision, and it wasn't long before he was doubled over on his knees, trying to move away from the random kicks to his side.

Renna's sobs for them to stop broke him more than the

punches and kicks. A voice screamed back at Renna to be quiet, followed by the sound of a stinging slap. With whatever strength he could find, he jumped to his feet and rammed his shoulder into the closest Guardian, knocking the man to the ground. Miles landed on top of him, but another Guardian grabbed his hands, binding them behind him before he could lunge again.

Miles headbutted the Guardian, causing blood to pour from the man's nose. A flurry of movement happened all around him, and two pairs of hands pulled him towards a utility truck.

He fought both of them. Wiggling and kicking the best he could to loosen the grip they had on him. But it wasn't any use. His only hope was to stall them long enough his uncle could save them. Doubt filled his mind, though, rising to panic. What were the chances Mack made it out of the tunnel alive?

Two metal doors opened, and the Guardians lifted him over the truck's hitch, tossing him inside the enclosed box. Moments later, a third Guardian carried Renna over, her hands bound in front of her. The man climbed up in the truck and set her on one of the benches lining the wall. At least he heeded Mile's warning that she was injured.

"What are you doing? Where are we going?"

"To Official Grant." The Guardian frowned, turning from Renna to Miles. "For her execution." He grabbed Miles and drug him to the bench, picking him up and dropping him beside Renna.

"What happened to kill on sight?" One of the Guardians called.

"Official Grant changed the orders. Now we are supposed to bring her to him, so that's what we are going to do."

"What about the boy?"

The Guardian jumped out of the back of the truck. "That's for Official Grant to decide." The metal doors slammed, locking them both in darkness.

"Renna? Are you hurt?"

"No more than usual. You?" Her voice was quiet and dull. Most likely in shock from what the Guardian just told them.

"We're going to get out of here." Miles spoke the words for his sake as much as Renna's. He needed all the confidence he could get. Somehow, they would make it out of this alive.

"I hope you're right."

"You just have to hang in there a little longer, okay?" He nudged her with his shoulder. "Do you think if I turn around, you could untie my hands?"

"I can try."

Miles shifted around on the bench and waited for Renna to find his hands in the dark. He jerked when her cold fingers found his wrist.

"Sorry." Her hands circled his wrist. "It's not a rope, Miles. It's more like little grooves and notches." Her fingers tugged and pulled around the contraption, and it slipped tighter.

"Ouch!"

"I'm sorry!" She let go of him. "I think we need a knife."

Miles closed his eyes and groaned. "It's in my bag ... with the Guardians."

Silence filled the small truck bed before Renna spoke again. "Maybe Mack will come for us."

"Maybe."

"But if he doesn't?"

"I'm still working that one out."

"Why aren't we moving yet?"

"I don't know."

What were the Guardians doing out there? Contacting Official Grant and awaiting orders? Or were they just messing with their heads? Some sort of psychological torture?

"I wish I had a flashlight." Renna shook, her breath coming out in short gasps. "If I live through this, I think I may have developed a fear of the dark."

An image of Renna surrounded by Guardians sent shudders down his spine. After all she'd been through so far, he was surprised she hadn't fallen apart yet. Most people would have. "I don't blame you."

A gunshot erupted outside of the truck. Then shouting and return fire. Renna let out a sob, and Miles tried to comfort her the best he could without the use of his hands. There was another burst of gunfire then ... silence. Miles held his breath, waiting to see if his uncle would open the back of the truck.

Nothing.

Minutes crept by, then finally, a door opened and the engine roared.

"Miles, we're moving."

The truck lurched forward, picking up speed only to slow back down again. Every bump and hole in the road sent them bouncing on the bench. With no windows in the back of the truck, Miles lost track of how long they drove or how fast they were going. It was impossible to tell.

Without warning, the truck lurched to the left and then to the right. Miles flew off the bench and landed on the floor, his side taking the brunt of the fall. Renna shouted, and within seconds a thud hit the metal surface near him.

"Renna? Are you okay?"

"I think so." Her voice was shaky, but he didn't hear any panic or alarm in her voice.

A sudden stop sent them careening towards the front of the truck. There was no way to stop the movement, and Miles flinched, bracing for impact. He hit the wall first, then Renna.

Had they wrecked? Miles slowly sat up as the doors of the truck opened, banging against the side of the vehicle. No time to check for injuries.

"All right, kids, you are walking the rest of the way."

44

"Uncle Mack, I can't believe it's you!" Miles scooted across the truck and hung his legs over the hitch. "You're bleeding!"

"I hit a large hole and overcorrected." His uncle leaned on the truck, hunched over in pain. Blood soaked the front of his uniform. "I think the axle snapped."

"I don't care about the truck. I'm worried about you. What happened?"

"I managed to get out of the tunnel but wasn't so lucky in the gunfight."

"How bad is it? Can you get me free so I can look at it?"

"I think so." He reached in his pocket and withdrew a knife. "Renna, are you all right?"

"I'm more worried about you."

Miles turned around so his uncle could cut the binds on his wrist. Once he was finished, he grabbed the knife and freed Renna. Guiding his uncle to the edge of the truck, he helped him pull off the uniform jacket.

"We need to get you somewhere safe." He listened for the sound of vehicles before focusing on the gunshot wound. This couldn't be happening. He gently leaned his uncle forward and checked his back.

No exit wound.

"We need something to stop the bleeding. Were our packs in the cab of the truck?"

His uncle nodded. "I believe so. But you know it's not going to help."

Miles ignored him and ran to the front seat. He grabbed both bags and hauled them to the back of the truck.

"You're going to be just fine." Miles's stomach roiled, but he tried to suppress it and get to the task at hand. He dug through his pack to find the first aid kit. He pulled out a roll of gauze and lifted up Mack's shirt.

"The bullet is still in there, and we don't have any tools to remove it." Mack's breath came out in shallow gasps. "Or sew up my wound."

Miles's mind was already making plans. "Then we will get you to the Forest Community. Elaine can fix you."

He applied the bandage to the wound. Blood soaked it in seconds.

"The Guardians will be here any minute. I couldn't stop them before they radioed Grant for backup." His uncle coughed, and blood coated Miles's hand.

"We will figure something out, okay?" Panic welled up in Miles's chest, and he looked over at Renna, who had tears pouring down her cheeks.

"You can't carry Renna and me." His voice was calm, which just made Miles want to shake him and try to make him see reason. There had to be a way to fix this. He just got his uncle back. He couldn't lose him again.

"I don't have much time, son. Listen to me." Miles wanted to look away, but his uncle grabbed his hand.

"In my jacket, I have a grenade."

Miles shook his head, not wanting to listen to anything else. "That's out of the question."

"Miles—stop! This is what we are doing. It's the only way to buy you enough time to get out of here. When the Guardians surround the truck, I will detonate the grenade."

"There has to be another way!" Miles wanted to scream at his uncle and make him see reason. To pick him up and throw him over his shoulder, to make him come with them anyway. His mind whirled with ideas and possibilities, but nothing he came up with solved the problem of all three of them leaving together.

"You know this is the only way." His uncle's grip on his hand tightened. "Your dad would be so proud of you. To see the man that you've become."

Beside him, Renna cried, and Miles's throat burned. There was so much he wanted to say, so much he still had to learn about his uncle's time away. There was so much he wanted to tell him about his life at the Forest Community. But no words would form.

"I can't wait to tell him all about you."

Miles closed his eyes, tears burning the lids. Renna's sobs became louder as he wiped his tears with his free hand. He finally found his voice. "You can't ... do this. I'm not going to let you." Miles sent a glance toward Renna. "Hand me another bandage, and then we are going to start moving."

Renna covered her mouth with her hand and averted her eyes, trying to quiet her sobs.

A small smile spread across his uncle's face. "You don't want me to bail on my promise to your father, now do you?"

Miles shook his head. "But ... I can't leave you. I won't."

The sound of engines rumbled in the distance. They were out of time.

"I know you won't. That's why I made the decision." He let go of Miles's hand. "Left jacket pocket."

He pressed even harder, trying to compensate for his uncle's hand moving away, but the blood already soaked through the second bandage and covered both of his hands. If he pulled away to reach for the jacket—heaven help him—he couldn't do it.

Mack gave a quick nod. "It's time."

Miles blindly grabbed for the jacket, tears blurring his vision as he fumbled for the grenade. Mack held out his hand, waiting. But Miles couldn't get his feet to cooperate.

"It's okay. I'm ready." His uncle sighed. "You're going to keep your promise to Renna, do you understand?"

"Yes, sir. I'm going to get her home."

Shaking, he placed the grenade in his uncle's hand and helped Renna down from the truck. She hobbled over to Mack and wrapped her arm around him in a hug. When she pulled away, they both had tears in their eyes.

How did he say goodbye? What words could he use that would make any of this okay? Nothing about this situation was right. He leaned down and embraced his uncle.

"I'm glad it was you driving that jeep. That you found me after all these years."

"Me too, son." His uncle's voice faltered. "Me too."

45

"How do you know where to go?" Gabbi adjusted the reins in her hands, trying to get used to the feel of movement underneath her. She'd never been on a horse before, and every sway of the beast made her think she was going to fly off.

"When Miles didn't come back, I decided to sneak into Thomas's office. He's the leader of the Forest Community, and I've never approved of Miles working under him." Keegan pulled out a map from his jacket pocket. "I dug around until I found this."

"What does it show?"

"For lack of a better description, meeting places. They are scattered all along the forest."

"And you think Miles and Renna will be at one of them?"

"I don't know. Maybe." He sighed and put the map away. "I've already checked a few closest to the Forest Community, but no luck. So we will go toward the next one on the map and hopefully find some sign that they are or have been in the area."

Gabbi nodded. It was better than the plan she had—which

was nothing. She almost wanted to laugh out loud at the absurdity of it. What was she thinking? Other than wanting to find Renna. She had never in her life been so impulsive. But if Renna was still out there, trying to make it back, she had to do what was necessary to bring her little sister home.

Even though she was uneasy riding the horse, it didn't change the fact she was grateful for running into Keegan. He might be big and burly, but the way he talked about Miles, she could tell he thought of him as a son, and that was good enough for her.

"How long have you known Miles?"

This brought a smile to the man's face. "I think he was about fifteen or sixteen. He just marched straight up to the Forest Community and asked for someplace to sleep." Keegan chuckled, a big, boisterous laugh that made her smile. "Our healer, Elaine, lost her husband years ago, and she had an extra bedroom, so she took him in. I think she hoped Miles would become her apprentice. But he can't handle sewing people up."

"So, you took him under your wing?"

"I guess you could say that. I taught him how to hunt and what I knew about tracking. It was Thomas who noticed how much he cared about people and how the community would flock around him."

"I still can't believe there's a whole community of people in the forest." When Gabbi first connected the dots, she didn't want to believe it. But the more Keegan talked about his home and people, the more it sounded just like the Outpost—only without the Guardians and the Officials looming over them.

"Renna was the same way." He looked over at her, his eyes concerned. "You know Renna didn't want to leave the Outpost. She wanted nothing else but to go home."

His words were a soothing balm to her soul she hadn't realized she needed. She'd always told herself Renna wouldn't want to leave, but there was a small part of her still worried. If

Renna got a taste of freedom, would she take it and decide not to come back? "I don't understand why she didn't come straight home then."

Keegan called out for his horse to stop and motioned for Gabbi to do the same. She pulled back on the reins and closed her eyes as the horse followed her prompting. Gabbi didn't know quite what to expect, but the animal stopped much more gracefully than she thought it would.

"It's not really my story to tell, but she injured her foot and needed stitches. Miles brought her back for medical care."

A surge of panic overwhelmed her, and she turned to look over at Keegan. "We have to find them."

"We will."

A thunderous boom shook the ground, and Gabbi's horse whinnied, tossing her head and stepping backward. Fire lit up the sky, and her heart nearly pounded out of her chest. Was Renna involved? Was she hurt?

"Keegan?" She barely got the words out before Keegan was flicking the reins and yelling for his mount to run. His horse galloped off in the direction of the explosion, and Gabbi gripped the leather straps as her horse raced after him.

"Keegan!" Gabbi hollered into the wind, but he didn't look back at her. His horse continued to run the best it could over the forest floor, and hers followed, seeming to enjoy pursuing the other animal.

The closer they came toward the commotion, the more the smell of smoke and gas clung to the air. She drew the neckline of her shirt over her nose to block some of the odor.

In front of her, Keegan slowed his horse down and then came to a complete stop. She did her best to follow suit, but her mount was more in tune with following the other mare's example instead.

"What is it?" She asked, afraid to speak louder than a whisper. Keegan's eyes narrowed as he studied their surroundings before climbing off the horse. He tied the reins to a nearby tree. "I'm not sure. But I think I hear running."

Gabbi tried to mimic his motions but getting down was just as hard as climbing up in the saddle. She misplaced her footing and crashed to the ground in a heap. Her horse turned to her and snorted, flicking her tail as though laughing at her.

Scrambling to her feet, she dusted off her pants and followed Keegan's lead, tying her horse next to his. Reaching behind his back, he slid a bow off his shoulder and motioned for her to be quiet.

She did her best to put her feet in the same places he stepped, but there wasn't any other way around it. The leaves crackled with every step, and sticks snapped under her shoes.

They walked a few more paces before Gabbi could distinctly make out the sounds of leaves rustling. Whoever it was, they were in a hurry.

And headed straight for them.

Keegan grabbed her arm and guided her off the beaten path. He nocked an arrow, pulled back his arm, and took aim.

As the rustling grew closer, Gabbi's heart beat harder.

Two figures emerged from the thicket, one clearly injured.

"Miles!" Keegan lowered his bow and started running towards the pair. Her eyes moved from the boy and locked with Renna's.

Renna!

Keegan was already pulling Miles into a hug before her brain got over the shock of seeing her sister. Alive. She wanted to scream at the top of her lungs that she had done it. She'd found her sister!

Renna's face was full of relief at the sight of Keegan, and then they widened when she looked in Gabbi's direction. "Gabbi? Is that you?"

At the sound of her sister's voice, Gabbi's feet unthawed, and she rushed to her, tears coursing down her cheeks. "Renna!" She flung her arms around her thin shoulders and pulled her close. Renna clung to her, sobs quietly soaking her jacket.

Finally, she pulled back slightly to look at Renna, her heart aching at the sight. Dirty and ripped clothing, most of her hair out of her braid and in desperate need of a brush. Tiny cuts marred her forehead, cheeks, and chin. A palm-sized bruise lined the side of her face. And her foot—well, Renna couldn't even stand on it.

She swallowed the lump in her throat. "I thought I would never see you again."

"What are you doing here?" Renna leaned more heavily on Miles. "How did you get here?"

"That is a very long story." She peeked over at Keegan and grinned. "I'm just so happy we found you."

"It's really good to see you, Keegan." Miles added, but Gabbi couldn't miss the grief that lined his voice. "But we can't stay still. We're being Hunted."

Keegan's face went pale, and Gabbi replayed the words over in her head. It didn't make sense. Who was hunting them? Why? "Wait, you're telling me someone is trying to kill you?"

"Yes." Renna's voice trembled. "Welcome to my never-ending nightmare."

46

"I can't believe I found you." Renna did her best to stand as Gabbi clung to her. It was as if her sister was afraid if she let go, Renna would disappear.

"What are you doing in the forest? Are Mom and Dad all right?" Renna pulled back from Gabbi, worry taking center stage.

"They are both fine. Well, Dad is sick, and I had to get Zeke's help to dig him out of a tunnel."

"A tunnel—Zeke?" She shook her head. "I think I need to sit down for the conversation." Renna wobbled, and Miles's arm tightened around her, balancing her, keeping her upright.

"I'm not sure this is a good time to stay still and talk." He sounded exhausted and probably needed the break much more than she did. Nevertheless, he was right. They needed to put as much distance between them and the Guardians.

"Miles is right. We'll have to talk later." Renna wiped her eyes with her free hand. "The Guardians won't be far behind, so we need to move."

Keegan and Gabbi exchanged a look but nodded, and a smidgen of anxiety eased.

"Please tell me you have horses nearby," Miles asked, hope hanging onto every word.

Keegan rubbed his hands together. "You know I do." He motioned for them to follow him. "This way."

Miles bent down, and Renna climbed onto his back. It was becoming easier to do so, but she knew he had to be exhausted at this point.

"How bad is your foot?" Gabbi asked, keeping step beside them. "Keegan told me you injured it."

"It was almost better, but with all the running through the forest, I've hurt it again."

"The stitches have probably worked themselves out at this point." Miles huffed, strained from carrying her. "Elaine is going to throw a fit."

"Sounds like we have a lot to tell each other."

"But how about we get home first?" Keegan led them off the path and stroked his horse's neck. "Gabbi, how about you ride with me, so Renna and Miles can ride the Appaloosa. I think she likes Renna."

For the first time in a long while, she smiled at the memory of the Appaloosa stopping and nibbling on grass the whole way to the Forest Community.

Keegan effortlessly placed Renna in the saddle so she could avoid further injury to her foot. He handed her the reins, and Miles swung up behind her.

Once Gabbi and Keegan were in place on the other horse, they were off. "How far do you think we are from the Gates?"

"With the horses, a few hours."

Renna turned to grin at Miles, and he beamed back at her. The first light to enter his eyes since they left Mack at the truck. "We're going to make it before the Gates re-open."

"Was there any doubt?"

She wanted to pinch him. "Don't jinx us now."

"Guys?" Keegan's voice rang out in alarm. "Look."

Renna followed his gesture out in front of them and gasped. Guardian trucks and jeeps were in the distance, heading right for them. "What do we do?"

Keegan peered back toward Miles. He gave a small shake of his head, and Renna's heart sank. "Considering how often you two have gotten lost this week, we need to stay on the trail, or we won't make it before the Gates close again."

There wasn't anything for them to do but run.

He spurred his horse forward, and they followed suit, staying a little behind them on the uneven trail. Renna worried the Appaloosa would slip or fall, but she gracefully kept her footing, and somehow Renna stayed upright. Last time, she hadn't had a saddle horn to hold onto. Or Miles supporting her back. After a few minutes, Keegan held up his hand, signaling them to stop.

"What's wrong?"

"We can't keep pushing the horses this fast on the trail. It's not safe."

"What do you suggest?" Renna asked, eying the oncoming vehicles. "Wait. Is it just me, or are they driving away from us?"

"It's not just you," Keegan called back to them. "I don't understand."

"Why aren't they coming for us?" Panic crept in. "They wouldn't have given up."

"No, they wouldn't," Miles said behind her.

"Perhaps they thought you died in the explosion?" Gabbi asked, her voice quiet and calm.

"Maybe." Renna's stomach clenched at the sight of the Guardian's trucks driving away from them, disappearing over the horizon.

"They know you weren't killed in the explosion." Miles stiffened, and Renna turned slightly in the saddle to see his face.

"It's too easy." She murmured the exact words he said about the boat.

"Well, let's quit wasting time and keep going. It will be a while before we get to see the tops of the walls."

The sun was bright over the trees, beautiful rays of light filtering through the canopies. The closer they came to the Gates, the more her stomach churned. What would everyone say when she returned? Would they hate her? Welcome her back with open arms?

Miles sighed behind her, and her thoughts drifted to him. Would she ever see him again? The ache in her chest grew with each step the horse trotted. There was no way Miles would leave Elaine and Keegan. Or his people. Just like Renna couldn't leave hers.

And there was the fact that at one point, Miles used to live at an Outpost. Once you desert it, you could never go back.

Which only sent her head spinning even more. Why did the Guardians suddenly drive away? They knew she was within shouting distance. She had technically won the Hunt, even though their trucks were moving away from her.

Renna leaned back into Miles and closed her eyes, letting her tears fall. What if she made it to the Gates only to have it ripped cruelly away again?

47

Day Nine

Golden strands of light glistened through the trees as the sun slowly rose. As they neared the Gates, Renna wiped her tears away and sat a little taller in the saddle. This was what she had wanted. To go home.

No matter what they found when they got to the Gates, she would meet it gracefully.

They slowed to a walk as they neared the thinning of the trees that bordered the grassy meadow around the Gates. No one was outside, of course, and Renna's stomach lurched at the reason why. They were still locked in their home because of her. Not even able to briefly enjoy the freedom the open Gates allotted during this time.

Nine days of being locked inside.

"It's so quiet." Gabbi echoed Renna's thoughts.

"I kind of figured Grant would be waiting for me." She breathed, taking in the area surrounding the Gates. What if he was in the tree line waiting to ambush her?

Miles swung down from the horse and tied her to a maple

tree. "As I said, this last part's been too easy. There wasn't anyone stopping us for the last few hours. It was like there was an open invitation to go back."

"But you've made it." Keegan urged. "And that's what matters."

It was true. She had made it home. She grinned at Gabbi, who returned the smile. If her sister risked everything to go out into the forest to find her, then maybe, just maybe, the people of the Outpost would forgive her.

Keegan and Miles helped her off the horse and put her gently on the ground. She wrapped her arm across Miles's shoulders as she'd grown accustomed to the past few days and then wrapped her other arm around her sister's.

They came out of the clearing, and once they were right up on the Gates, her unease started to subside.

Gabbi stepped back and allowed Keegan room to hug Renna. "I'm so glad you are all right."

"Thank you for everything." Tears started to threaten, and she tried to push them away. "Take care of Miles for me."

He pulled back and laughed. "I'll try, but you know what a handful he is. It's a full-time job in itself."

"That I do."

"I'll give you two a minute." He waved goodbye to Gabbi and then slipped back into the trees.

"Thank you, Miles, for taking care of my sister." Her voice broke. "And for bringing her back to us."

"That was always the plan."

Gabbi nodded and walked to a nearby bench. Renna hobbled on her foot, turning around so she could face Miles. She leaned into him, allowing him to hold her up.

"Miles—" She stared up at him, soaking up every fleck of gold in his eyes. "I don't want to say goodbye—"

He leaned down and kissed her, silencing every thought that tried to steal away the contentment of his arms around her.

She focused instead on how perfectly safe she'd felt since the moment he helped her up off the ground that first day. How he'd fought to protect her ever since.

Much too soon, he pulled away from their kiss. "Then we won't."

She wrapped her arms around his waist and laid her cheek on his chest. She nodded, not able to work past the burning of her throat to speak.

"Here. I want you to have this." He pulled the colorful corded bracelet from his mother out of his pocket and tied it around her wrist. "Something to remember me."

"I can't take this, Miles. Your mother gave that to you."

"That's right, she did. So don't lose it." He laughed. "I can get it back next time I see you."

"There will be a next time, right?" This time her tears did spill down her face.

"You can't get rid of me that easily." He wiped her tears away with his thumb. "Besides, now you know there's a secret tunnel going outside."

As if in protest, the warning alarm for the Gates closing blared around them. Gabbi got up from the bench and made her way to them.

Miles rested his forehead against hers before kissing her one last time. He transferred her arm to Gabbi and stepped back. Squeezing her hand, he gave her a crooked smile and then let go.

At the entrance, he pulled something out from under his collar and held it up.

Her Speaker necklace. Renna laughed aloud, swiping her tears as he walked away from the Gates, taking a piece of her heart with him.

EPILOGUE

Renna opened the door to the Monitors building and hobbled up the stairs on her crutches. Her foot had slowly started to mend over the past few weeks, and she wished she could say the same about her relationship with the people of the Outpost.

And her heart.

While the people were happy to be out of their homes, they kept their distance from her. Anytime she was out on the side-walks, or if they came into the bakery, they avoided her and refused to talk to her unless she asked them a direct question. Even then, it was quick, one- or two-word replies.

Of course, her parents were thrilled to have her home and forgave her as if nothing had happened, but some shunned them and their years of friendships in light of what Renna had done.

Mother said they just needed time. But Renna didn't know how much more she could take of the endless stares, whispers, and snubbing. There were two bright spots, though. Her actions hadn't seemed to harm business at the bakery—the people still had to eat and, well, they were the only bakery at the Outpost. And her relationship with her sister had never been better. At first, Gabbi went overboard, fussing over her every minute and taking it upon herself to care for her injured foot. But then they sat down and discussed everything that happened while she was gone.

The Runners didn't say much to her each morning, either, with the exception of Porter. Renna was surprised to learn he had helped Gabbi escape into the woods. But them not speaking to her wasn't any different than before she left.

Each morning Renna sat in her chair—earlier than needed —waiting for the Runners to pass her the sealed envelope. And each morning, she recited the rules to the people of the Outpost and then went to the bakery. It was a never-ending, monotonous routine she couldn't escape.

She missed Miles. And Keegan. And even Elaine.

A few days after she got home, there was a note from Miles taped to the entrance of the hidden passage outside the Gates. Telling her they made it home without an incident and that Thomas was furious with Miles about running off and helping Renna escape. They hadn't received any word from Grant on if or when their usual arrangements would resume, though.

Renna pulled the note out of her pocket and traced over the letters of his name with her finger. She had opened it so many times the folded creases had started to tear.

The door swung open, and she quickly closed the letter and stuffed it back in her pocket. Renna brushed away a tear and turned her chair to face the door. They were earlier than usual.

"Was it your turn this morning? I thought you were here yesterday?"

Porter waved a hand and took a seat in front of her. "No, it's not my turn, but I wanted to stop by and see how you were doing."

She raised an eyebrow. "Really?"

"Don't be surprised. I helped your sister after all."

"I heard." Renna smiled. "Thank you."

He leaned back in his chair. "Believe me, I think she would have made it with or without my help." He laughed. "She's stubborn."

"Yes, she is."

"Well, in any case, I'm delighted everything worked out and you're back."

"Thanks. But I think you may be the only one, outside of my family."

"I don't think that's true." He frowned. "People are just afraid. Afraid of things they don't understand."

Renna sighed, rubbing her hand over her face. "I wish I knew how to help them. Believe me, I understand they are mad, but I don't know how to make it right."

Porter nodded, taking a moment to reply. "I think you just have to give them time."

"You sound like my mother."

"Well then, she must be a very wise woman."

Renna laughed, the sound echoing in the old building. "You would not be wrong."

"What do you think about these tunnels?" He leaned forward in the chair, dropping his voice to a whisper. "I hear there was a community? In the forest?"

Renna froze. What did she think of the tunnels and Forest Community? She scarcely had time to process being back before hearing about the tunnels and everything Gabbi and Zeke accomplished while she was gone. Guilt churned in her stomach at the thought of her sister and Zeke.

Her heart ached for her sister, who had grown fond of Zeke, yet the two still had not resolved their argument from the day Gabbi left. Several times Renna caught her sister with red, puffy eyes.

"Well ...?"

Porter's voice cut through her thoughts, and she nearly

jumped out of her seat. "Sorry." She cleared her throat, trying to come up with something to say. What could she tell him about the tunnels and Forest Community? Gabbi trusted him enough to let him show her the hidden passageway, but how much else could they trust him with?

She opened her mouth to answer, and the door opened again. This time, the Runner with the morning's reading walked in. He frowned when he noticed Porter sitting across from her.

He walked over to the front of the table and held out an envelope.

"What is it?"

"It's thicker than usual, isn't it?" He placed the envelope into her waiting hand, and the weight felt like lead in her palm.

"Yes, it is."

Eyes full of worry, he exchanged a look with Porter and backed up but didn't leave like they usually did.

Renna gaped at the envelope and, with shaky fingers, ripped open the flap. Several sheets of paper fell out on the desk, bound together with the waxed seal of the Officials.

Chimes went off in the Monitors, a signal to everyone in the Outpost that it was time for the Reading. She quickly broke the seal and opened the papers, a cry ripping from her throat as she skimmed the page.

At the top of the page, it said, "Read out loud to the Outpost in its entirety."

Renna pushed the intercom button and the second Runner pulled up a chair beside Porter. His eyes were concerned. She looked away from both of them and down at the page. Her throat was dry.

She cleared it. "Good morning, people of the Outpost. At this moment, this Reading is announced at each Outpost and the Forest Community." Renna's voice faltered for a moment, but she kept going. Her heartbeat pounded in her ears.

"As you know, I left the safety and protection of the Gates several weeks ago. The Guardians captured me and issued a challenge for my crimes against the Government and the sacred position of Speaker."

She raised her eyes to glance at Porter, and he nodded for her to continue.

"What I didn't know is that when I brutally attacked a squadron of Guardians with a grenade, it killed Official Grant's one and only son."

Renna covered her mouth with her hands. Her eyes were thick with tears, and the words blurred on the paper. "The result of such a horrendous crime against the Guardians is a life for a life.

"Each Outpost Speaker and the Forest Community leader will choose one child to send outside their Gates, taking Renna's place in the Hunt. Since Official Grant is a just man, he will allow you time to say goodbye, even though Renna and her partner did not give him that option."

The paper fell from her hands and, seeing Porter's horrified brown eyes, she let her tears fall. "You have three weeks to choose."

End of Book One

ABOUT THE AUTHOR

Erin R. Howard is the YA urban fantasy author of The Kalila Chronicles. She is also a content and acquisitions editor for Expanse Books, an imprint of Scrivenings Press.

She loves playing video games with her husband, watching movies with her children, and fueling her many craft addictions.

Erin has a Creative Writing degree and is a member of Realm Makers, RagTag Writers, and Once Upon a Page. She resides in Western Kentucky with her husband and three children.

ALSO BY ERIN R. HOWARD

The Seer

Book One of the Kalila Chronicles

Viktor has one order to follow:

Kill the girl before her eyes are opened.

For thousands of years, his job has been to torment and kill seers: humans that have the gift of seeing the spiritual realm. So it was no surprise when his brother Matthias was once again sent to stop him and protect the girl.

Now the last of the seers' bloodline hangs in the balance, as the estranged demon and angel brothers are forced to work together to save a girl's life and escape to the sanctuary city of Bethesda.

∾

The Soul Searcher

Book Two of the Kalila Chronicles

Elnora's parents gave her one rule:

Stay hidden away at all costs.

Elnora Scott is used to her survival depending on the decisions of others. Locked away in her safe house, it is easy to follow her parents' dying wishes until an angel, demon, and seer show up on her doorstep. Now, waking up in a dirty cell, she wishes she would have gone with them when she had the chance, because the ones who unknowingly ushered the kidnapper to her location may be the only ones who can save her now.

When Thea learns that Elnora may be in danger, she doesn't hesitate to find her. Thea thought stepping through the portal would be her greatest obstacle, but it only reveals a more sinister threat.

The Silencer

Book Three of The Kalila Chronicles

Sam's parents asked him to do the unthinkable:

And it cost him everything.

When Sam Hart was forced to walk away from everything and everyone he knew, The Kalila became his new home. He thought he could keep the past buried but after an unexpected visit from his brother, a family secret is revealed.

Already reeling from a murder of one of their own, an unimaginable chain of events leaves everyone questioning each other's loyalty. Will Sam, Viktor, and Matthias be able to stop this newest threat before they lose another?

MORE FROM EXPANSE BOOKS

The Girl with Stars in Her Eyes by Dawn Ford

Eighteen-year-old servant girl Tambrynn is haunted by more than her unusual silver hair and the star-shaped pupils in her eyes. Her uncontrollable ability to call objects leads the wolves who savagely murdered her mother right to her door.

When she's fired and outcast during a snowstorm, her carriage wrecks and she's forced to find refuge in an abandoned cottage. There, her life is upended when the magpie who's stalked her for ten years transforms into a man, Lucas. He's her Watcher and they're from a different kingdom. His job is to keep her safe from her father, an evil mage, who wants to steal her abilities, turn her into one of his undead beasts, and become immortal himself.

Can they make it to the magical passageway and get to their home kingdom in time for Tambrynn to thwart her father's malicious plans? Or will Tambrynn's unique magic doom them all?

Shadows at Nightfall by Brett Armstrong

The shadows of Jason's past have caught him. Having stepped into the Quest of Fire, Jason is pursued by a league of assassins formed of pure darkness. To his horror he discovers these creatures also were contracted to eliminate Anargen and his friends as they sought to understand the Tower of Light's oracle. To unravel the mystery of who wants him dead and how he fits into the ages old quest, Jason must travel the lengths of the Lowlands. In the Ziljafu deserts a secret awaits him that will shake him to his core. He'll have to move fast and cling fiercely to hope, as Anargen's story twists down a bleak path to almost certain failure.

The creatures of darkness in the Lowlands have long waited for men to spurn the High King's laws. With few concerned for the light and everything falling apart around them, Jason and Anargen will face the shadows of night's falling as their world hangs in the balance.

Expanse Books is the speculative fiction imprint of Scrivenings Press LLC.

ExpanseBooks.pub

Stay up-to-date on your favorite books and authors with our free e-newsletters.

ScriveningsPress.com